CYRUS DARIAN
and the Technomicron

CYRUS DARIAN
and the Technomicron

Raven Dane

The Misadventures of Cyrus Darian Book 1

First published in 2011 by Prosochi

This Edition, 2017 by Telos Publishing Ltd
5A Church Road, Shortlands, Bromley, Kent, BR2 0HP

Telos Publishing values feedback if you have any comments
about this book please email feedback@telos.co.uk

Cyrus Darian and the Technomicron © 2011, 2017
Raven Dane

ISBN: 978-1-84583-965-9

Cover Art: 2017 © Martin Baines

British Library Cataloguing in Publication Data. A catalogue
record for this book is available from the British Library.

To Darren Jack Powell, icon and inspiration.

Prologue

The Persian Gulf 1862

Cyrus Darian, alchemist, thief and fugitive leaned on the taffrail of a swift steamship and watched the waters of his homeland merge into the choppy green/brown of the open Indian Ocean.

Everything that was familiar, the scents and sounds of the bustling port of Chabahar were already lost to the horizon. The ship's wake in its relentless conquest of the water had caused havoc among the dhows and small boats in the crowded waters. There would be casualties from the steamship's brutal, indifferent passing but life was cheap in this region.

Darian gave a humourless grin: perhaps none was cheaper than his.

Ahead lay an uncertain future, one he had considered forgoing but for one stubborn spark of hope in his heart. That and the priceless stolen artefacts strapped to his chest. His destination lay far to the north: England – a society in the fevered grip of a technological revolution, mesmerised by the wonder of steam power and startling new inventions. It was a bright, whirring future of grinding cogs, billowing steam and flashing lights. However, none of this was of the slightest interest to the twenty-three year old fleeing his Persian homeland. Darian intended only to seek out the occult, the supernatural underworld of England's capital, London. A city with the highest accumulation of the mysterious and the strange in the world. A city that may have the one answer he needed: could he find a way to turn back time?

He became aware of another traveller approaching him in a casual stroll. Alert for danger, Darian studied the middle-aged foreigner. He was European by his pale features and wealthy by his immaculate western garb. His tall, lean frame was clothed in an exquisitely tailored long frock coat of cream linen with a silk embroidered waistcoat, and cream trousers. In his hand he carried an ebony cane with a clear quartz crystal orb handle. The man stood beside Darian at the rail and glanced across the Gulf.

'Mr Darian, I hope your intentions up on this deck are purely observational,' the man spoke in perfect English. Too perfect, it was not his mother tongue. 'It would be such a waste to the world to lose such a promising young man.'

Darian feigned incomprehension, shrugged and moved away, muttering in Farsi. Inside panic spread through him. Had the Shah's agents tracked him down so quickly? The man held him by the arm.

'Now, now. There is no need for concern. I am not your enemy. And do not feign ignorance, your English is better than mine, Darian.'

The younger man was not easily fooled by the soft words of strangers. A nomadic life spent surviving on the world's meanest streets and occasionally time living in palaces had prepared him well. He shook off the restraining hand with a low curse and continued speaking in Farsi. '*My name is Farid Rostam ...*'

Darian attempted to move away, his head down but the unknown man stepped in front of him. 'You will need western clothes, money, recommendations and a place to stay in London,' the man insisted, refusing to accept that Darian could not speak English. 'All of which I can provide – in return for the Samandar feather.'

He leant forward and winked. 'I am aware that you have it, Darian.'

How did this insistent stranger know about the phoenix tail feather, a vital ingredient in creating resuscitating elixirs? A precious thing once on show in the Shah's private museum. Darian had stolen it not from greed but from need. Having a close look at the iridescent blue and silver Samandar feather was one thing, helping himself to it quite another. One more priceless rarity gathered to help his greater plan. In fact, it had been so easy to take. Darian had also helped himself to an early Pharonic ring with an image of the Goddess Isis in lapis lazuli, carnelian and gold. That was greed.

He had no intention of relinquishing either to this man.

'Where are my manners, my name is Tobias Delany, a citizen of the world, like you. And most certainly not an agent of the Shah or any law enforcement organisation. I am an avid collector of the strange and the interesting. In fact, we should be business partners.'

Darian glanced around: the man appeared to be alone. Would he be missed? Again he tried to walk away, muttering. *'You are mistaken. I do not know you. My name is Farid Rostam, leave me alone.'*

Delany refused to let him slip from his grasp and his veneer of bonhomie disappeared, replaced by a furious snort of frustration but he swiftly recovered his composure though not his smile.

'There is no need for any hostility or suspicion Mr Darian. We are both businessmen. In return for the sale of the feather, I will give you everything you need.'

Darian stopped trying to get away from the man. Maybe this was the break he needed. He looked at Delany and smiled. Then, speaking in perfect English, Darian replied, 'I couldn't agree more – I believe you will, Mr Delany.'

London 1864

It had to be here. Just had to be! He had followed every clue, spent much time in the unsavoury company of London's criminal underworld, and even more with its supernatural denizens. All leading up to this appointment with a female fae in a basement beneath a row of ruins in Southwark.

Cyrus Darian, aged twenty-five, alchemist, amateur dabbler in the occult, collector of antiquities and murderer, hesitated. Before him, lit by one flickering candle was a stone step, glazed with green algae slime, one of many that would take him far down below the city, away from the safety of the crowded street, the everyday bustle of people going about their daily business. One loud shout away from help.

He was alone, the scrap of torn parchment slid under his hotel room door had insisted on this. If he wanted possession of the Sumerian lifestone, he had to come here alone. That was not difficult, since moving to London Darian had made no friends: all his acquaintances were as treacherous and untrustworthy as he was.

His heart hammering loud enough to wake the dead floating in the many underground rivers beneath the city, Darian tightly wound up a Luxis device and was rewarded with a beam of soft light. Modern technology triumphing over the candle's fragile glow. Instinct told him that this choice of meeting place was not right, that no fae would ever dream of meeting so deep beneath the city with the weight of dead stone pressing down on the hidden earth. But desperation drove reason from Darian's mind. This was the last object he needed, the one thing that could help him defy every rule of the universe, to undo what could not be undone.

Ignoring the stench of stagnant water and the claustrophobia, he descended, every sense alert for danger. Known for their disdain for humans, the fae, though not malicious by nature, could lead people into danger through their indifference to the consequences to mere mortals. Despite his quick wits and courage, that included mere mortals such as Darian.

At the base of the steps, he raised the Luxis by its polished wood handle to sweep the wan light around, illuminating a series of narrow corridors extending from a circular central hub. It was no more mysterious than an abandoned icehouse, one no doubt belonging to a grand mansion, now demolished. Dozens of fat rats scuttled away from the beam, Darian exhaled with relief … no unnatural vermin … so far …

In fact there was nothing and no sign that anyone or anything had entered these chambers for some time. The coating of algae on the flag-stone floor had no footprints beyond the trails of busy rats. He turned to leave and noticed something nailed to the wall close to the stairs. It was a scroll of parchment with a few words scrawled in a shaky hand.

I admire the brave and the bold. You came here alone and therefore, Mr Darian, you have passed my test. Here is the address and key to my home in Mayfair. What you seek and far more is waiting for you there.

Cursing, Darian left the icehouse, furious at the slimy green mess on his shoes. If this was someone's idea of a prank … he considered abandoning the search for the fae female but yet … with the lifestone so close … still within reach …

The address turned out to be a fine, tall Georgian townhouse overlooking a neat and prettily planted garden square. With the key in his possession, Darian expected no staff in attendance and let himself in. He was immediately surrounded by a soft scent of meadow flowers – the signature smell of a Fae. He put down his gloves and crystal-topped ebony cane and followed the trail of the perfume, leading him up the elegant curve of the stairs and onwards towards the inevitable bedchambers. Darian grinned; his dark good looks enthralled and repelled females of many species with equal passion. Why not this fae? Cautious, aware but with growing excitement, an open door and the scent at its strongest lured him forward.. Could the lifestone really be so close? Might the frustrations of false leads and the pursuit of fakes be over?

He stepped inside the chamber: a bright, feminine room, delicately decorated with taste and decorum. Less decorous was the fae female, a petite yet voluptuous form. She lay on the bed clad only in a wisp of silver gossamer voile. A magnificent mane of golden hair framed her elfin face, illuminated by huge green/gold eyes. Cold but beautiful in a way only those of the magical fae race could ever be.

'My brave human adventurer, shall we celebrate the success

of our business deal with some shared pleasure?'

Darian's gaze scanned the room for signs of treachery but saw and heard nothing untoward. He had never bedded a fae before and a dangerous curiosity began to take over his mind. But not completely. 'First, let me see the stone and then I will be at your fullest disposal.'

'Ah, Cyrus, you disappoint me. Business first?'

The fae sighed, unfolded herself off the bed, and went to a bedside table. She took out a red velvet pouch inside which was what looked like a piece of dull basalt. She handed it to Darian.

His hand shook at he cradled the lifestone, immediately realising that it was genuine. It had an inner pulse, a heartbeat, steady and eternal. His mind reeled at what this deceptively simple thing could do – it could break the laws of the universe, shatter that which could not be broken.

Forgetting the fae female in his joy, even for a few seconds as he held the stone, was a serious mistake. One small hand reached over and caressed his face, the other stroked his inner thigh but Darian's mind was too full of what this stone could do once added to his other treasures. Absentmindedly he brushed her hand away.

'Give it back to me!' The fae's voice was strident – too strident. He spotted a large cut crystal bottle of French perfume on the bedside table, this was puzzling. Fae had no need of artificial fragrance. Recovering from his surprise at her change in attitude, Darian apologised profusely and tried to summon up the enthusiasm to entertain the now furious female.

'We had a deal. I kept my side of the bargain and will happily join you in an amorous celebration.'

The fae grabbed back the stone and threw him onto the bed, this was wrong … very wrong. The fae were not that strong, the scent of flowers had gone and in its place something earthy, fetid. She pinned him down, clawing and tearing off his clothing, the coldly beautiful eyes becoming harder, more yellow than gold. As she straddled Darian, he could feel the soft fae skin become coarse. He swore and struggled to free himself – this was no fae!

Her thighs tightened like a vice around his hips, the pain making him gasp: there was no possible way he could perform now. Her face elongated and hardened, casting aside all illusion of a fae and becoming fully demonic. Darian's fear tumbled out of control. This was a demon, a succubus. One that by forgoing the usual form of a beautiful, seductive woman meant not to drain his life energy during sex but to kill him outright.

Long needle-like fangs dripping a vile green venom grew from now slavering jaws. Her tongue emerged, small and pink at first before lengthening, splitting into a thin, forked red protuberance that licked his face and neck.

'Pretty human, have you no loving kiss for Bruxa?'

Her fingernails had become long curved talons which raked down his body, drawing blood, one hand heading dangerously low down. Using all his strength Darian fought back but the succubus was too strong, her desire to play with him before ripping his body to shreds, too determined.

'Tell me, I need to know before you kill me, who summoned you to do this execution?'

'Pretty boy, such a pretty boy. Bruxa knows you will taste so sweet. As does this.'

The demon popped the lifestone into her mouth and swallowed it. Throwing back her head, she howled in victory knowing that the last fading ember of hope was dying in Darian's soul with the loss of the stone. Her eyes glowed with triumph, now for her reward. She leant down, sucking and licking Darian's neck, taking her time to savour his taste before devouring him – body and soul.

All too aware that he had but seconds to live, Darian made one last, desperate fight back. As he forced his head away, the tip of one fang pierced his neck, deep enough to drip venom directly into his bloodstream. Not enough to kill him, but enough to give him a brief burst of Bruxa's own strength. He heaved the startled succubus off him and sprinted to a full length mirror, smashing it into shards with one well-aimed kick. Grabbing the largest piece of jagged glass, he held the crude makeshift weapon before him.

The room boomed with mocking laughter. 'Pretty boy, you have made so many enemies in this life but you are going to die without ever knowing who sent me to kill you.'

Bruxa confident in her superior strength and speed rushed forward and found only air. Darian had sidestepped with his innate agility honed on the back street slums of Tehran and using all his strength swung the glass shard in a tight arc, decapitating the succubus in one stroke. Her body crumpled, erupting into a writhing mass of agonised flesh, other forms she'd assumed, including the fae, appearing and merging back into the mangled abomination. With eyes glaring with shock and hatred, the head screamed and screamed, a horrific sound that could curdle even dragon's blood.

'Die you bitch,' Darian managed to mutter as he fought to stay conscious, the venom already surging through his bloodstream like liquid fire. Instinct screamed that he should flee, find some dark safe place. His mind fought back, desperate to retrieve the lifestone. Swallowing back bitter bile of revulsion, Darian approached the now twitching body with the glass shard, preparing to crudely dissect the succubus' carcass to find the stone.

The head stopped screaming, now laughing with Bruxa's baleful, mocking triumph, knowing the stone was lost to her assailant. Both parts of the succubus' body collapsed into thousands of squirming slug-like sections that burrowed through the floor and disappeared – taking the lifestone with them.

Darian fell to the floor, searching with desperation for the precious lump of enchanted basalt but it was gone. He lay there clutching his stomach as the venom fire in his blood stream intensified, too weak to move, in too much despair at the loss of the stone to care.

He had no idea how long he had lain on the floor. Early morning daylight streamed through the bedroom, he had been there for at least a day and night. Shivering with cold, stiff and aching, Darian rose unsteadily to his feet and attempted to leave the room. There was no doubt that the succubus venom had affected him. He felt different as a human being, changed. Darian's hand went to his chest, felt his heart beating slower yet his agitated, colder blood seemed to speed through his veins. Curious. He staggered out of the room and down onto the street, seeking a Hansom cab but the weakness returned and he fell to his knees on the cobbles.

'Sir, may I offer some assistance?'

A couple of well meaning passersby, spotting his confusion and shaky gait and then his fall, had paused to help him. Darian looked up and at the sight of his face, the woman screamed and swooned back into her partner's arm. The man hurried her away, muttering, glancing back at Darian with fear in his eyes.

Darian spun around, at every turn people shrunk back in horror at the sight of his face. What in Hades had the demon done to him? Somehow, he found the strength to get back into the house and sought out a mirror. He paused at first, what would he see? A monster? Bracing himself, Darian approached the silvered looking glass. Though gaunt and marble white from the trauma of the poisoning, his good looks remained but none of that mattered.

Not with the extraordinary change to his eyes.

1

Cyrus Darian: hedonist; philanderer; alchemist; necromancer and now possibly near immortal adventurer; stifled a yawn of boredom and did not vary his pace. Using mirrored side lenses, he could see furtive assassins behind him. What a disappointment, three ordinary rogues with appalling tailors, hardly worthwhile adversaries to a man who faced down a reanimated Berserker horde single-handed, armed only with a swordstick and a glass of cognac.

He wasn't sure yet about the last part of his *curriculum vitae*. The purple-lensed, brass rimmed spectacles he wore were not an affectation but a necessity. The venomous 'love bite' by the succubus had left his eyes changed, no longer a piercing but normal blue but curious ever-swirling hues of violet and silver. The lenses gave the outside world an illusion of normality. He also recovered more swiftly from injury and had not appeared to age since the vicious attack ten years before. He looked and felt twenty-five and maybe always would. This did not alarm him. Cyrus was vain, as elegant, handsome and as highly-strung as a fine-bred racehorse. He enjoyed his lean good looks, the thought of them surviving the cruel passage of time delighted him. The thought that those around him would age and die gave him no lasting concern.

Greenish yellow fug from the Ephesysium Gas Works blended with vapour rising from the Thames to weave through the narrow streets in a foul miasma. Most passersby hurried home, the fog burnt throats and made eyes stream and it stunk of rotting flesh. In such situations many still favoured wearing cumbersome contraptions – Dr Mirabillis' Patent Respiratory Facilitators – to help them breathe. The whirring cogs and flashing valves were flim flams, the devices were as bogus as was their inventor, Dr Mirabillis aka Ernie Snudge.

Darian had exposed the devices as fraudulent and had added Snudge to the growing number of his enemies.

The fug also brought flocks of breeth rising from the sewers, their fragile spirit forms strengthened by the gas. Darian was unbothered by the supernatural vermin: he wore the Talisman of Greel around his neck, a trinket worth losing two stalwart companions to acquire from a haunted monastery in the Ukraine.

He glanced again for signs of his pursuers, they were still there behind him and closing in, apparently immune to the stinking fog. This did not surprise Darian, these men were no doubt born and raised in the riverside slums of Lambeth where rats and breeth where everyday companions and the fog never seemed to clear whatever the weather.

Darian had no intention of leading the men to his destination, not out of any gallantry, he suspected that she could deal with them better then he could. No, he didn't want to be robbed of the fun of dispatching them.

He paused to let his pursuers catch up, amused at their clumsy attempts at subterfuge. Darian casually wandered into an alleyway which led to a well-known opium den. As a man notorious for indulging all his whims and vices, this was normal behaviour and unlikely to put off his adversaries. Even with the sound deadening effect of the fog, their footsteps clattered on the damp cobbles, proving they were all too human. Darian couldn't be bothered to find out who sent them, clearly not much of an adversary to have such lowly minions at their disposal.

Once in the alley, they rushed him in a sudden burst of angry energy finding only fetid air. Darian re-emerged from the shadows and ran one through with his swordstick. Another he despatched with a cunningly concealed pearl handled Deringer. The last he used magic to destroy, sending a brief flash of ancient power from his Asgard ring evaporating the attacker completely. An indulgence: it would take many months of blood and moonlight for the ring to renew its power.

Long slivers of green phosphorescence insinuated down the alley, five of them, all hungry for life to contaminate. The breeth found Darian cleaning his sword on the clothes of one of his victims. They tried to approach but the talisman's subtle power kept them well at bay yet they circled him with low hisses of thwarted malevolence.

Darian looked at the breeth. 'Too late, my disembodied friends, there's nothing left for you to possess. You need to be quicker when I am around.'

Darian stood up and strolled away from remains of the would-be ambush.

He did not find the Emporium, it found him. The shop was never in the same place, nor did it ever look the same twice. Like its owner it had many faces. There was a shimmer in reality close to the Embankment and the Emporium appeared wreathed in its own silver mist. This time its façade was of well-faded Venetian Renaissance splendour, the peeling paintwork crackled and distressed. Verdigris tarnished the metal scrollwork and corrosion etched the classical statues. The theme continued inside its crowded interior though the deep blue and gilded hues of the walls were less faded. Hundreds of arcane and obscure fantastical objects gleamed and flickered filling every shelf and most of the floor space. Other strange forms and curios hung and spun glistening from hooks hanging from the tall ceiling. The proprietor eschewed gaslight preferring gilded sconces of warm candle glow to illuminate her esoteric wares.

As he expected, Lady Teknoligi chose the appearance of a Venetian courtesan to match her Emporium. Her damson silk, extravagantly bustled gown was low cut, revealing a glimpse of ample creamy breasts adorned with a necklace of huge rubies. Her classically beautiful face was framed with tumbling ebony curls artfully escaping from her immaculately coiffed hair. Her black eyes gleamed with desire and delight but for what purpose was yet to be learnt. Sometimes a deadly adversary, other times an ally, always a passionate lover. Darian did not know her true form nor was he interested in discovering whether she even had one. All that mattered was her mood: Darian remained on his guard expecting the kiss of a blade as much as her wine red lips. Her clientele were the elite of the world's adventurers, occultists and alchemists but also criminal masterminds and evil mavens. He liked to think he was her only lover but that was unlikely. The Lady lived beyond the rules of any society.

'*Amore mio*,' her voice was low, warm and redolent of sensuality, 'why has my beautiful one taken so long to return to my embrace?'

Darian shrugged. 'Possibly because last time we met, you tried to kill me with the Agis Dagger?'

Her laughter echoed around the stacks of artefacts. 'That would not have killed you. Not the great Cyrus Darian! Merely slowed you down by a few decades. I needed that statue of Bastet for a client I could not afford to disappoint.'

'You only had to ask, *belleza*.' Darian shrugged, the gold and lapis lazuli figure of the Egyptian Cat Goddess was desirable for its great beauty but more so for its repelling powers against the reanimated dead. He had no doubt he would reacquire it one day soon. Cyrus Darian did not lose.

'I have brought quite a shopping list, *tesora*.'

The Lady held out her hand towards him, her voice slurring with need. 'I require payment up front tonight.'

'It is my pleasure to accommodate your terms.' Darian smiled and kissed her hand and though ever wary, allowed himself to be led to her bedchamber high above her wares, the ceiling lit magically by a full blue moon.

During the night, the Emporium changed appearance, as did its proprietor. Darian awoke to find his arm around a luscious silver-blonde girl, elfin in appearance, her beauty provoking his renewed desire. This trip to acquire some useful artefacts was going to take longer than he planned. Not that he was complaining.

As she slumbered, he took in the fairytale décor: the shimmering gauze curtains; the sparkling crystal chandeliers suspended in thin air; the delicacy of the light; exotic flowers that scented the room. The girl's eyes opened and they were huge and green, her smile innocent with an enticing glimmer of secret knowing. He wanted her but not without a price. The Emporium had moved again as he had slept. Darian could not hear the many pounding heartbeats of London life: the constant drum of the gas works; the hammer of iron foundries; the rattle of steam Hansom cabs; and the huff and screech of locomotives. The everyday sounds of the million humans and uncountable non-humans that inhabited or infested the capital.

In its place, there was the unmistakable sound of calling sea birds and the rhythmic pounding of high surf on a beach.

With one hand, he caressed the softness of the girl's porcelain pale skin, lingering on the small, pert breasts, her flat stomach and neat mound of silver-blonde down, pleased by her responding quiver of desire. His touch became more insistent until she began to beg him to take her again. Then his other hand tightened around her fragile slender neck.

'My angel, I will give you all you desire and much, much more but not until you have taken me home.'

The Lady's eyes narrowed, their colour turned from warm green to glacial jade, she hated to be bested by Darian in anything be it business deal or in the bedroom. The atmosphere in the bedchamber changed, darkened, became a far grimmer fairytale. Cobwebs draped the ceiling and over the now fading, broken furniture, the flowers withered and stank of decay, sinister furtive shapes moved among the shadows.

None too gently, she traced the outline of his spine with fingernails now closer to steel tipped talons. 'As you wish, my beloved, though what you see in that stinking corrupt city defies me.'

What indeed was it that drew him to remain in London? Though deeply unpleasant, it was also a lodestone, a magnet for intrigue, adventure and trouble … the things Darian thrived on. Without dropping his innate wariness, he concentrated on pleasuring the Lady.

Otherwise it would be a long walk home.

For once she was good as her word, and equipped with some new exotic objects from her collection, Darian sauntered out of the Emporium. It had reappeared in Russell Square at three o'clock in the morning startling only some roosting pigeons and a gang of brown scaled blaggers fighting over the corpse of a cat. The minor demons were a step up from rats, there was a better class of vermin in this district.

He returned to his home, unhindered but certainly not unobserved, the constant price of his infamy. Darian whispered some incantations and the front door of his Georgian townhouse opened as he reached it.

As he lit the corridor candles, an agitated scatter of nails on the parquet floor greeted his arrival home, Misha, his only permanent companion, scrambled hissing with pleasure around his feet. Though he had no clue to the beast's gender if it had one, Darian considered the sinuous dragoncat to be female. He did not know her species either; extensive searches in every known bestiary had left him baffled. Her body was a kaleidoscope of black, red and gold soft fur, a long mane of glossy black hair grew down her spine from forelock to the tip of a long tail. Her eyes glowed green as if lit by an inner fire, useful for navigating his house without candlelight.

Leaping to his arms then settling to her favourite place curled around his neck, Darian and the creature went to his study. He was eager to examine his acquisitions and quickly lit the candles and a fire in the hearth. Darian, like the Lady, was no supporter of the gas company's dubious wares. The price to pay for the light and warmth the Ephesysium Gas Works supplied could sometimes be death due to the inconsistency and impurities of the chemical brews they made. Londoners stoically accepted the risks in return for cheap and plentiful fuel.

Darian no longer hired staff for his London home, too many had betrayed him or lost their lives defending their master. He poured himself a generous tumbler of fine single malt and began to examine his purchases. The Emporium's visit to the Far East had paid dividends. He picked up a delicate red lacquer and bronze mirror – Japanese, at least three thousand years old. A harmless trinket at first perusal, a sideways glance at its reflective surface revealed symbols etched into the polished metal in quicksilver. Its sole purpose was as a defence against Kubikajiri: headless ghosts seething with hatred for the living. The mirror could shatter the evil spirits into a thousand harmless pieces. In Darian's life, he could never discount the possibility of encountering Kubikajiri.

A smoky green, gold topped, glass phial was believed to contain distilled mermaid tears, a vital ingredient in creating many useful healing elixirs. He had tried in vain to acquire some for many years and hoped the Lady had not duped him with another fake. She did not do refunds.

A slim ebony, lead-lined box slid open to reveal small nuggets of rare ores, xilaniun, triallion and glowing deborite. Darian grinned with delight. His experimentation with inanimate metamorphosis could advance further now. He admired the ores but did not touch them: such substances were highly toxic and volatile. He had not long finished rebuilding the room after the last explosion.

Another object had defied explanation when he found it in the Emporium but had intrigued him greatly. Even its seller had no idea what it was and she never revealed how and where she acquired her stock. A matte grey box forged in a metal that he did not recognise, had a delicately wrought fretwork on one side which revealed a tantalising glimpse of the contents: a deep blue gemstone that pulsed as if alive and seemed to be singing with a curious small voice that reached across some unfathomable distance in time and space. Darian would not attempt to open the box until he had done some research. He did not want to emulate Pandora and release some great evil onto the world. This one needed careful guarding, so the alchemist hid it in plain sight on a high cabinet filled with Haitian guardian totems blessed by houngan devoted to the voodoo Goddess Erzulie Dantor.

Once there, only he could remove it. Anyone else attempting to touch it would at the very least lose a hand. Another reason not to keep staff, he did not want any diligent maids being attacked while dusting the shelves. According to the voodoo priests, Erzulie Dantor had favoured Darian. To have the Goddess of wealth, vengeance and protection on your side was never a bad thing.

The final object was a gold embroidered turquoise velvet pouch containing rare semi-precious stones from secret mines deep in the Amazon jungle. Darian raised each one in turn to the candlelight, enjoying their individual beauty. Each would have a useful purpose in his experiments.

The warmth from his hearth, the fine whiskey and pleasurable fatigue from satisfying the Lady's voracious desires were adding lead weights to his limbs and eyelids. He sank into the depths of the soft leather armchair by the fire and drifted off to sleep, Misha curled protectively around his feet.

2

Darian awoke with shafts of dawn's wan light in his eyes, the fire had long gone out and he was stiff from sleeping in the armchair. It was times like these he was relieved not to have kept staff, keeping up the appearance of being a gentleman at all times could be wearying. His clothing was dishevelled, a night's growth of rough stubble was on his face, his shoulder length black hair was messed and wild. He arose, stretched and glanced out of the window. There was little to see: the overnight fog had not cleared but a slight breeze rising from the Thames Estuary created swirling patterns within it that looked alive. Ethereal forms with a beauty they didn't deserve.

He had just finished his morning ablutions and sat down to a quick breakfast of buttered rye bread when Misha gave him early warning of trouble. She raced around the kitchen hissing and spitting, giving his ankles sharp little nips to get him to arise from the table. The creature never gave false alarms: Darian always listened to her warnings and armed himself with discreet weapons.

As he strode into the main hall, a shadow darkened the windows as a whirring, wheezing and billowing dirigible descended, brazenly anchoring on the gaslight outside his home. Trouble indeed. Only the richest could afford a private airship and the richest tended to be corrupt and venal in Darian's circle of acquaintance. Arrogant men who called without prior notice and would bring plenty of private muscle.

He returned to his drawing room as if there wasn't a large airship tethered outside his home. Darian now regretted not having a butler to announce to the unwelcome arrival that the master was not at home to visitors. He quieted his dragoncat as the doorbell rang several times wondering how long he could ignore this intrusion. The possibility of them breaking down his front door was considerable. When the doorbell ringing changed to furious pounding by many fists, Darian sighed and finally deigned to open the door.

Outside stood four henchmen identically garbed in aviator clothing, their eyes hidden by thick brass and glass goggles. They bristled with weapons and exuded mindless menace. Behind them was a small, rotund man in an immaculate morning suit. Darian recognised him straight away: Sir Vivian Crimm-Smythe. His oleaginous and fraudulently unctuous manner hid a sadistic monstrous nature. He had openly boasted that he never had blood on his hands but his minions had rivers of the precious liquid on theirs. He had made his fortune in property and coal, owning highly profitable mines in Wales and vast swathes of London's dockside industrial region. That gave him the influence and financial clout to run his private army of Mechmen virtually unchallenged, Crimm-Smythe had a way of silencing his critics – permanently.

'Why, Cyrus, my dashing Prince of Persia, anyone would think you had no wish to speak to me.'

The alchemist chose not to rise to the thinly veiled taunt. The man was a known racist and unashamed xenophobic as were most of the English establishment. Darian was proud of his ancestry; he owed his lush good looks and love of escapades to his mixed genes. His mother had been a vivacious Irish witch, a great beauty. His father was indeed Persian of noble blood. An adventurous, devoted couple who had gone missing while sailing in the Bermuda Triangle when Darian was twelve. His search for them was in vain but he would never give up the hope they were still alive.

'I don't,' Darian replied, controlling his voice to feign indifference, 'so take your big bag of wind and blow away.'

The industrialist raised one hand and from the side streets came a familiar marching sound so fearsome, it froze many in their tracks. Crimm-Smythe's private army – Mechmen. A dozen of the metal and clockwork enhanced soldiers stomped towards Darian's home, sending startled passersby running away. A carriage horse reared in terror and bolted, oblivious to its driver hauling on the reins.

As one, the Mechmen halted in silence around their master and his henchmen.

'As you see, Darian, I am taking this meeting seriously and I suggest you do the same. You have a reputation for laughing in the face of danger. My associates will wipe any smile off your face – lastingly.'

'Why don't you just bugger off, Vivian old thing, you are trespassing on private property and boring me to tears.'

At the insult to their creator, the Mechmen whirred into action, part human, part clockwork they were far more formidable foes than the fools Darian had dealt with the night before. Their leader halted them with a muttered command. This was too public a place for a bloody, one-sided confrontation. The sight of the Mechmen was usually enough to reduce people to quivering compliance, clearly this alchemist was made of sterner stuff. Or too stupid to realise how much danger he was in.

'Leave him for now. I would not expect a lowbred mongrel cur like Cyrus Darian to behave like an English gentleman.'

'Of course not, I would never stoop that low,' Darian returned with a humourless grin. 'I take it this is not a visit to exchange pleasantries.'

Crimm-Smythe winced and his hand involuntarily went to an old scar across his cheek. 'Nothing concerning you will ever be a pleasant experience.'

His eyes narrowed, already tired of this delay. 'I believe you have something of mine. You visited your shape shifting whore and did not leave empty handed.'

Darian considered his options. The oligarch in person was no threat but his powerful minions were, their vulnerable human organs protected by thick steel armour.

'I have no wish to emulate English manners if slurring the reputation of a lady is considered acceptable.' Darian made no attempt to hide his contempt. He should have called Crimm-Smythe out to a duel after such an insult to the Lady but he knew the man was a coward and would have him assassinated long before the event.

'A lady?' Crimm-Smythe snorted. 'You two are well matched. A pair of thieving, rutting gutter-snipes.'

The open derision did not concern Darian, the insults were tame. He had been taunted by much worse jibes, usually by demons with their extensive, multi-lingual, multi-speciel vocabulary.

'And this from a man who will turn poor families onto the street without a farthing in compensation and demolish their homes to make way for more factories.'

The industrialist ignored him, his patience worn thin. Darian re-assesed his situation. The Mechmen were powerful but cumbersome, the heavy energy packs on their backs would slow them down. Perhaps he could outrun them after a suitable distraction. Such as a huge hole appearing in the dirigible.

'I am no thief and have nothing of yours. So if you will excuse me, I have no further interest in your company.'

The industrialist sneered. 'If you have the Thebus scroll, then you are indeed a thief.'

Relieved that none of his latest acquisitions included a scroll, Darian continued, 'In that case, you have wasted your time and vexed me for nothing. I have no knowledge of this scroll nor did the Lady show me any such artefact at the Emporium nor did she mention it in passing.'

Darian turned to walk back into his home, the man knew enough about his famed occult knowledge and use of alchemy not to risk entering his home uninvited. If it wasn't for the gathering public scrutiny, Crimm-Smythe would have no hesitation in sending in his Mechmen, prepared to sacrifice them all in the hope that one would succeed. One day soon, he would be too powerful to care what anyone thought.

'You cannot remained holed up in your haunted bolthole forever Darian. Unless you return what is mine, your life will be under great threat.'

'When isn't it?' Darian shrugged and slammed the door behind him.

Intrigued by this unknown scroll, Darian headed to his extensive library stocked with works of great antiquity and rarity, working all day, through the night and onto the next dawn, searching for any mention however obscure of the Thebus scroll. Unsuccessful, he dropped his glasses onto his desk and rubbed eyes made painful by the marathon investigation. It was no use, if he wanted to learn more, he would have to ask his wife.

3

A few hours of deep, dreamless sleep and a refreshed Darian saw the light of reason. He could not find a trace of evidence that any such item as a Thebus scroll ever existed and there was no need to take a perilous and emotionally fraught journey in search of some possibly non-existent artefact. Men like Crimm-Smythe were easy victims of extravagant frauds: one promising him weight loss or hair re-growth would hook him in as easily as a hungry trout after a mayfly. One day, if sufficiently jaded with life, Darian decided he might even construct such a fraud himself to entrap the industrialist, it would be amusing to lead the man and his brutish minions a merry dance.

In truth, Darian admitted to himself that he too had momentarily fallen for the allure of the unknown and wasted a day and night in searching for what may not exist or be worthless if it did. Darian recognised the symptoms. He had too much time on his hands and needed another adventure. In the meantime, he decided the best use of his day was a brisk ride on his favourite horse around Rotten Row followed by a Turkish bath and some time relaxing at his club. Any of which activities could produce the start of an escapade as well as being pleasurable. A stronger wind from the South West rolling in from the vast Atlantic Ocean had dispersed the fog and he now looked out at a crowded London landscape where the sun sharply defined every building and glinted off the recently constructed overhead tramway.

This early morning clarity would not last. Once the factories opened for the day and poured forth their clouds of foulness, another obscuring haze would accumulate. Now was the time to enjoy the brightness and nearly breathable air. The wind was too strong for a public dirigible and he loathed the crowded steam omnibuses. He felt compassion for the hard working, wheezing beasts pulling Hansom cabs through crowded streets and breathing in the foul London fog and would never hire one. He decided to walk.

As Darian entered the livery yard where his horse was stabled, the ostlers ran to greet him and to hear his instructions. His wealth brought their diligence, his ethnic background their barely hidden contempt. He tipped them handsomely but declined their services. Getting the Akhal Teke stallion ready was part of the enjoyment of the day. The horse, a snake necked whippet that gutted curiosity among the English horses, whickered in delight at his approach. To the eastern and far eastern realms of the world, the Akhal Teke, bred in the harsh mountains of Turkmenistan, was a horse without equal. Once treasured by the Chinese as a 'Celestial Horse', and sought after by travellers along the Silk Road, to many of the English, it was a worthless oddity far inferior to the exquisite Arabians who were the ancestors of their own thoroughbred hunters and racehorses. Darian took some delight in the fact that one of the thoroughbred breed's illustrious ancestors, the Byerly Turk, could well have been an Akhal Teke.

'Hello my handsome man,' Darian whispered in the Turkomen dialect from where the horse was foaled. 'I hope none of these overbred equine fools have been giving you a hard time.' Darian caressed the fine, silky, golden hair of the beast's neck and it nuzzled his face, its intense metallic sheen a unique and beautiful aspect of the breed. Nobody else rode the horse – as a breed they were known as 'the horse with one master' – and Maksat was no exception.

Like Darian it was sensitive, intelligent and highly-strung. Like him, it was a tough and courageous foreigner, an outsider in London society, stabled with English thoroughbreds and the source of much derision. Darian could live all his life in London yet still be looked down on as a foreigner, hated equally for both sides of his racial background.

This horse from an exotic location, a breed with an ancient, illustrious past, was the perfect choice of mount for Darian. It pleased him to think that his noble Persian ancestors would have ridden similar horses and the warrior horsemen among his Irish forebears would have appreciated the breed's qualities.

The sunny, late autumn, day brought many riders to Hyde Park for exercise and socialising. A brisk south westerly wind had given the people of London a short reprieve from the endless industrial smog and many of the wealthy celebrated by a ride in the park though it was a sad shadow of its former glory with stunted, dying trees and blighted, grey-leaved undergrowth. Every shower of rain brought more stress to London's trees and plant life, the chemical brew in the air mixed with the rainwater and soaked into the soil, poisoning from the roots upward, while the acidic rain corroded the leaves. Yet Londoners persevered in the illusion that Hyde Park was a pleasant slice of the countryside in the centre of the capital.

Despite the sorry state of its greenery, the park was considered a much-needed haven in an increasingly chaotic London. By the personal edict of Queen Victoria, no dirigibles overflew it in case they startled the fine-bred horses nor were steam Hansoms allowed in the park itself for the same reason. She also forbade any building of overhead steam trams near the park. Personally Darian agreed with the Empress, he would have built the new system in tunnels beneath the city.

Darian ignored the other horsemen; they would openly snub any attempts at pleasantries from him. He concentrated in gently controlling his over-fresh mount eager to gallop and cause chaos scattering the placid park hacks.

As he reached a steep hill where cantering was allowed, galloping hooves and a female's shrill scream came up fast behind him, making Maksat whirl and spin eager to join the bolting horse. With a firm hand on the reins and a curt command, Darian stilled his golden stallion and waited to watch the drama unfold.

A trim young woman sewn in to a tight navy velvet habit galloped past, hauling ineffectively at the mouth of a dappled grey park hack. The horse passed close enough for Darian to easily grab the reins but he let it pass. Inevitably, another horse galloped in pursuit. A man on a fine bred bay hunter chased after the runaway, catching it at the top of the hill. Once he had settled and calmed down horse and rider, handing the reins to a conveniently waiting groom, the man cantered back down to confront Darian.

'What sort of cowardly cad are you?' he thundered, round face florid with rage and brandishing his whip. 'How could you ignore the plight of a lady in peril?'

A lady? Darian considered warning the man about Lady Arabela Grayshott aka Libby Jenks, clever little minx and conwoman extraordinaire. Instead he shrugged and attempted to continue on his ride. The man was having none of it.

'I am addressing you sir, have you an explanation for your disgraceful behaviour?'

'None whatsoever,' Darian replied with a provocative grin and a deliberately exaggerated Persian accent.

It worked, he had lived up to the Englishman's low opinion of foreigners and with the man's curses following him up the hill, he allowed Maksat his head to gallop briskly away. As he passed Libby at the top, he doffed his hat to her. She was a delight in bed but not worth provoking a duel over. 'He's all yours, ma belle.'

'I'd rather 'ave you, Cyrus!' she returned with a saucy wink.

With the horse safely returned to its stable, Darian hailed a steam cab and gave directions to the baths. The weather-wizened driver hesitated, tugging at his cap in abject apology and disappointment. With so much competition between the steam and horse drawn Hansoms, it was never a good idea to turn down a fare from a well off toff.

'Sorry m'lud. Can't get through to there, terrible riots all around the 'ouses of Parliament. A right to do. They have sent the troops in.'

Darian sighed, another regular vexation of London life.

'What is it this time, my good man? Taxes? Anarchists?'

'No, m'lud. Air, or the lack of it. It's the poor folk who live dahn low wot suffers the most. Toffs, begging your pardon, sir, can afford to live up 'igh or well out of the stinkin' Particular.'

Another riot over the polluted air. That could only turn nasty with the emotions of the ordinary people running high, they were the ones who coughed and wheezed their way through a short miserable life, burying their sick and young early from corroded and poisoned lungs. Pitching these desperate people up against nervous young troops armed with hair trigger circadian repeater rifles was a massacre just one wrong move away. Already an ominous plume of smoke arose from Westminster.

'How vexing,' Darian sighed, 'well, get me as close as you can. I do not mind a longer route but I cannot possibly attend my club reeking of horse sweat.'

Much later, ignoring news urchins running around the streets waving lurid pamphlets telling of how the riot was bloodily quelled, a well pummelled and thoroughly clean Darian left the Turkish Baths and took a steam Hansom to his club in Ormond Yard off St James Square. No other London gentlemen's club would accept his membership, nor would he want to join them. The Iblis club was a private and safe sanctuary to some of the most disreputable of the capital's occult and adventurous society. It welcomed men and more unusually for London clubs, also women, mavericks who lived by their own rules.

Built in 1710 in a discreet corner of the Yard, the building was unremarkable. The dimly lit entrance, up a set of narrow steps, was illuminated by a flickering oil lantern. His approach was well observed and uncontested by vigilant eyes within the building. Once inside, he was required to hand in all weapons, mechanical and supernatural, his progress watched by a silent giant of a doorman holding a slavering breeth-possessed wretch on a leather lead and chained collar. Any attempt to smuggle in occult weapons would be accompanied by screeches of recognition from the breeth-man hybrid. A complex device over the inner entrance corridor scanned for any suspect technology. With his Asgard ring drained of power, Darian passed through unhindered.

This vigilance was a major reason for the club's popularity: many mortal enemies met and shared civilised conversation while sipping from lead crystal balloons of cognac within its walls. The club's staff and members would robustly and lethally deal with any attempts at creating mayhem within its walls. A cellar full of hungry blaggers disposed of any inconvenience. A service Darian believed the club offered to Her Majesty's Government's Secret Service in return for protection. It was simply not done to ask questions.

Darian went straight to his retreat in the library: his favourite comfortably overstuffed oxblood leather chair set by a cheery hearth well stocked with apple-wood logs. Within seconds a valet brought him a tumbler generously filled with a fine old cognac and a fat Havana cigar he didn't smoke. A curious custom that never changed. At nine o'clock in the evening it was early and Darian was able to peruse the newspapers uninterrupted. The usual war news around the Empire, public announcements, royal court news and politics were of little interest, Darian was more interested in details of new inventions and reports of strange occurrences. Best of all were accounts of the latest scandals, he found these enormous fun, reading about salacious details were a personal weakness of his and a source of facts he could often use to his favour in future encounters.

That night, the newspapers made disappointing reading. Apart from yet another objection to a plan to build huge turbines to blow London's industrial fog out to sea, there was nothing worth spending time on. By midnight the club was busy, most were familiar faces he could ignore, a mixture of humans and a handful of low caste demons in human form: the usual crowd. He was enjoying a light supper of roast guinea fowl and considering joining the gaming tables when a new arrival caught his interest: an imposing figure in a floor length maroon cape. The middle-aged man had strong features, a prominent nose, a white-streaked black beard and matching long hair, worthy of a biblical patriarch. His fingers bore many large rings and one hand gripped an ebony cane topped with a silver bulldog's head. Theatrical, most likely a charlatan, but interesting nonetheless.

Noticing his curiosity, the man approached smiled and held out his hand.

'Zachariah P Dedman, at your command, sir.'

An American. That explained the brash appearance and forward nature. Darian rather liked Americans. He introduced himself and beckoned for the newcomer to join him beside the fire.

'Interesting name, you have there, son. Persian and Irish?'

Darian nodded with a smile of respect, this man was well educated. Few had heard of his middle name: Kavan.

'You probably already know it means handsome,' Dedman continued, 'as indeed you are.'

Darian took the compliment with a smile and slight incline of his head: he was used to attracting the attention of both sexes and of many species.

'I will not insult you by pretending this was a chance encounter.'

'Is there any other sort?' Darian replied evenly.

Dedman nodded, unsure what to make of the confident young man opposite him. Graceful in manner and movement, his pale skin contrasted with the luxurious jet hair, his fine boned features lean to the point of aesthetic but with a well-defined and sensual mouth. Dedman found the hidden eyes frustrating. It was hard to read character when the windows of the soul were shuttered. Darian wore languid Bohemian style garb favoured by the Pre-Raphaelite Brotherhood of artists. A burgundy velvet frock coat, loose cream silk shirt, pewter silk brocade waistcoat and dark grey trousers. It was difficult to imagine such a man capable of anything more strenuous than lifting an opium pipe. But Dedman knew different.

'Mr Darian, I am a private collector of obscurities. Objects whose purpose has baffled mankind and demon horde alike.'

'Don't tell me … you are looking for the Thebus Scroll?'

The American laughed, full bodied with genuine mirth. 'I take it you have also been harassed by that poisonous little jerk with his army of clockwork soldiers.'

At Darian's bemused nod, the man continued, 'A diversion, I arranged it through a discreet third party to keep Crimm-Smythe well occupied while we are conducting business.'

'Are we?'

'I hope so, Mr Darian, or may I call you Cyrus? You come highly recommended by a mutual acquaintance, the beauteous and bewitching Lady Teknoligi, though from what I have heard she may be a tad biased.'

Darian did not answer. It was a cause of wonder and some concern that his private business was such common knowledge among London's more mysterious community, its secret world of the occult and strange.

'I wish to acquire a certain item of interest and I know you are the man to get it,' Dedman announced. 'I have hand picked excellent operatives to help you achieve this.'

'I work alone or I select my own team,' Darian insisted, his voice cold, brooking no argument. For the first time, Dedman could see the steel behind the louche appearance. 'If that is not acceptable to you, walk away now.'

'You will give me no say in whom I employ?' the American argued.

'None whatsoever.'

Dedman laughed, this time with no mirth. Many had warned him against contacting this man. The best in his field but uncompromising and unpredictable. As likely to waste his wages in a brothel or opium den as buying equipment for the expedition. Dedman had to have at least one of his own people on the team.

'Why in tarnation, man, you can have whoever and whatever you want. But Cyrus, there is one condition on which I will not back down. I insist on one team member of my own choosing.'

Darian shrugged, appearing indifferent. 'And if I refuse?'

The American prepared to leave, using his bulldog cane to help himself up, standing with a noticeable twinge of pain. 'Then I will find another expedition leader and mention to the odious Crimm-Smythe that I saw the Thebus Scroll in your hands at the Emporium.'

'So be it.' Darian took another swig of his brandy, picked up a newspaper and pretended to read. 'Don't let me stop you.'

4

Maybe the vast turbines would be a good idea after all, Darian wondered as he took a steam cab to a corner of Soho. With the loss of the brisk south westerly, the industrial fog descended again, shrouding London's streets in swirling, stinking filth. He suspected their champions had not properly addressed the fact that the machines would blow away far more than the noxious fug. For one thing, English gentlemen would have to adopt their ladies' use of hatpins to secure their bowlers and top hats. The skies would also fill with fleeing newspapers and baffled pigeons.

He still had an amused grin at this image when he alighted at his China Town destination and walked the last hundred yards to Madame Xiu's Retreat. Superficially a Chinese teahouse, those allowed into the secret inner-sanctum were offered a haven to 'chase the dragon' in a safe and protected atmosphere. Darian had, however, no interest in seeking the oblivion of opium that night, not with the addictive excitement of a new adventure coursing through his veins. He was there to find the first member of his team.

Well known to Madame and her discreet staff, Darian was politely ushered through narrow winding corridors to the opium den. As they entered the main rooms, the dry, burning, odour permeating the walls and furnishings stung the eyes and throat of even Darian.

On this occasion, Darian declined the wares and glanced through the dense curling smoke to the still figures lying on piles of Chinese silk cushions or chaises-longues. Some with pipes in their hands, others in a stupor. It was not the done thing to disturb the dreamers but Darian lived by his own rules and walked openly through the rooms on his search, the smoke swirling around his coat as he moved. The man he sought was a muscular and blond and in his mid thirties, a near handsome face marred with a nose broken many times.

As he suspected, the broken-nosed man was indeed there. Adventure seeking inventor, penniless aristocrat Sir Miles Hardwick lounged deep in dreams, lying on cushions on the floor, his head resting in the lap of an exquisite Chinese girl in a turquoise cheongsam embroidered with gold dragons. She was gently stroking the man's forehead.

'Ah, Li Mei, and I thought your heart belonged only to me.'

As he expected, the girl's eyes widened in alarm, she stood up abruptly, and Hardwick's head thudded against the floor.

'So sorry, Cyrus, I am devoted only to you.'

She flung her arms around him and kissed him with passion.

'I need to borrow sleeping beauty here,' Darian laughed after returning her kiss. Li Mei's perfect face grew sad as if she knew this meant both men were off on some dangerous adventure, one they may not return from.

'I will bring you back something pretty.'

Kissing him again, Li Mei said, 'Forget any trinkets, Cyrus, just bring yourself back unharmed.'

Rubbing his head and groaning, Hardwick stirred, fighting the effects of the opium. 'How the hell did I end up on the floor with a sore head?'

He glanced up at the familiar tall figure beside him and groaned again. Cyrus Darian. No other explanation needed. 'When are we leaving?'

Darian smiled, relieved that the narcotic had not yet stifled the man's spirit of adventure. He reached down and offered a hand to assist Hardwick to his feet. The young aristocrat refused the help at first but after a couple of unsuccessful attempts at getting to his feet, reluctantly accepted Darian's help and left the premises on unsteady legs.

'Are we bringing the mesmerist?' he asked.

'Dead,' Darian replied with a slight shrug. 'Not my fault this time, he had a run in with some Russian icon thieves in St Petersburg.'

'Ronny Barlow?'

'In prison – and before you ask, I am not springing him out again.'

Hardwick shoved his fists into his duster coat as they walked through Soho. They had never seen it so deserted. Even the ubiquitous street urchins that pestered every passerby for loose change were missing. The reason was obvious: the industrial fog was at its worst. Both men quickly produced respirators from their cases, respirators that actually worked and which were a little less cumbersome than the fakes. They had been invented by Hardwick, and should have made him rich but for his heavy addiction to gambling. The machines whirred and wheezed as they fought to filter out the noxious gases from the air, and their sounds attracted attention. Soon someone or something was following them through the gloom.

Darian caught a slight whiff of sulphur beyond the scope of the respirators or the senses of an ordinary human. The entity stalking them through the narrow, gloom-laden streets was demonic.

'Keep walking,' Darian signed, a language of subtle gestures only known to his inner circle. The two men kept the same pace – there was no point in quickening their steps – concentrating on finding a suitable place for a confrontation with their unknown pursuer. There was no time to prepare a protective pentacle within a circle even a symbolic one using an athame. Demons were quick, clever and hard to deter.

Footsteps behind them quickened, paused and became the four beat clop of hooves. A shapeshifter. Another change to padding near-silence broken by the pant of a large dog or wolf.

Darian realised what was happening. He halted, spun on his heels and dropped to his knees and greeted a grey timber wolf which emerged from the smoke behind them. 'Cambion, always the show off!'

The beast's appearance shimmered, became cloudlike then reformed into the shape of a small, wiry man of undetermined age and mournful appearance. There could be no man less likely to be accused of show boating than Cambion in his human form. He was so meek and retiring as to be practically invisible in a crowd.

'I sought you out, Cyrus, as soon as I heard you had a visit from that industrialist and his Mechmen. Father had one too, luckily I was there to protect him.'

Cambion's father was a kind, elderly man of science who had taken in Cambion, a half-human, half-incubus hybrid, abandoned by his own mother, and raised the infant with love and care.

Hardwick grinned and shook his friend's hand with genuine warmth. 'And what could you do against those mechanical menaces? Fangs and talons cannot dent thick layers of bronze.'

'But their human skin can react to flea bites!' Cambion laughed, a rare sound for he was a doleful individual, loathing his hybrid inheritance.

Darian and Hardwick laughed with him as the London Peculiar swirled around them.

5

Back at Darian's home, Hardwick and Cambion made themselves comfortable in the drawing room, indulging themselves sampling vintage bottles from their host's well-stocked wine cellar. Darian was a generous if indifferent friend and allowed them any choice of fine wine and the contents of his kitchen. They warily avoided his dragoncat, remembering the sharpness of its teeth and shortness of its temper, and were relieved when Darian confined it to its own room in the cellars

The team was not complete, not for Darian at least. Finding Hardwick and Cambion was the easy part. Now Darian chose to move into the most dangerous realm possible for any mortal being.

As the others relaxed, unaware, their host sought the privacy of a secret chamber. No one but Darian could enter this place built deep in the centre of his home. Ancient talismans set into the windowless outer walls and old earth magic spells gave the circular room some protection from occult attack. As a concession to the modern age, it also had one of Hardwick's patent visualising alarum devices above the only door for surveillance. Nothing – in theory – could break in or out.

Darian removed all of his everyday clothes and put on a simple white silk robe before entering the chamber. He carried a ceremonial dagger: an athame made from intricately worked gold, studded with an emperor's ransom of finely cut rubies. Inside, a permanent pentacle within a circle made from clear quartz was set in the centre of the otherwise empty room. It also had black granite walls devoid of decoration or gaslights. Darian did not need light, his altered eyes were able to navigate easily to the centre of the protective pentacle, where he sat and began to meditate.

Time ceased to matter as his mind focused on contacting one particular entity. There was great danger in this as he prepared to lay his soul open to attack and possession from all the forces of Hell itself. A gamble whose odds even Hardwick would consider too high to consider. However in the infinite dimension of Hell, there was one and only one powerful entity which Darian could call on. He was gambling thatthis one being would answer before other monstrosities invaded the portal that he had opened and destroy him.

Already, earth-bound human souls crowded outside the door, desperate for either communication or malice. Darian ignored them. Some of their heartrending entreaties would have moved a lesser man to tears of pity. Spectral children crying for their mothers, damned souls pleading for release, lost lovers seeking their beloved – these Darian mistrusted the most. Earth-bound spirits were nearly always liars and mischief-makers. Others claimed to be the souls of those he had killed, furiously clamouring for revenge. That these were likely to be real was a possibility but again, Darian ignored them.

He concentrated on contacting the more perilous, highest dimension of the Fallen. Protection was paramount, Darian focused his entire being on surrounding himself with spectral light that flashed and glittered off the quartz pentacle. He made symbols in the air with the athame then began a whispered incantation, one taught to the Sumerians by the ancient civilisations of Africa who learnt them from the shamans of Atlantis. The words had great power and as his voice grew louder, the cadence of the primeval language echoed around the room becoming a continuous ribbon of sound. No demon, however exalted, could cross the resonance of the sound barrier uninvited – at least in theory.

Twisted shapes appeared as dark shadows, trying but failing to breach the wall of sound. Their hissing, spitting frustration poured forth in a rain of demonic curses and their sharp, venom-tipped claws raked in anger and frustration along the chamber walls giving off sparks. From their sharp-fanged mouths issued foul-smelling steam, glowing lurid yellow in the darkness. The nightmares encircled Darian, their indistinct forms sometimes merging to briefly form a greater horror before splitting apart again. Darian caught glimpses of their horrifying, evil-distorted faces, eyes wide with hate and madness before they were thrown back, screaming in rage. And these were only lowly minor demons.

One form became more distinct than the others, bent low, its limbs charred and distorted, bone-like fingers ending in cruel talons, its barbed, black bat-like wings torn and ragged. Despite the horror of its form, it was different from the others, and moved with an innate majesty of bearing. As it approached Darian, the others scuttled away cowering in submission.

The lesser demons had eyes that glared a sickly venomous green. This new arrival's eyes flashed and flickered with fiery red Hellfire. The demon passed through the incantations without hindrance and stood before Darian, just beyond the protective circle.

Slowly, painfully, it began to rise from its crouching stance. Its charred hide healed and skin of a shining golden hue formed. It finally stood upright, a noble form surrounded by waves of scintillating light. Briefly a celestial being from before the Fall stood before Darian, an angel as beautiful as anything in creation. The fiery eyes softened first to a kaleidoscope of colours from an unearthly spectrum then settled to a human shade of dark amber. Hair, more liquid silver than blond, fell to the creature's waist. Within seconds, Darian witnessed the eternally damned become briefly the angel he once had been and finally an exquisite human youth.

Belial. One of the seven High Princes of Hell.

Now came the tricky bit. Darian had to risk leaving the protection of the pentacle and cease the incantation. He held out his arms towards the demon in human form and took a leap, or rather a step, of faith. Was the old, curious and precarious bond between them still in force? If not, Darian's life was now at an end as was his immortal soul. He held his breath and waited for the answer.

All was well, Belial hugged him then turned and with a powerful, contemptuous roar dispersed the lowly demonic minions which in turn chased away the lingering earth-bound human spirits. When all had gone, Belial turned back to Darian and attempted another embrace.

'Sorry, old chap,' Darian muttered to the being with a rueful grin. 'We have visitors, I'll find you some clothes.'

Resplendent in one of Darian's charcoal silk suits with an embroidered blue waistcoat complete with gold fob watch and double Albert gold chains, the demon prince in human form sauntered into the drawing room to greet the others. His silken voice could not totally disguise the hell-spawned snarl beneath. 'Cambion! Good to see you on two legs for a change.'

The little man sighed, fighting to find a civil reply. 'Belial.'

Hardwick gave a curt nod of greeting in his direction. He never could understand the friendship between Cyrus and this monstrous being and no matter how many adventures they went on together, would never trust him. According to ancient grimoires, the demon Belial was the prince of trickery and of unnatural sexual practices among men. Hardwick would rather do without this exceedingly dubious help and not have the mocking, dangerous creature amongst them. In human form, most of Belial's great infernal power was weakened or absent, but even so, Hardwick shuddered at the thought of the terror and destruction this being could wreak on Earth as a demonic High Prince.

'We have our Fallen Angel and now we are a team.' Darian raised a glass of ruby red wine in a toast.

'Who else are you gathering?' muttered the shapeshifter to

Darian while doing his best to avoid the insolent twinkle in the full demon's amber eyes.

Darian ignored the tension: it was always the same at the early stages of a reunion. Once they had made plans and the mission was underway, these people would gel into a tight and supportive team. Well, at least they had done in the past.

'I'd like to have Mercedes with us. But I think she is out of the country.'

'Shame,' replied Hardwick, 'I always feel better with that Argentinian sharp shooting firecracker watching out for my back in a battle.'

'Pity that is all she will do for you,' added the demon, amused by Hardwick's flush of anger. 'Nothing like the pain of unrequited lust.'

'You should know all about that, Belial,' Hardwick snapped back.

Cambion's face briefly flickered with relief when he heard that the Argentinian woman was not part of the team. He lived a monk-like existence, avoiding all contact with women. He was half-incubus and though he did not suffer the uncontrollable slavering lust typical of such a creature, Cambion was certain it was deep within him, lying dormant. The thought of his demonic nature ever surfacing appalled and haunted his every waking hour and tormented his dreams. He did not trust Darian, a human who willingly and cheerfully consorted with the forces of darkness but if anyone could find a cure or a means to successfully cage his inner demon, this man could. It was the only reason he tolerated his irreverent and louche company.

'Gentleman, it is time I explained why I have brought you here tonight,' said Darian, settling down in an armchair. He waited until the others had found seats before telling them about his encounter with Zachariah P Dedman.

'He will finance this escapade but only if we have one of his team with us. I told him to take a long walk off a short pier.'

'Cyrus!' exclaimed Cambion in exasperation. Darian was wealthy and could afford to turn down remuneration for a mission but the others were not.

'Hear me out, gentlemen,' Darian raised an elegant hand then continued. 'Once I know the object of Dedman's desire, there is no reason why we cannot take it for ourselves.'

'Cyrus Darian!' Again the shapeshifter admonished him. 'Haven't you made enough enemies!'

'There are some things a gentleman cannot have enough of: beautiful women; fast horses; fine wines; and mortal enemies.' He raised a glass in Belial's direction, 'And of course ...'

'A night on the town! That is what we need to celebrate our reunion,' Darian suddenly announced, ignoring the despairing groan from the shapeshifter and uneasy sigh from Hardwick. Only Belial had leapt to his feet, eager for action. His assumed human form could experience sensations his demonic one could not and he fully intended to make the most of every moment of his summoning.

'Come now, you two,' continued Darian, 'why the dour expressions? We ought to have some fun before this adventure gets too dangerous. Or we may get too old and cynical to enjoy ourselves.'

'That is the problem, Cyrus,' the inventor interjected. 'Your idea of a good time is usually more dangerous than the adventure.'

'Like the time you thought it would be a lark to gatecrash a reception at Windsor Castle for Sultan Zog of Albania.'

'How could I resist meeting a monarch with a name like that?' Darian grinned.

'It wasn't meeting the Sultan that nearly got us all clapped in irons, it was bedding his new young wife in our own dear Queen's private chambers,' muttered Hardwick, his skin crawling as the flood of uncomfortable memories filled his mind. He had been within a hair's breadth of the Castle guards capturing him as the team fled through the Queen's gardens, pursued all the way to the River Thames and an awaiting swift steamboat.

'Did the poor lass a favour, my sterling effort for international détente and goodwill,' Darian continued, 'and we are all still here to tell the tale.'

'And who cares if there is a price on our heads in Albania? It's easy to avoid one country,' added Belial.

Darian leapt to his feet, clapping the demon on his shoulder. 'Come on, let's all head off to the city of sin and depravity. It must feel like an eternity since you had any mindless pleasure, old chap!'

Cambion visibly appeared to shrink into the chair, his morose demeanour deepening. 'Count me out, Cyrus. You would have to drag me in chains to go out with you.'

'Oh, I am sure that can be arranged, you might enjoy it.' Darian answered with a wink. 'And you, Miles – time to shake free of that ghastly English gentleman repression for a few hours?'

Hardwick muttered something under his breath; he was no stranger to the company of damsels of the night but on his own terms. An evening with Cyrus and the demon would end badly, how couldn't it?

Darian ushered them towards the door. 'That settles it. The Steam Citadel, that's the place for us tonight.'

Hardwick groaned. Just when he'd thought things could not get any worse, an evening in London's most notorious house of ill repute became Darian's agenda for the night. Of course, there was a plan behind this; the alchemist would be seeking tongues loosened by pleasure and alcohol among the Palace's wealthy but corrupt clientele. Any careless mention of Dedman's elusive object of desire could give them a useful advantage. Darian grabbed the inventor's hat, gloves and cane and threw them to him, it seemed dissent was out of the question, as usual.

Leaving a deeply grateful Cambion behind with the dragoncat as company, the three adventurers braved a walk through the deepening fog to the nearby Strand. Despite the Steam Citadel being situated in a side street it was not a discreet address that was made impossible by a near permanent crowd of protestors picketing outside the distinctive doors. A secret entrance existed for the better-known and more eminent customers but Darian enjoyed making a bold and shameless arrival through the main doors.

Many would-be visitors baulked at the prospect of fighting their way through the thronged and determined crowd. Their strategy to shame people from visiting the Citadel was an effective and successful one. Unseemly fights often broke out on the street outside, not between the protestors and customers but between protestors and the working girls furious at losing clients thanks to their interference. Luckily for all concerned, the London Constabulary turned a blind eye to these dramatics as their commander in chief was an enthusiastic regular visitor to the bawdyhouse.

For Darian and his friends, passage through the strident placard waving, churchgoing picketers was easy. Belial led the way and the malign power of his diabolic aura cleaved a path through the angry righteous mob. Whatever evil they thought was going on inside the bawdy house was nothing to his powerful demonic presence. Like Moses parting the Red Sea, they moved away from him with silent shudders without knowing why.

The front of the Citadel was infamous for a pair of steam-driven pistons, scandalously designed to be phallic in form, that pumped in and out of equally suggestive containers either side of the main door. It was impossible to openly complain about them without admitting to an impure mind. It was just working machinery after all.

Darian waved cheerily at the silenced protestors, even stooping to kiss the hand of one hatchet-faced matron armed with a mouth like a gin trap.

'That should give the baggage some interesting dreams tonight,' he joked with the others as they strode into the Citadel.

The décor inside reflected its celebration of the wonderful world of new technology with glistening whirligigs and geegaws of every shape and size whizzing with mechanical and clockwork enthusiasm. Some gizmos could even be used for pleasure among the more adventurous of the clientele. Jaunty music from a steam accordion gave the Citadel a carnival air which was also reflected in the bright, gaudy colours and many mirrored surfaces of the décor. The Steam Citadel was unashamedly designed to celebrate human vice and pleasures, cheerily cocking a snook at the sensibilities of English society and was therefore the most popular and most hated brothel in London.

Warmly greeted by the buxom Lolita Du Pinero aka Sally Lumb, the middle-aged and yet still-handsome Madame, Darian opted for a hookah and cognac in the well populated lounge while Hardwick disappeared immediately with a saucy, raven-haired stunner clad in an unfeasibly tight corset, bustle and little else. Belial after the physical deprivations of Hell, whispered in Lolita's ear and was escorted arm in arm by the Madame herself to a suite of private rooms reserved for her most athletic and adventurous customers.

Slumped across a burgundy velvet chaise longue and feigning narcotic intoxication, Darian's sharp hearing was attuned to the murmured conversations of the guests, relaxing before or after their horizontal – and sometimes vertical – exertions. After an hour, he became fascinated by a huddle of men clearly making the most of the facilities. Three were curiously wearing the same black suits, almost as a uniform. The fourth was well known to Darian, a stage magician known as The Amazing Bizarro and Fanny. Who was of course not with him tonight.

As the evening wore on, the black clad men began to angrily berate Bizarro who had sobered up and now looked trapped and afraid. One grabbed his arm in a tight grip and tried to manhandle him out of his chair causing the magician to give a high-pitched shriek of fright. The fraught transaction triggered Darian's curiosity. He wanted to know what these men wanted with a harmless chap like Bizarro. Pretending to struggle to unsteady feet, Darian lurched over and flung his arms around the magician in a display of inebriated affection, pulling him away from the others.

'Bizzy old chap! How long has it been? When was the last time we met?'

Surprised and relieved to see Darian, Bizarro returned the embrace like a drowning man grasping at straws. 'Cyrus, my dear, dear friend, how wonderful to see you.'

The other men stood and tried to step between Darian and the magician but he was too quick and manoeuvred Bizarro out of their reach.

'Come along with me, old chap,' Darian insisted loudly, 'Madame Lolita has two new ladies to entertain us, a pair of luscious Siamese contortionists that will put a smile on both our faces.'

Turning to the infuriated bullies, Darian quipped, 'Sorry gentlemen, we are taking our leave of you to find some more fragrant company. I am sure you will find something amusing here to while away the time.'

A thug reached inside his coat for a weapon but one of his companions stopped him with a curt instruction. 'Not now, Poole, we can wait until later to question Fleming about the Technomicron. We are in no rush.'

Once out of earshot, Darian relaxed. 'So old chap, what mess are you in now? I know! You have upset Fanny again and she has set her unpleasant, dark clad cousins on you.'

Still alarmed, his eyes darting around for danger, Bizarro answered, 'I have no idea who they are, Cyrus, they barged in here tonight, stopped my liaison with the lovely Agnes and her snake. They keep calling me Harry Fleming.'

Darian thought for a moment. 'There was a Harry Fleming recently at your Music Hall. He had a pathetically inept Spiritualist act. Got pelted with rotten tomatoes once too often and bolted leaving his assistant to face the torrent of abuse from the audience.'

'I can empathise with that, both me and Fanny have felt that abuse for ourselves. They don't just chuck tomatoes – had a brick once.'

Flinching at the sound of footsteps, Bizarro continued. 'Anyway, those brutes keep demanding to know the whereabouts of the Technomicron. I have no idea what they are talking about.'

Darian bustled the magician through the corridors of the Steam Citadel and out through a back exit. 'Time to make yourself and Fanny disappear for a while.'

Keeping a tight hold on his swordstick, Darian returned to the main rooms but the men were gone. Well-paid inquiries of Lolita and her girls brought no answers, nobody knew who the men in black were nor had anyone heard of the Technomicron. Intrigued, Darian waited with a bottle or two of cognac for company for Belial and Hardwick to finish their night's entertainment before tipping them into a steam cab and returning home to Mayfair.

When they arrived, the three men retired to Darian's parlour for a nightcap in front of the fire, though dawn was but an hour away. With no further information to impart over this latest quest, the evening ended with increasingly slurred remembrances of wild adventures past. Darian made an excuse and left the others to it. Such was the volatile nature of their relationship with each other, they were as likely to end up trying to kill each other as fall asleep in their chairs by the dying fire. Either way, he wanted some time alone to think.

6

The next morning, dawn attempted to break through the sullen pall of lead-coloured rain clouds. It failed. The street lights stayed on to aid workers rushing to their posts as the skies threw down a torrent of acidic rain which at least temporarily cleared away the poisonous fog. The cobbled streets were soon covered with a greasy wet glaze that caused draught horses to scrabble for footing and steam cabs to skid. The driving rain and high winds grounded all the dirigibles and only the overhead trams seemed oblivious to the weather. It was another typical October day in the capital.

Dedman arrived before noon and pounded on the front door with the brash confidence of a wealthy colonial. With his guests still alive but worse for wear for their wild night on the town, Darian answered the door after an unseemly long delay and, taking his wet coat and hat, ushered his guest into a morning room.

'So, my fine fellow. What is your answer?'

A hung-over Darian poured out strong black coffee for himself and his guest and answered, shaking his head with feigned regret. 'Same as it was before. Mr Dedman.'

'Zachariah, please …'

'Mr Dedman, I cannot put this any clearer, if I cannot choose my own people, then you will not have my services.'

The American put down his coffee cup in a brusque manner, causing the silver spoon to rattle against the bone china. He appeared to be afraid. No, more than that, terrified. His eyes darted towards the windows and doors as if afraid something would burst through at any moment. He composed himself to continue but there was no disguising the waver in his voice.

'But that is my problem. You will not be just choosing people to help on this mission. There will be *others* in your team.

You live on a dangerous edge, Darian, openly flirting with the dark side of the occult. It means nothing to me, of course. I am no saint.'

Darian was aware of a considerable change in the man's demeanour since their first encounter. The air of bonhomie had gone and in its place was a haunted wariness. He had been a big man with matching personality but he now seemed diminished in body and spirit. What had changed in such a short time?

The man continued, his once booming voice now had a nervous tremble. 'My sponsors will have nothing to do with association with "a man in league with accursed demons or their half-bred spawn". My apologies, these are their words not mine. But I do agree that the object is too dangerous to fall into the wrong hands.'

Darian's first encounter with this man was on a one to one basis. There were no others, no sponsors. Whoever these newcomers were, they had badly frightened Dedman. He laughed without humour and for added shock effect removed his tinted spectacles to reveal the full eldritch strangeness of his altered eyes.

'By Hades, you really have approached the wrong man, Mr Dedman. I am part of the forces of darkness, I am the wrong people!'

Dedman fell back in his chair and shook, only composing himself when the alchemist put the shaded glasses back on. His desperation became evident when instead of walking away, he continued to try to win Darian over.

'Just for once, could you not comply with another's demands? You will be well paid. A fortune: that I can promise you.' The man was now openly pleading and close to tears. 'This is no longer a matter of acquiring an interesting curiosity just for my collection. This object is of world threatening importance!'

'I might have dealt with you directly,' Darian lied. 'But not with mysterious sponsors who are clearly prejudiced against my colleagues.'

Defeated by Darian's intransigence, the American slumped, the picture of a broken man.

'This is worse than I thought. I have been gravely misled, sir.'

Dedman rose, preparing to leave but not before turning with a parting shot.

'I was told you were pure human, a skilled and resourceful adventurer, a man who did not mind bending the rules to achieve his ends. Someone who could accommodate my simple conditions in return for a generous recompense.'

At that moment, Belial appeared in the doorway. Wrapped only in a blood red velvet dressing gown, he languidly draped one arm around Darian's neck before speaking, his words a sultry slur. 'You did not tell me we were having guests for breakfast, Cyrus.'

'Mr Dedman was just leaving,' Darian replied, amused by the flushed expression of outrage and disgust on the man's face.

'You will regret this, Darian. My sponsors are expecting quick results. If you try to pursue this item yourself, you and your unnatural *friends* will incur the wrath of the Brothers of Satarel, they have many ways of eliminating a noisome sorcerer.'

'Alchemist, actually,' Darian corrected but was probably unheard as the man swept out of the front door clearly terrified of his own failure to raise a suitable team to find the object. With good reason, Darian had heard of the Brothers of Satarel, religious zealots operating under the name of the angel of hidden knowledge and secrets. Fanatical 'Men of God' who would not be concerned with the loss of innocent life in pursuit of their aims. Neither would Darian but at least he made no pretence of being anything but a ruthless, cold-hearted bastard. He found the Satarelites' hypocrisy loathsome.

As he turned back to the demon, Darian raised his eyebrows in amused exasperation: Belial was spinning the American's silk top hat around his index finger. With a flash from his eyes he set it on fire.

'What an ill mannered oaf to leave a gentleman's house in

such a hurry. He has not finished his coffee and left his hat and cape behind.'

Darian ignored him and sought out the shapeshifter. Cambion was still asleep, but Darian roused him by shaking his shoulder, ignoring the little man's wincing as he woke. 'Your first task in this mission, old chap. Follow Dedman and find out what it is he is seeking and anything else that can help us.'

Appearing to be glad to do something more useful than waiting around in the company of the scornful demon, Cambion readily agreed and left Darian's home.

By now the alchemist's curiosity was at an all time high, eager to hear what Cambion could discover on his flight. Whatever this thing was, Darian was determined to have it now; there was nothing so delicious as possessing something that so many others desired.

7

Cambion waited in the shadows: there must be no observers to his shameful transformation, his human form giving in to the legion of demonic beasts locked within him. How he longed to be without this curse, this foul inheritance: just an ordinary human being.

He crouched low and first became smoke, then the smoke coelesed into a peregrine hawk, swift and sharp-sighted. He flew fast and high above the crowded streets, soon catching up with Dedman's conveyance. Cambion hoped the journey would be short. The longer he remained a hawk, the more the alien mind of the bird merged with his. This sense of losing his precious humanity terrified the shapeshifter. What would happen if he stayed in beast form too long? Would the animal, at ease in its own skin, overcome the haunted, unhappy human? It had nearly happened before when in wolf form. The confidence and fearless courage of the wild predator was intoxicating, it would have been so easy to remain a wolf.

To his relief, Dedman's carriage pulled up outside an imposing fortress-like edifice. Once a well-appointed Knightsbridge mansion it was now an ugly block of complex defences all designed to keep brute force out. A crude mishmash of heavy steel mechanisms, hissing blue-grey steam and oily grey smoke. Nothing like Hardwick's beautifully designed and crafted works: his devices were effective and efficient works of art forged from bronze, brass and copper, finished with polished mahogany. The American obviously believed he had something significant to fear if it necessitated living in such a cold bleak place.

Armed servants hurried out to meet the carriage and a well-dressed, statuesque young woman greeted Dedman with a kiss on both cheeks. The peregrine swooped low and perched close to the main door, well hidden by profuse bushy laurel growing around the outer marble porch.

Cambion listened as Dedman and the woman spoke but did not change form and follow them inside as a mouse or fly. That is what Darian would expect him to do, but the shapeshifter was not a risk taker or an adventurer. He only cooperated with the man's wild schemes in the desperate hope that Darian might find a cure for Cambion's affliction. Who else could?

The Technomicron. That word again was all Cambion brought back from his eavesdropping flight following Zachariah P Dedman. Something the American whispered to a young woman, possibly a lover, at the door as he hurried back into his London home. Cambion had flown back swiftly, returning to human form to ring Darian's doorbell. As he did so he steeled himself for another encounter with the caustic-tongued demon, the alchemist's pet, friend, lover? Whatever Belial was, he was an unwelcome presence. A constant reminder of Cambion's own loathed mixed heritage. Darian ushered him in with much enthusiasm, his hands shaking as he guided him into the drawing room.

'Technomicron. I had never heard that term before this week,' Darian said, 'but it does sound fascinating. Dangerous even.'

'And anything the Brethren of Satarel wants, Darian just has to have,' Belial added as he sauntered into the room causing the shapeshifter to shudder involuntarily.

Shards of glass window shattered into the room, one explosion then another and another from three small spherical grenades, their clockwork mechanisms clattering a countdown to detonation. Belial's demonic speed saved them: he scooped up the explosive devices and returned them at speed back through the shattered window. They exploded a few feet in front of Darian's home, incinerating a large plane tree which had been there for many centuries. Darian and the demon ran out into the street, rapidly joined by a well-armed Hardwick. He threw a differential combustium to Darian but there was no sign of an assailant.

'There must be someone close by!' snapped Hardwick. 'There was nothing occult about those bombs.'

Apart from startled locals, the street was empty. Hardwick and Darian questioned anyone prepared to stand still, but most had scurried away in fright and confusion. None of those left remaining to gawp had seen anything untoward or were prepared to be witnesses to anything.

'That alone is a clue, I suspect,' ventured Darian. 'A Mechman or something occult would have stood out, there would always be a frightened person ready to speak after seeing something like that. It must have been an attacker able to blend into the crowd, someone well dressed, possibly hidden within a passing carriage.'

Hardwick looked about. 'Where is the shapeshifter?'

Concerned, he abandoned the search for the attackers and ran back into Darian's house. He found Cambion collapsed on the floor with a jagged shard of glass buried in his chest. The shapeshifter was alive, just, with an alarming amount of blood spreading from the wound.

'No doctors,' Cambion gasped, 'even if it means I lose my life. I beg you, no doctors.'

Hardwick nodded a curt assent with great reluctance: any man of medicine would swiftly detect the man's demonic hybrid metabolism.

The others joined Hardwick in the fight to save him. Darian rushed to his laboratory and returned with phials of elixirs. One he poured down Cambion's throat straight away sending him into a deep, death-like sleep.

'That will buy us some time to fix him up ourselves,' Darian muttered as he looked around at the glass-showered mess and smoking ruin of his tree. But for Belial's swift reaction, this could so easily have included their smoking bodies as well.

'It wasn't the accursed Satarel zealots.' Darian's lean face tightened in fury. 'This has all the signs of clumsy operatives. The holy madmen would know how to correctly wind up simple detonation devices and get the timing right. They have been operating long enough to learn.'

He looked across to Belial and Hardwick. 'Whatever this damned Technomicron is, someone else other than the zealots does not want us to have it.'

'Or live,' added Belial with a demonic snarl, temporarily marring the illusion of human beauty.

The team volunteered Hardwick with his skill at precision engineering to try to repair the shapeshifter's wound. It was a deep gash but had not punctured any vital organs. The greatest danger to his life was from blood loss and infection. Darian sterilised a needle and some fine sewing thread and handed it to the inventor who glared at him in frustration.

'This is insane, man. I make mechanisms. You are the one with scientific knowledge.'

'I am an alchemist, not a physician,' Darian replied with a bored sigh, this was getting repetitive. 'You make highly balanced, complex mechanisms. Sorting out the working of Cambion's flesh and blood will be easy for you.'

Muttering curses, Hardwick continued to do his best for the amiable Cambion. The mildest, kindest man he had ever met despite his terrifying parentage and someone who should stay well away from Cyrus Darian, preferably by at least a whole continent. Hardwick's innate neatness, precision and courage was put to its ultimate test, he repaired what he could and sewed Cambion's wound up with great skill.

Darian patted him on the back. 'You are in the wrong profession, old chap. I doubt if a Harley Street quack could have done such a fine job.'

Hardwick glared up at the alchemist with a look close to hatred. In fact he'd decided long ago it was impossible not to love and hate the man at the same time. Perhaps it was only hate combined with fascination: the lure of Darian's deadly charisma. And shamefully also wealth, Darian had paid off the inventor's debts many times.

'You should have found some sort of medic among your unsavoury contacts, a bit of mumbo jumbo might have a better prognosis than this bit of ham-fisted butchery!'

'I doubt whether I would reach the end of the street alive, Hardwick,' Darian countered. 'I suspect all of London's sub strata is being ruthlessly scrutinised by the forces after this Technomicron.'

'So you will let him die?' Hardwick thundered.

'You have done your best, Miles. That is the nature of how we live our lives.' Darian turned to walk away, 'Or have you lost your edge and become a mild mannered pen pusher?'

He walked to a cabinet by the furthest wall, brushed away the shattered glass and found himself an unopened and intact bottle of cognac. He took a generous swig from the bottle and threw it across to Belial.

'We will keep Cambion's wound clean and give him a place to rest and recover. The rest is up to his hybrid metabolism. Incubi are tough bastards and Cambion also has his unlikely but strong faith in the Christian God.'

Hardwick and the demon carried the little shapeshifter up to a spare bedroom and made him as comfortable as they could. The sleeping draught was still in command of Cambion's mind and body which eased their task.

Darian did his best to tidy and repair the damaged room but the ease and near success of the attack concerned him. He had spent too long protecting his home against occult attacks and the brute force of the human world had exposed his vulnerability.

No sooner had he cleaned up the last fragments of glass and helped Belial secure stout wooden planks over the open window when they heard the loud hiss of steam brakes outside the house followed by a man's frantic exhortation for someone to make great haste. Darian recognised the voice as a deeply frightened Dedman. He reached his front door just as the American began to pound away at it with the force of the pursued.

'By all that you hold dear, I beg you let me in,' Dedman pleaded unnecessarily, as the alchemist calmly opened the door and ushered him and his companion inside. A young woman, her face shocked and starkly pale, accompanied the American. Her hands trembling as she clutched a small carpetbag in front of her like a shield, one that could fight off nothing beyond a few desultory wasps on a picnic.

'I implore you to give sanctuary to my daughter!'

Darian shrugged and took them through to a drawing room. 'Sanctuary? Have you seen the mess made of my home not an hour before your arrival? I doubt if my protection will be of any worth.' He paused before adding, 'If I was offering it.'

As he settled them in the room, Darian took notice of Dedman's daughter. She had inherited her father's haughty patrician presence but there was no doubting her Junoesque femininity. Nor her pride as she became aware of Darian's scrutiny and returned his interest with a flash of withering contempt. Darian liked that. The woman was no simpering hothouse flower. Clearly she had fled her home with no preparation, her copper and russet hair had become unpinned and tousled, her day gown partially unbuttoned, and she was wearing neither a coat or gloves.

'Athena and I thought nothing could get through our defences,' Dedman began, his whole body shaking in delayed shock. He paused to give Hardwick a wan smile of gratitude as he entered the room with a tray of strong spirits and a pot of coffee.

Hardwick decided to tell the newcomers of the attack on Darian's home, to give them time to recover. If only there was a female, even if only a maidservant in this household to help Dedman's daughter.

'Such a brutish attack would have made little impact on my home,' the American ventured after hearing the man out, 'nor was it the work of those religious maniacs. Someone had the power and ability to summon up Wraith and force them to do their will.'

All eyes involuntarily went to Darian who raised his hands in mock surrender. 'Caught red handed. What else could I do? I was bored.'

'This is serious man,' an unimpressed Dedman muttered, 'we would not have fled here if we thought you were involved.'

'What happened?' Hardwick urged, eager to take the attention of the alchemist and not a hundred percent certain he was not involved in the attack on Dedman. Darian was perverse and unpredictable at all times even towards his allies, Hardwick would never use the word 'friends'.

Athena answered, her voice had a melodious low timbre and she was clearly recovering from her fright.

'It happened so quickly, gentlemen,' she began, pointedly addressing Hardwick and not Darian. 'We were dressing for breakfast when the whole house began to freeze. The hearths were lit, flames still flickered but could not combat the terrible cold.'

She shuddered at the memory before continuing, 'An unbearable feeling of terror descended on us. We lost poor, faithful old Jeffries straight away to a fatal seizure.'

'Your dog?'

'Our butler, Mr Darian.'

Athena sighed and shook her head, 'We could hear the servants screaming from the floors below, such a terrible sound. Then the, the *things* came, straight through the floors and walls. They looked like living black smoke with hideous, tortured faces filled with hatred and spite.'

'Wraith,' Dedman took up the story before his daughter's pretence of steely composure crumpled. 'The spirits of evil magicians who tried to extend their lives by unnatural means and have become little more than hate incarnate.'

'And harmless,' interjected Darian. 'All they can do is whoosh around looking insane and malevolent. They are only spooks.'

'How dare you sir!' Athena was furious; she thought about slapping his smirking face then remembered they were seeking this infuriating man's help. 'They killed Jeffries!'

'Jeffries' weak heart killed Jeffries,' Darian answered with indifference. 'The greater danger is that there is someone out there with the ability to raise and control Wraith. That might have been just a warning to back off, as was our barrage of grenades.'

Darian returned from his place by the fire and sat opposite the Dedmans. 'It appears we have another player in the game. Isn't it about time you told me all about the Technomicron?'

'I will tell you what I know, Darian, and it is not a great deal.'

Darian signalled to Hardwick to bring in the demon. Up against at least three sets of foes, he had to work with a team, and with Cambion's injury, he was already likely to be one man down. He enjoyed Dedman's discomfort at the arrival of Belial, his illusion of humanity did not convince them nor did they approve of the demon's over familiar and unseemly manner as he perched on the edge of the settle and draped an arm along the back of it behind Darian, an almost possessive and provocative gesture.

'My sources told me about a book. Discovered recently. Full of old magic. Deep, deep old magic. Its finder died recently before he could use it but rumours say he planned to fuse the book with modern technology to greatly enhance its intensity. It would then become world threatening. Now there is some deadly scramble to find it.'

Dedman leant forward, his hands together in a prayer like gesture. 'And it must be found and destroyed.'

8

A vertical travelator carried Darian to an observatory built above the main house. He needed time and space to think but neither was forthcoming anywhere else in his increasingly crowded home now it was under near siege conditions. Here he could ponder his situation without distraction.

It would take too long to make Dedman's home safe against occult attack and the same level of difficulty applied to the effort required to make his own home proof against man-made force. The only safe place on Earth was the Lady's ever-moving Emporium: surely it would be impossible for any enemy to predict where it would materialise next? But Darian did not trust any alliance with his lover. He had left her with a satisfied smile on her lips, her body still quivering with pleasure but ice in her eyes. Darian knew that Lady Teknoligi would want the Technomicron just as fervently as he did.

That left him all but trapped in a damaged house with a gravely wounded shapeshifter and two vulnerable civilians relying on him for protection. Beyond what little knowledge he had on the mysterious book, Dedman was of no further use. His daughter would have made a challenging conquest but there was no time for dalliance. So she too was out of the equation for the moment.

It worried him that the religious lunatics had not yet made a move to neutralise his team. Their prime target would be Belial: high in the upper echelons of Hell and therefore a trophy to hunt and destroy. With the demon out of the way Darian's chances of staying alive would decrease dramatically and his hopes to obtain the book even more so.

What to do, what to do? His mind raced but found no answers. This vacillation had never happened before and he had to fight hard to prevent it from triggering a crippling panic attack, a scourge that had plagued his life.

With perfect timing, a figure appeared in the doorway and golden eyes gleamed from the threshold.

'You are tense and troubled my friend,' Belial murmured, voice silken, seductive. Soundlessly he crossed the observatory and began to massage the tense muscles in Darian's shoulders. 'Do you want the woman, would that help you relax?'

'The only thing that will help me relax is to know exactly who is attacking us and how to stop them.'

The demon stopped working on Darian's shoulders and stepped back. 'Then I suggest you stop sulking up here with the pigeons and their crap and help me and Miles decide how to take the battle to our enemies. Flush them out and look them straight in the eye.'

'Know thine enemy?'

'Of course,' agreed the demon. 'And then destroy them.'

Downstairs, the troubled fugitives were in dispute with each other. Left alone while Hardwick went to check on the injured shapeshifter, the Dedmans, father and daughter, began to argue.

'This is a mistake, Father. That man is a nightmare and will not protect us. In fact, I do not want his dubious help.'

Athena Dedman had recovered enough to want to leave. Whatever nightmare her father had got them into, Cyrus Darian was no knight in shining armour and had made no promise to help them. The aristocratic Miles Hardwick seemed decent enough and appeared to be a gentleman but she doubted appearances stood for much in this deviant household. The inventor was allied to Darian and his strange 'companion' and that made him equally suspect.

'My precious, what else can we do?' Dedman had not regained his imposing stature. Love and fear for his daughter had further weakened him. In truth, he had fled his home with no plan but to escape the Wraith, assuming them to be supernatural foes the alchemist could easily deal with. To discover that Darian also was under attack had been another blow.

'Cyrus Darian is a degenerate and oblivious to anyone but himself.'

'True, Athena, but he has so many darned useful resources to call on when dealing with the occult.'

An elegant eighteenth century skeleton clock on the mantelpiece chimed. It was one am. With no sign of their reluctant host, Dedman made his daughter as comfortable as possible on a velvet upholstered Chesterfield before settling for what was left of the night on a nearby armchair. He had thought he would feel safer in Darian's house but the opposite was true.

At some time during the night, Hardwick slipped out of the house and by less conspicuous horse drawn Hansom cab, returned to his workshop built on all that was left of the once generous London estates of his family. The workshop, fabricated by knocking through a row of Regency mews, once served one of Hardwick's mansions near Hyde Park.

Throughout the journey, he questioned his motives for getting involved with Darian and his insane, dangerous world again. Hardwick was on edge, suspicious of every vehicle clattering or huffing through the near empty late night streets of the capital. There was every chance some dastardly foe followed the cab, waiting for some idiot to leave the Mayfair stronghold alone. Of course he had to be that idiot.

Though an undisputed genius in his world of engineering marvels of new technology, Hardwick was no match for the quick wit and mercurial brilliance of the alchemist. Using some magic of personality, Darian always managed to talk him into tagging along in his wake. This time was no different – or was it? Could the presence of the beautiful and fascinating Athena Dedman be another deciding factor?

This adventure or whatever it could be more accurately

called – suicidal folly being the first to spring to his mind – was unlike any other he had undertaken with Darian. This was no thrilling excursion to foreign climes to obtain some rare and esoteric artefact. No seemingly endless days and nights spent in his workshops and the alchemist's laboratory seeking some new and exciting discovery. This was all about being the vulnerable centre of attention from malign forces from throughout London. This was no fun at all.

Tapping on the roof with his cane, Hardwick halted the cab some distance from the workshop and after paying the driver, waited until the Hansom had rattled out of sight. Slipping into a shadowed doorway, he waited and listened for any sign of a pursuer. Satisfied he was alone, Hardwick walked to the well-protected mews and with an ingenious wrist device of his own invention, unlocked the tall, wrought iron gates. Nothing else would allow them to open – in fact any form of brute force only strengthened their resistance. The treated metal bars were another Hardwick/Darian collaboration, one they were keeping for themselves for now.

Once inside, Hardwick wound up the trigger mechanisms that brought the building to life. From this one action of manpower, powerful generators hissed and began to turn, cogs ground into life, rows of lights flashed and flickered. This was his world, a gleaming palace of shining copper and burnished brass, of measured forces and rational calculations. As far from the bizarre, irrational occultism surrounding Cyrus Darian as he could be.

This was the only world Hardwick wanted to inhabit, one considered unseemly for an English aristocrat. Not for him the mud and blood of the hunting and shooting season, the brain-sapping tedium of the summer cricket field or languorous days at sailing regattas at Cowes or on the higher reaches of the Thames. The river still clear of the industrial poisons poured into it further down. He could not abide the prissiness of ballet or comprehend the caterwauling of opera.

The only music which was pleasant to his ears was the chugging rhythm of smooth running pistons, the thrum of finely tuned machinery and the hiss and whistle of controlled steam. Hardwick loved the smells too: the tang of polished copper and brass, pungent aromas of oil, smoke and steam. Nothing could compare to the satisfaction of taking an idea, developing it into models and then watching it become full size, shining, functioning reality. So much so, that he would always do the final polishing of every machine or device himself, enjoying the sensation of bringing the metal to a mirror-like shine and satin smoothness beneath his fingers. Darian had often joked that the inventor loved the feel of polished metal as he revelled in a woman's soft, warm skin: an exaggeration of course.

By day, the workshops were a bustle of industrious activity, the finest artisans and smiths Hardwick could gather from throughout the United Kingdom and Empire all working to bring his inventions to life. All paid for by Cyrus Darian. Hardwick realised he was being a fool questioning why he always fell into line with the alchemist's adventures. How could he refuse the man who held the purse strings? The alternative was ruin and penury or becoming a drone of the government. Many times they had offered him generous financial backing: how could they not want a man of Hardwick's genius? Forging a growing empire needed new weapons, new means of transport and communication.

Hardwick knew this would be a form of financial slavery for him, no longer owner of his creations, no longer master of his conscience. Cyrus Darian gave him complete freedom to work on what he wanted to, when he wanted to. The only thing he asked in return was Hardwick's company on the occasional expedition. It was a price he had willingly accepted and never questioned. Until now. Now, some deep, self-preserving instinct cried out in warning. Anything to do with this book was iniquitous.

He walked through to his research area and, using the same wrist device, opened a sturdy cabinet where he stored weapons of his own design. Cause and effect. These beautiful, deadly things had a purpose and their effect could be predicted and measured. They were an antidote to the bizarre and irrational world of Cyrus Darian.

By five am, the inventor returned to Darian's Mayfair home, waking the fitfully slumbering household and no doubt most of the street with the explosively loud mechanisms of his steam coach.

Bleary eyed, the others greeted him in the hallway.

'I bring an Accelerated Momentum Fragmentiser for all of us,' announced Hardwick with some pride. 'Perhaps the right talisman or spell can block all this airy-fairy stuff of yours, Cyrus, but nothing stops a finely tuned AMF!'

9

Darian berated himself as he went through another marathon session locked in his library. 'Focus man. Focus!' He did not expect any mention of a Technomicron in the ancient grimoires – it was clearly a recently fashioned name – but he strove to find details of any missing ancient book. Something of enough power to attract so much attention.

Downstairs, the formidable Athena Dedman attempted to take over the household. She had ordered in a supply of food, hired a cook and a nurse to take care of the recovering Cambion, but had at least stopped short of taking on a lady's maid and a valet. Darian was furious but accepted that the siege-like situation needed the practicality of order and some decent food for his assistants. Even Belial in his human form needed to eat. Leaving her to it and therefore too preoccupied to meddle or annoy him, Darian was free to study.

He reconsidered the name Technomicron, so close in structure to the Necromicron. The Necromicron were ancient tomes, the most feared of which being four copies of an original pre-Sumerian grimoire containing demonic secrets and incantations. Many believed a demon wrote the first book but Darian had never believed this, his theory later backed up by Belial: demons had far better ways to torment humanity and were not known for their love of literature.

What was certain was that the grimoires were created to bring great occult power. But it was also said that they would cause insanity in anyone too weak who attempted to possess them. Legend said the first – and thankfully lost – book was written on the skins of the first humans and written in their children's blood. The four copies were no less dramatic in origin and manufacture. Savonarola had burnt one in 1497 at the infamous Bonfire of the Vanities in Renaissance Florence along with countless other precious works of pre-Christian art and learning. Darian frowned as he considered all that had been lost in the flames of ignorance and bigotry. Savonarola – What a sanctimonious rear end of a pig!

One book remained locked securely in the Vatican and the others? Darian knew one copy was in the safe possession of a wise and beneficent mage, Artor Voravian, whose location was unknown to anyone. The man was, however, in frequent correspondence with Darian and he had made no mention of the loss of something so dangerous. The other, the notorious missing Necromicron of Zurich, remained undiscovered despite Darian's best efforts over many years. Could this terrible tome be at the heart of the Technomicron? One central theme of the Necromicron was rumoured to be ultimate control of the souls of the dead: literally turning spectres into slaves unable to refuse any command.

A chill passed across Darian's heart. All he had to work on was a fanciful name, but if allied to what was known of its potential antecedent, then the world was indeed in serious trouble and his desire to possess it grew.

A shimmer of familiar chill air beside him announced a visitor.

'Cyrus, you look like a muck snipe. Take a bath, change your clothes and join us for luncheon. You haven't eaten for days. Or bathed … and they say the denizens of the Inferno smell bad.'

Ruefully, Darian rubbed a hand over the growth of stubble on his chin. 'Who exactly have I summoned from Hell? A mighty fallen angel or a fussy old nurse maid?'

'You know exactly who you have summoned – and why.' Belial's voice became a low purr, 'But none of that will happen with you looking like this!'

Darian raised his hands in mock submission but before he attended to his ablutions, he drew Belial closer.

'Do not alarm the others with this knowledge yet, but I think the missing Necromicron of Zurich could be at the heart of this book.'

A flash of hell fire briefly flickered across Belial's amber eyes and his smile widened.

'A compendium of ultimate wickedness. No wonder so many humans want it for themselves. Now, this could be fun!'

Darian took his place at the head of the table, suddenly ravenous as delicious cooking smells wafted up from the kitchens. Maybe it was time to rethink the no staff rule.

'How long have I been up there?'

'Three weeks,' stated Belial solemnly.

'Liar!' exploded Hardwick.

'Er, demon?' returned Belial with a grin.

Exasperated, Athena Dedman turned to her host. 'You have been locked away for three days, Mr Darian.'

A selection of hot food arrived via the dumb waiter and with no one else volunteering, Athena distributed it around the table with barely disguised ill temper. As soon as it was placed before him, Darian began to wolf down a thick broth generous with lumps of good beef.

'Mr Darian, please!' Grossly affronted, Athena slammed down a bowl. 'My father hasn't said grace yet.'

'Don't let me stop him,' Darian replied without raising his head, continuing to devour the soup.

Dedman did his best to sooth her. 'My dear, this is not our home and we have no right to impose our beliefs on our host and his guests.'

An ear-piercing scream from upstairs followed by frantic footsteps interrupted further discussion. Athena leapt to her feet in concern but the men, including Dedman continued their meal. Whimpering in distress, the nurse rushed down stairs and past the dining room doors. The front of her dress had been ripped and torn. Hauling the front door open, she fled into the street.

Darian paused from his broth. 'I see Cambion is recovering well,' he observed.

Hardwick stifled his amusement, not wanting to upset Athena further. He found her both fascinating and beautiful.

Belial didn't and laughed out loud.

'If you want to run after her, don't let me stop you Miss Dedman,' the alchemist continued. 'It was your choice to hire a female nurse without consulting me. Her distress is therefore your responsibility.'

'You are a heathen, a cad and a coward, sir!'

Darian answered her with a broad, dazzling smile and continued his meal. He would need his strength. Later that day he planned to slip away from the others and enter the curious world of the grotesque.

Another scream, this time from the kitchens. Cyrus put down his spoon and sighed.

'Which dolt let Misha out?'

10

The phrase *There is a new exhibit at Randalfo's* was used by respectable gentlemen as a euphemism for visiting their kept women or 'dollymops'. When challenged by suspicious wives, these men could bring them to Randalfo's Astounding Museum of the Macabre as proof of its existence. Its curator had cunningly placed some of his most ghastly exhibits in the first hall, the jars of preserved deformed babies, sad little souls with two heads or eight limbs floating forever in cloudy formaldehyde. Their sightless eyes turned to gaze at the daily lines of horrified gawpers. This was enough to send the wives scuttling out holding their hands over their mouths, looking for somewhere to be sick or faint. The wives never questioned their husbands again.

Darian decided to forego his open and vocal dislike of the steam trams and endure the journey across town from his Belgravia home to Southwark and the museum. His enemies would not expect this – at least he hoped not. Every step towards the gigantic travelator that carried passengers up to the station was unpleasant. As he neared it, he could hear the steam wheeze and deafening chug and clang of two enormous wheels that propelled people vertically to the station in an open metal cage.

They were not infallible, only six months before, an explosion at the Embankment station had sent one of the huge steel wheels toppling onto nearby tenement homes, killing a hundred people. Another dozen were hurled to their doom from the travelator cage. The highest death toll was on the tram system itself as fully laden carriages toppled into the Thames taking a thousand people prematurely to their maker.

Pushing aside morbid recollections of this tragic event, Darian steeled himself to enter the cage, joining a long queue of people sharing his unease. The system was the fastest and cheapest way to cross the capital, it also had an added bonus. On this cool October afternoon, a passenger could rise above the city's near permanent gloom and see blue sky, white clouds and distant views of green from Epping Forest and Hampstead Heath. For many, that was worth enduring the added frisson of possible danger. Darian took an inner seat in a first class carriage and gritted his teeth as he prepared to travel above London's rooftops.

As the carriage rattled and swayed its way above the city, Darian amused himself by openly reading other people's newspapers. The English always hated that and huffed and shuffled their periodicals in wordless disapproval but were usually too repressed to actually voice their disapproval.

Every headline told the same story: the plans by a consortium of businessmen and members of the aristocracy to build vast machines to blow the poisoned air away from London and out to sea. Such grandiose and often absurd schemes were commonplace and like most, would come to nothing. It gave the English something to moan about beyond the weather, Darian mused, giving a cheeky wink and grinning at a puce-faced businessman sitting opposite. That was another thing that reduced them to apoplexy, over familiarity from someone they had not been formally introduced to. The English were so easy to annoy.

A chill ran up his spine as one lurid headline caught his attention – the alarming murders of three performers from the Jolly Japes Music Hall in Clapham. The mutilated bodies of spiritualist Harry Fleming, a magician known as the Amazing Bizarro and his glamorous assistant Fanny, aged fifty-four, were all found on the same day but in three different locations. Suspicion was focused on any jealous rivals eager for a headline spot at the popular Jolly Japes. Darian doubted the constabulary would be looking for a man named Poole and the two other sombrely clad villains. He could not envision what manner of music hall act they could be part of. Knife throwers? Mentalists? Corps du Ballet?

Poor old Bizarro and Fanny, harmless wielders of playing cards, strings of coloured handkerchiefs and scruffy, laudanum-quietened doves. As for Harry Fleming, couldn't one of his spirit guides have warned him of the danger? Clearly they were keen for him to join them on the other side.

There was a whoomp and a dull bang, and all heads turned at the sound of a distant explosion. It was another everyday aspect of London life: a dirigible collision. Passengers gasped in horror as the gondolas of two high-speed private airships entangled high above the fog line, an explosion of highly inflammable gas illuminating their death throes. They were too far away to hear the screams of the doomed aviators, their crew and passengers or even those from the people down below hit by burning debris. Luckily it was above the fog. A dirigible exploding at low level igniting the fog when at its most toxic was a nightmare which haunted every Londoner. Maybe the timing of this latest accident would help the consortium get approval for its vast artificial gale machines.

Like everyone else in the carriage, the businessman opposite stood up to watch the unfolding aerial drama, dropping his newspaper onto his seat. Darian casually picked it up and sat back, legs crossed, and perused the pages for scandal, confident that this scion of the English middle classes would do nothing to object beyond tut tutting under his breath. A member of the upper or lower classes would attempt to knock Darian's block off. The alchemist reasoned he was doing the man a great favour. Another long, tedious day spent scratching in ledgers with a quill pen transformed into a talking point. The day some wretched street ahab had ignored a human tragedy to steal his newspaper.

On alighting from the travelator, Darian pushed through the milling crowds of passengers, all busy recalling the horror they had witnessed above the city. Southwark was an old part of

London, untouched by the Great Fire and still in possession of some half timbered buildings and the narrow streets that went with such an old heritage, all overlooked by the medieval Southwark Cathedral. It was not a picturesque area, with squalor and overcrowding and many buildings in parlous states of ruin and decay. It had improved greatly though, Darian recalled a time when vast heaps of human ordure lay piled on every street and cess-filled drains flooded to knee height on the streets.

Reaching London Road, Darian paused to read the latest bill of performers on the newly rebuilt South London Palace, a popular music hall. The original had burned down, no doubt because its design, curiously resembling a Roman Catholic chapel, had offended the large Irish populace of the area. The new building could seat four-thousand people and was rightly famed for its excellent circuses, ballets and spectacles which Darian enjoyed greatly. He was well acquainted with many of the performers – dogs, acrobats and magicians, alongside operatic tenors and marvels such as Otto the Bicycle Wonder of the Age – including, of course, the prettiest chorus girls.

His destination lay down the same road, one already filling up with a queue of people waiting to be shocked and appalled. On arrival at Randalfo's, he strode past the queue, ignoring the harrumphs of disapproval, and walked straight through the turnstile without paying. He headed directly to Randalfo Walpurgis' private sanctum in the basement level beneath the exhibit halls.

To get there he needed to pass through the chambers of exhibits but Darian was well used to the horrors on show: real and cleverly bogus, he had no interest in them. He passed without viewing the mermaid babies and embryo dragons in glass jars, the zoological displays of stuffed unicorns and a minotaur, the cases of biological deformity and gruesome instruments of torture. Oblivious to the display, depicting victims of the guillotine and the death of Joan of Arc. Popular with the paying public and the most visited was a graphic recreation of the fate of Guy Fawkes as they hung, drew and quartered the wretch. Ghouls, Darian called the gawpers: they should be on display themselves.

Randalfo was born to be master of the grotesque. Any other profession would not have suited his cadaverous demeanour, with a pale, white face and dark, shadowed, sunken eyes. Bald for many years, he was tall, with a pronounced stoop and an unfortunate habit of wringing his long bony fingers. Despite his unfortunate appearance he was proud and vain and no longer mixed with his visitors after being mistaken for an exhibit one time too many. The man was surprised but not alarmed at Darian's abrupt entrance through a hidden door.

'Ah, Cyrus my dear boy, are you still holding a candle up to the Devil?'

'Of, course. I never change, Randalfo, old chap,' Darian answered truthfully. He flinched away as the man's bone-like finger attempted to touch his face and hair.

'Not one wrinkle, not one grey hair,' Randalfo mused with a dry chuckle. 'Carry on like this my lad and you will be welcome to join my little family.'

Shuddering, Darian shook his head. He would cut his own throat before becoming one of Randalfo's Family of Others, a secret troupe of living exhibits who spent their lives in the museum's basement catacombs on show to those who could pay a higher price. Whose bodies would carry on making Randalfo rich long after their deaths by joining their compatriates in jars.

'Was there anyone in particular you have come to see?' Randalfo bade him sit down beside his impressive seventeenth century walnut desk. 'You are not a man who comes here to gawp at my poor unfortunates.'

'Is Aayushi still alive?'

'Just.'

Darian fetched a bag of gold sovereigns from his coat and dumped it in front of the museum owner. 'There is extra here if I can see her in a private room.'

The thought of walking through a throng of lost souls, kept safe and well but as curiosities did not appeal, but high though the cost of Randalfo's protection was, Darian needed it. He did not wish to be *changed* by the souls. To end up with another head growing from his chest or a single central eye. To have scales and gills and be forced to live in a tank of seawater. Or to be recreated as a snake man with no arms and legs and with an elongated sinuous body.

Aayushi entered on Randalfo's arm, her head and body shrouded in layers of faded, ragged grey sari silk. Her hand was as thin, brown and withered as an Egyptian mummy. Once made comfortable on a chaise longue, Randalfo discreetly left. Cyrus Darian paid well and was not a man to be crossed or short changed.

Darian took Aayushi's hand and spoke to her in her native Hindi.

'*Aayushi, is that man treating you well?*'

The old woman nodded, but her movements were frail, faltering as was expected of the oldest living human, the oldest that had ever existed. She gave Darian's hand the slightest of squeezes.

'*Beloved boy, I continue to exist as my punishment from the Gods. You have not forgotten your promise to me when they finally relent and give me peace?*'

'*Never, mother, you know I will keep my word.*'

Aayushi gave a sigh, the sad sound of a breeze sifting through a ruined temple. '*You give my life its only ray of hope. How can I help you today?*'

The old woman produced a small bowl carved from clear quartz from her robes and waited for Darian's questions. Other petitioners to the once famed Oracle of Varanasi were allowed only one. There would be no limit of questions to the man who promised her a respectable Hindu funeral. Cyrus Darian had vowed he would never allow Randalfo to make her one of his post-mortem exhibits. He looked away discreetly as the old woman moved her veil aside and, lifting the bowl to her eyes, wept tears into the crystal.

There must be great mystic power in the Oracle's tears, but any temptation to take them was tempered by the knowledge that any thief would be cursed. A terrible punishment from the gods that not even Darian could deflect. While she lived, Aayushi's knowledge was freely given to him, there was no need to risk the wrath of deities. He had to be careful, Aayushi's answers were always truthful and there were questions that he did not want the answer to: the true fate of his parents; when he would die; and whether he would ever be reunited with his wife.

'What do you seek, my son?'

'Madhu, you already know.'

'And that gives me great sorrow. Continue on this path and you will indeed possess the Technomicron but it will destroy you unless you destroy it first.'

'Was I right about its origin: the Necromicron?'

'Yes.'

Darian was knocked to the floor as a huge explosion shook the museum, followed by an eternity of shocked silence, and then terrible screams. Darian swore. The Oracle had also fallen. He scrambled to his feet and helped her to rise as he tried to work out what had happened. The sound came from upstairs at the front of the building, and a fire could trap the Family in the basement and burn them to death.

Something approached on swift, hammering feet, a Mechman? No, he was wrong – many Mechmen. He had left his home armed only with the hidden Deringer and a swordstick. And a powerless Asgard ring. God's Teeth but he could be a fool sometimes.

He had a choice, let the metal-enhanced power of mighty minions beat him to a pulp, or hide. Not that much of a choice in fact. Darian gently scooped up the Oracle and hurried to the secret door to the home of the Family of Others.

11

As Darian burst through the door, the swipe of a tree branch sent him sprawling. His head spun as he saw Aayushi being gently ushered away by the Others and a furious tree man standing above him. The unfortunate's skin was covered in a rock hard coating that looked for all the world like the bark of a tree. Across the hall, a fragile voice called for calm.

'Our mother says you must not be harmed.'

At least that was what Darian thought he said through the heavy growths covering his face. Darian ignored his assailant's proffered hand and rose unsteadily to his feet. Of course the members of the Family of Others were on their guard. They had heard the explosion and, unable to leave their sanctuary, waited, guarding the door. Ruefully rubbing a growing lump on his head, Darian looked for anyone that might be their leader.

'Is there another way out of here? Not just for me, but for all of you?'

'I suspect it is you that they want, Mr Darian. We will be safe if we give you up to your enemies.'

Darian looked for the speaker – a deep, booming male voice, strong and determined – but could not recognise its origin among the throng of frightened people, including many children.

'It is the fire in the museum that is our mutual enemy, my friend,' Darian addressed his unseen interrogator, 'though I am certain the Mechmen won't be averse to breaking heads and limbs in their progress through the building.'

'He is right, Leonora,' another answered, this time identifiable as a timid living skeleton whose clothes hung loosely off his bony frame. Eyes made huge by his natural emaciation were teary with fear. 'We will have to flee through the catacombs.'

'To what?' Leonora stepped forward, curvaceously female but with more than a hint of a five o'clock shadow: a hermaphrodite. 'A life of despised fugitives hiding from the Normals?'

She glared at Darian with defiance and pride. 'And what of Sebastien? Our merman. How can he be rescued? He will die out of water. We are a family, we do not leave one of our brothers behind to die in the flames.'

Darian could detect the build up of acrid smoke seeping through the building, the thought of flames reacting with so much formaldehyde made him shudder. It would ignite in a massive fireball and release deadly poisonous gases. Not how he intended to die.

'Anyone who wants to live can come with me. Otherwise, enjoy the inferno! Those babies are going to blow!'

'*I am staying here Madhu. Maybe this is my time.*'

Aayushi stepped up to Darian, pressing a jewelled metal vial into his hands. '*Do not open this until the right time. You will know when.*'

He pocketed the object quickly before arguing with the old woman in Hindi. '*No! I will not let these cowardly flames take you, mother. I promised to take you back to India, to the Ganges, so you must endure living a little longer.*'

Darian scooped her up once more and strode through the increasingly smoky hallway. 'Which one of you people will show me the way out?'

Seeing this stranger handling their venerated Oracle stoked up the Family's rising fear and anger. They surrounded him in a tight circle, unable to attack without risking harm to the old woman. A dog-faced boy of no more than seven or eight growled and tried to bite his ankles. Darian stepped back to avoid him. Right into the reach of the long fingertip tendrils of the Incredible Octoman who tried to prise Aayushi from Darian's arms.

A billowing waft of heavy smoke behind them announced an arrival from the blazing museum. Randalfo Walpurgis pushed through his living exhibits, foul smelling soot covered his clothes and face.

'I will, Cyrus, these are my beloved family, much as you despise how I employ them. These are my people, I will lead them to safety. Boys, I am certain we can carry Sebastian's tank between us, no one will be left behind.'

Never one to embrace responsibility, Darian gladly handed over the Oracle to Randalfo and stepped back. As the Family moved away, someone screamed as a large clanking figure followed Randalfo into their domain. A Mechman reached down and grabbed Darian's shoulders, holding him fast in his augmented mechanical grip.

Randalfo shrugged apologetically. 'You are just a client, Cyrus. A good one but nothing more. My Family have to come first. No hard feelings?'

'None whatsoever, old chap,' Darian replied, he would have done the same in Randalfo's shoes. To his relief, the Mechman only saw human freaks and not the true value of the shrouded figure in Randalfo's arms. Unable to free himself from the Mechman's vice-like grasp, Darian allowed himself to be hauled away. A faint voice called after him in Hindi: '*Remember my child. For once forget your contrary nature and curiosity. Do not open the vial until the right time.*'

12

Darian was thrown onto the floor of Crimm-Smythe's large dirigible.

'You are beginning to irk me, Mr Darian,' said Crimm-Smythe, sitting in some comfort on a large gilded throne-like chair, richly upholstered in blue velvet.

'Only beginning to irk you? I must be slipping.' The alchemist steeled himself for the blow or kick that would accompany his response.

A Mechman stepped forward, fist raised, but the industrialist waved him back with a curt, dismissive gesture.

Crimm-Smythe was dressed for a night at the opera: cape; top hat; cane; and smug smile. The perfect end to a day where he had ordered the burning alive of some humanity's most vulnerable wretches, and was about to torture and kill an unarmed man. Why not end the day with a light supper at Claridges followed by *Die Fledermaus*?

Darian tried not to laugh at the sight of Crimm-Smythe's small feet in black patent shoes dangling, unable to reach the floor of the dirigible gondola. Decked out like an audience chamber in a palace with gilded walls and unlit crystal chandeliers, it was complete with large ornate decorations. Darian decided it looked like a room in a gin palace.

'Firstly, you try to trick me over the whereabouts of the Thebus Scroll and now you are openly seeking another object of my desire.'

'A smaller chair?'

That did provoke a hard kick in the stomach.

'I was puzzled at finding you at Randalfo's freak show, the man has no interest in our shared obsessions. You seemed at home with the monsters. My Mechmen can re-arrange you, help you fit in better with your unfortunate friends.'

Darian struggled to get up despite his stomach cramping with fire. 'Those people were no threat to you nor had anything you needed. Why try to incinerate them?'

'Mr Darian, what kind of inhumane monster do you think I am?'

The alchemist remained silent, in too much pain to risk another kicking by answering. Instead he studied his surrounding for signs of escape.

'It was nothing, a diversion to flush you out. A show of smoke and alarums. Nothing more than one wall part-demolished and halls full of smouldering ash.'

Darian glanced out of the gondola's windows. Night had fallen and the dirigible flew above the fog line, revealing the thin, wide smile of a new moon. He could see nothing funny about his situation.

'Of course, you may not relish becoming a member of the Randalfo Family, you are known for your vanity as well as your arrogance,' Crimm-Smythe continued. 'Your continued existence is vexing to me. I think a tragic fall from an unknown dirigible is in order.'

He signalled for the nearest Mechman. 'It is time our modern day Icarus met his fate.'

Darian had nothing to lose, he leapt to his feet and grabbed the industrialist's ebony cane, rightly gambling that it was also a swordstick. Pushing open the outer door of the gondola, he gained a few precious seconds as the shock of night air rushed into the room. Lithe and faster than the Mechmen, Darian scrambled up the side of the gondola and unsheathed the sword from the cane. His moving weight on the roof caused it to sway further hampering the clumsy Mechmen's attempts to follow him outside of the gondola.

He could hear their boss squealing in terror, demanding they stop him before he compromised the stability of the dirigible and they all fell to their deaths. Darian intended more than compromising the airship, he was going to bring it down. Unable to fire their formidable weapons for fear of igniting the gas-filled canopy, the armoured minions clambered onto the rigging and tried to grab Darian any way they could. He ran to a chain winch and unwound the anchor until it dangled beneath the airship. At the moment it only touched air, soon, if his audacious plan worked, the anchor would be connecting to buildings.

There was only one chance of success, just one. Steadying himself as best he could on the swaying gondola roof, he aimed the sword up at the canopy and threw it as hard as he could. Rewarded by a satisfying long, slow hiss, one side of the airship began to dimple, billow and deflate. Darian slid down the chain, hand over hand, and held tight, a foot on either side of the anchor. The airship was dropping fast, the anchor chain swinging wildly. Beneath him the city loomed ever larger. Darian made out familiar landmarks lit by fog-softened gaslights. Just a mile or so to the east and he could drop in on his own home.

With the other inhabitants of the doomed dirigible occupied by their panic to survive, he concentrated on finding a way off the flailing anchor. This would not be easy, the airship was heading closer to the Thames. A plunge into that poisonous oily liquid would be fatal. The wild pitching and rolling ceased as at last someone in the gondola had enough sense to use the airship's combustium engines to bring it down in a more controlled descent. Darian had only punctured one section of the gas-filled canopy and it still had some buoyancy.

The pilot turned the wounded dirigible towards Crimm-Smythe's vast mansion on top of Parliament Hill, while one of the Mechmen leant out of the open door and aimed at Darian with his augmented fragmentiser pistol. Darian made an easy target. The only defence he had was his weight as he dangled from the front of the airship. Holding on tight and swinging on the chain, Darian began to push down onto the anchor with all his strength, getting it to move backwards and forward like a child's swing. The nose of the dirigible dipped slightly, enough to unbalance the Mechman whose shot went wildly off aim.

Panicked, a screaming Crimm-Smythe had the minion hauled back into the gondola and the door slammed shut.

Darian had won a reprieve but was no closer to getting off the airship with his body intact. The pilot descended again and brought the dirigible into the main flight path and for the first time, other craft shared the skies. Landing at the mansion would be death to Darian, he needed to get off – now.

Another dirigible, a private one passed close by, then another. If their pilots saw the hapless dangling traveller, they made no move to aid him. Then possible salvation came in the form of a huge public airship, like a vast leviathan of the skies it began passing slowly underneath. Darian swore in Farsi and leapt free from the anchor. Seconds stretched to infinity then the world became a vast canopy, cushioning his fall and enveloping his plummeting body in gas-filled canvas.

He paused for a few minutes to recover his breath and composure then clambered down the canopy rigging to knock on the door of the gondola.

An astonished conductor nervously opened up and fell back as Darian swung in.

'Thank you, my good man,' said Darian, dusting down his trousers. 'Tell me, are you going anywhere near Mayfair?'

13

Bruised and bleeding, Darian re-entered his home to the complete indifference of the others. Hardwick and a revived Cambion were fussing around a distraught Dedman while Belial stood in the background, arms folded, and an amused grin on his near-angelic face.

'You did what, Cyrus? Saved innocent women and children from being burnt alive? Took on six deranged Mechmen single-handed and unarmed? Dangled high above London from a dirigible's anchor?'

'Not now, Cyrus,' muttered a terse Hardwick without looking up. 'While you were gadding about town, Miss Dedman has been taken.'

'We didn't even know where you were,' spluttered an affronted shapeshifter. Clearly his incubus blood had speeded his recovery.

'I told you, dangling from … forget it. I need a drink.'

Belial went to fetch him a glass of cognac while the alchemist sat down.

'So, what are you going to do about it?' Hardwick demanded, pacing the floor. His eyes were bloodshot and bleary indicating he had taken something to soften the blow of the woman's absence. That was all Darian needed, the inventor was of great use when focused, now he was like a love struck youth, most unseemly in a man of thirty-two.

'Er – nothing? This has nothing to do with my search for the Technomicron.'

Darian thought both Hardwick, Cambion and the woman's father would explode with indignation. He pressed on regardless. 'By taken, if you mean Miss Dedman has been kidnapped, then I cannot see the problem. Once she starts correcting the kidnappers' table manners, they will send her back to you forthwith.'

He strode over to a cabinet and retrieved the Talisman of Greel, tossing it to Dedman. 'If by taken, you mean she has been possessed by breeth, wave this around her head and hey presto – end of your dilemma.'

Dedman marched over, his hands curled into fists. 'You, sir are an unmitigated ill-bred cad!'

'Cad, most certainly, ill bred? No. My father is directly descended from the great Persian King Xerxes, my mother is of the bloodline of the Irish King Cormac mac Airt.'

'A shameless liar as well as a cad,' thundered Dedman. He'd heard Darian's deceased father had been a dealer in stolen antiquities, his mother a gypsy fortune-teller. 'It is a source of wonder how you have survived your constant outrages!'

At that moment Belial arrived with two cut crystal balloons generously filled with cognac. Dedman backed off, after glaring at the demon standing at the alchemist's side. To think he wondered how had the man survived. Ha! There was no need for Darian to answer.

Darian took a big swig of the gloriously burning amber liquid, then, sighing, turned to his company. 'That's better. So, what exactly happened to the unfortunate Miss Dedman?'

'Misha took a strong dislike to her and she stormed out without a chaperone, the others went looking for her while I fed your dragoncat and put her back in her room,' Belial replied, clearly enjoying the human drama. They were such entertaining creatures.

'Wretched thing bit her ankle!' fumed Dedman.

She is a great judge of character, thought Darian but for once held his tongue.

'She was just playing,' Darian remarked, unhelpfully stoking up Dedman's fury. 'If she had meant it, Miss Dedman would be minus a foot.'

'We searched and searched but to no avail and when we returned to the house in despondency, we found this missive on the doorstep,' Hardwick continued. With ill grace, he handed a scruffy piece of paper to Darian.

Back off you Persheeyan bastid or the woman gets her gizzard slit. After she has earnt her keep wiv a spell rubbing giblets in the bawdyhouse. If you behave, once we get the book, we will give her back.

Darian tried not to laugh at the inept spelling as he read the letter out loud though Belial didn't bother stifling a loud guffaw.

'Let us recap who the players in this game are.' Darian announced. 'Us of course. And most likely the Lady. My night's near fatal adventure confirms Crimm-Smythe is now in the running. We have the still unknown controller of the Wraith. Then there are the religious nutcases: the Brethren of Satarel. Now this charming missive and the unfortunate abduction of Miss Dedman confirms that Mr Stanley Fogue, the East End Mage, is also in the chase for the Technomicron.'

'How could you possibly know that, Cyrus?' queried Hardwick, relieved they had a name and possible destination in their rescue of the beautiful Athena.

'Stanley is the only one who calls me "a Persheeyan bastid".'

Darian did not relish the thought of entering Old Nickol, the seamy underworld of London's criminal underclass. The area between Shoreditch and Bethnal Green in London's East End was the vilest, most soul-destroying slum in the capital. It was also Stanley Fogue's unchallenged kingdom, one he never left. A lawless section of the capital where no rozzer would dare enter, indeed her Majesty's Constabulary avoided it like the plague that probably still infested the populace.

A permanent shroud of industrial smog reigned over its narrow streets, the tightly packed bleak tenements poured out soot and smoke to cut out all daylight. Lurking blaggers cleared the filth strewn, muddy streets of dead cats, dogs, occasional babies and murder victims. Breeth possession was an every-night hazard along with betties, bit fakers, bludgers and shivering jemmies and other all too human low life. Many of the indigenous working people had moved away to London's crowded Seven Dials and St Giles areas leaving behind a seething melting pot of human and occult criminals and those fallen on hard times.

The overhead steam tram route did not stop anywhere near Old Nickol for fear its inhabitants would attack and rob the passengers and it was a no go area for any dirigibles to over fly, too tempting as targets to take pot shots at.

If Hell was found anywhere on earth, it was on the nightmare streets of Old Nickol.

'We go in hard and fast. That is, except you Cambion. Your task is to get better and feed Misha,' Darian announced. 'Miles, old chap, is the Brigantia still up and running?'

For the first time, Hardwick was able to raise a smile: his mighty steam machine was his pride and joy. 'She is by Gad, Cyrus, and eager for action.'

'This is madness, utter insanity,' a frantic Dedman interrupted. 'As soon as we make a move on them, they will kill my daughter.'

'Shock tactics,' Darian replied. 'Fogue expects us to be cautious, too anxious to risk the fragrant Athena's life. While Fogue throws everything he has at the Brigantia, Belial will find and rescue your daughter.'

'Why the demon?'

Belial was standing by the hearth, one arm resting casually on the mantelpiece, but in the next moment he was standing beside an astonished Dedman.

'*That* is "why the demon",' said Darian.

14

An hour before dawn the inventor returned having encountered no let or hindrance *en route*.

'She is a beast, a big beautiful beast!' Hardwick beamed with satisfaction as he strode into the hall.

'Oh come now, Miles, that is no way to talk about your heart's desire, Athena is a handsome woman most certainly but not ...'

Hardwick ignored the alchemist, fully aware Darian knew he was talking about his pride and joy, the *Brigantia*. His masterpiece of precision engineering, a marvel of steam powered, eutronically compressed energy, his patent Combustium Engine. This one fuelled by a gift from Darian's laboratory, a new element – infernion. An alchemy created from oil of such high flammability it could not be used by anyone without Hardwick's expertise. Darian had destroyed his lab's interior many times in the search for a commercial version of infernion but the wonder fuel still eluded him.

Despite the early hour, the machine had gathered a big crowd of gawping onlookers, many startled at each whirr and wheeze of the machine at rest. It was power combined with great beauty, a typical Hardwick design. The *Brigantia* was a one off, designed for his personal use. Its steel core hidden by shining panels of rich mahogany inlay and sweeping curves of polished brass: she was large but undeniably elegant. Darian could see why Athena Dedman had caught the eye of the inventor, there were certainly similarities.

'He'll never look at any woman with so much open adoration,' noted Belial. 'Who could compete with that metal goddess?'

Darian grinned in agreement before concentrating on galvanising his troops. Every second wasted here could lessen the element of surprise. Fogue had spies everywhere in the city, no doubt some were watching Darian's home. They had to be neutralised now.

'Have you come armed?' Dedman demanded of the alchemist. The others, including the demon, wore fully charged AMFs across their backs and pistols tucked into their belts. Darian appeared to carry nothing, wearing a long floor-sweeping duster coat over garb still grimy from his adventure above the capital's rooftops. With a flourish, Darian opened the coat to reveal a collection of small amber glass spheres on one side of the garment's lining and similarly shaped globes glowing with a green liquid on the other.

'Mesmerine for our human foes,' the alchemist explained, 'and ectophane for our otherworldly enemies.'

'You have been busy since our last encounter,' the demon noted, his eyes gleaming with a yearning he made no attempt to hide.

'Well, you wouldn't expect me to mope about pining for you,' replied Darian with a wink. 'Hard work takes my mind off the pain of your absence.'

Hardwick reached down into a carpetbag and produced a new device which he clamped to his wrist. He lifted a brass-mounted green glass lens from the front and wound up the mechanism, the instrument burst into life with a yellow light spreading to its many dials.

'Belial, my friend, I suspect we have unwelcome eyes outside peering at our little enterprise. This is a task for you and me. This metallurgical detector will single out those humans lurking in the surrounding streets with hidden weapons. I will leave tracking supernatural foes to your own unique detecting abilities.'

While they waited for the one-man, one-demon assassination squad to conduct their bloody business, Dedman pulled the shapeshifter to one side out of Darian's earshot.

'What is going on between Darian and that demon? Do they

have some sort of depraved and unnatural liaison?' Dedman's voice could not hide his disdain for what he imagined was going on between them.

Cambion shook his head. 'No, absolutely not. Never. And they never will.'

'You surprise me, sir,' replied Dedman. 'I have never seen such overt and licentious repartee. Between two males! An outrage.'

The shapeshifter nodded in agreement. 'It's a bizarre and dangerous game Cyrus plays with the demon, a playful dalliance that draws him ever closer to the edge of a hellish abyss.'

Cambion did his best to explain a complicated situation. 'In order to engage the demon's aide for his escapades, Cyrus plays with him, keeping the evil creature's hopes alive that Cyrus will give in one day to what he desires. It can never happen, they both know that. The moment the alchemist succumbs, he will be lost forever and his immortal soul, his humanity, everything that makes him Cyrus Darian will be destroyed. Tragically, Belial's punishment as a fallen angel is a cruel one. Everything he loves will become corrupted, ruined and die. So they play this game in the full knowledge of the dire consequences.'

'So Darian is shamelessly manipulating the demon's emotions, exploiting him?' questioned Dedman, surprised at his own pang of sympathy for a celestial being created to be pure love that could now only destroy.

'He does that to everybody,' Cambion replied with a deep, bitter sigh. 'I thought you knew that already. And we all have something we want from him, why else are we here?'

There was nothing Dedman could say to refute this statement. The shapeshifter was correct.

Hardwick concentrated on his task, seeking lurking human spies with hidden weapons. He had seen action with Belial before and it was not for the faint hearted. The demon was a swift and chillingly effective killing machine, not always for necessity: this was sport for the monstrous being.

The demon slunk into the crowd, soon lost in a blur of swift, surreptitious movement. Hardwick sought out a good vantage spot and found one on the steps of a close-by church and half-hidden by a pillar, scanned for signs of weapons.

He had designed the metallurgical detector well and did not have to wait long before it indicated where to find them. Three shabby, unshaven men, clearly uncomfortable in the well-to-do surroundings, harboured pistols under their jackets. Their eyes never shifted from Darian's front door and as they moved to get between it and the *Brigantia*, he was relieved to have Belial arrive at his side.

'Nothing to concern us from the spook realm, Miles,' a gleaming-eyed Belial reported, eager for a skirmish. The inventor sighed and pointed out the armed thugs to him, knowing he was sealing their fate. Not an easy thing for a man raised as an English gentleman, with muscular Christianity and a sense of fair play honed on the playing fields of Eton.

As the demon headed off to dispatch them, Hardwick considered that his only consolation was that these men meant harm to the innocent. Indeed these thugs could well be the very kidnappers of Athena Dedman.

15

Belial, wiping smears of still-warm human blood from his mouth and hands with a silk kerchief, returned with Hardwick. How he'd managed to dispatch the assassins without alerting the growing crowds admiring the steam coach was a mystery. One nobody wished to question. With the spies removed, the rescue mission began in earnest. Or more accurately in the *Brigantia*. They climbed into the steam coach's luxurious interior and took their seats as Hardwick took control of the machine's steering.

'You are going to have to get your own clothes after we get La Dedman back,' grumbled Darian to the demon, wincing at the fresh gore on his silk brocade waistcoat. Belial shrugged in rueful apology, he'd made two messy kills after getting carried away with the pleasure of the chase.

'At least it is not soot and gobbets of charred flesh,' countered the demon. 'Blood's easier to get out.'

Curbing his now momentous distaste for the man, Dedman addressed him directly. 'Darian, if this man is a mage, will thick steel and firepower be enough to overcome the bounder?'

Laughing Darian patted his coat on the side the green phials were stored. 'I can assure you sir, we have enough ectophane at our command to fend off all the breeth-possessed villains he has at his command. Men who weren't exactly that hard to control in the first place due to their general idiocy and greed. That my friends, is the full extent of his occult powers.'

'I do not share your arrogance and complacency,' Dedman argued. 'If Fogue has opened the door to the supernatural anything could happen. It may be something else we face, something powerful controlling him.'

'Doubt it,' returned Darian with an exaggerated yawn. 'At least demons can spell.'

He glanced at Belial for confirmation who nodded in mock solemnity and added, 'Especially our names.'

'And they usually have more interesting things to do than capturing young women as hostages for some human magician,' continued Darian. 'Rest assured, Dedman old chap, I invested the chassis of this fine machine with many high quality and potent talismans and spells from my extensive collection. You may remain inside in complete safety while we retrieve your errant daughter.'

Affronted, Dedman growled his insistence on being at the forefront of any assault on Fogue and his minions.

The journey across town to Old Nickol began with the surprisingly quiet engines springing into life, the *Brigantia's* momentum system was the most sophisticated ever invented, so much so, Hardwick had ensured it could only be controlled by him. Otherwise it would be yet another object of desire for the criminal wealthy or the downright just criminal. Secretly it was a war machine but disguised as a gentleman's large steam coach so the team travelled in comfort, fortified with the contents of a well-stocked drinks cabinet served by a discreet valet.

Far from being a tremulous victim quivering in fear for her life, Athena Dedman had found an inner strength and was furious. So furious in fact that her captor had insisted on her being gagged as well as tied up.

One of Fogue's punishers was now nursing badly bruised nether regions from a well-aimed boot after attempting to frisk Athena for weapons. Another sported an impressive black eye from Athena's elbow. Her fight back only ceased when the odious Fogue summoned breeth-infested thugs who swiftly overpowered her with their supernatural strength and foul breath.

'Believe me, m'dear, there is nuffink I want more than to see the back of yer and your sharp-tongued scorn.' Fogue moved across the room with considerable speed and grace despite his large frame, seemingly as tall as he was wide. 'The last missus of mine who spoke to me like that is now scolding flounders in the Estuary. So ill-advised in view of yer circumstances.'

Unable to talk, Athena kicked out, missing her captor's ankle by inches. Fogue's temper flared. He had a notoriously short fuse.

'Take the toffer away and shut 'er up. But no marking the goods now,' ordered Fogue, his corpulent form encased in a suit and vest which threatened to explode in a rebellion of pallid flesh. The chain links of his gold fob watch stretched to their limits across the expanse of his belly. Instead of a frock or sack coat, Fogue wore one of crimson silk, embroidered with occult symbols in pure gold thread, with a matching eastern skull cap in case his status as a mage was ever in doubt. Fogue attempted to adopt the manners and dress of a toff and a mystic with mixed results. The attention and considerable expense spent on his appearance was wasted as soon as he opened his mouth.

Athena Dedman raged in frustration at the gag as she was dragged kicking and flailing to a secure room infested with three breeth/human symbiotes. They circled her, hissing and gibbering in the voices of other humans they had taken in the past. It was Athena's first sight of the parasites and they were as foul as their reputation. The breeth were inside living human bodies and moved them crouched right over so their fingers trailed the ground, their flaccid skin an unpleasant shade of grey, their eyes lit with a green glow from the otherworldly leech controlling their minds and bodies.

Released from Hell some fifty years past by the inept dabbling of some unknown amateur occultist who was unable to reverse the tear in a dimensional portal and had let them loose on London, breeth were the lowest form of demonic life. Devilishly hard to expunge from their human hosts, sanatoriums had sprung up across London to house the possessed, usually run by kindly God-fearing folk, keeping them fed but safely contained. Those like Fogue with a little occult knowledge could control them as strong but stupid underlings. It was highly illegal and inhumane but effective.

Trapped deep within the underground rooms below Fogue's mansion amid the slums, Athena did not hear the shock of the *Brigantia*'s headlong approach into Old Nickol's crowded streets. Though her courage was sorely tested by her captors, she knew the stalwart Miles Hardwick would come to her rescue as a true blue English gentleman, an aristocrat steeped in old world chivalry. So unlike his odious companion, who was nothing more than a degenerate foreigner with the morals of an exceptionally libidinous alley cat.

16

The entrance of a gentleman's steam coach driving into London's slums was not an unusual sight. Areas like Seven Dials did not only house the poor but were packed with tradesmen and artisans. The premises of printers, goldsmiths and clockmakers rubbed shoulders with bawdyhouses and overcrowded tenements. All useful excuses for the wealthy to openly visit the narrow streets and indulge their many and varied vices after visiting their tailor.

Only the most ill-informed would enter Old Nickol on such a pretext, this was the cover that Darian hoped would get the *Brigantia* within striking distance of Stanley Fogue's lair. As the machine approached the top end of Nickol Street, he knew every inch of its journey into London's equivalent of hell was being scrutinised by greedy eyes sensing easy prey and with no worries about interfering constabulary. The *Brigantia* chugged across the filth–strewn cobbles at first unopposed but once she was within the narrowest winding of the street, the first stones rained down on her metal sides, a warm welcome from the local urchins.

Soon pot shots from better-armed older locals joined the stone throwing chavys but the *Brigantia* shrugged them off with indifference as no more hindrance than raindrops. The attacks were sporadic, random, but Darian and the team knew that heavy artillery would await them as they approached Fogue's domain, his vast fortified mansion built with shameless arrogance in the midst of the tenements of the desperately poor. Something no doubt Mr Dickens would have railed about had he not suffered a fatal stroke four years before.

The glare of an obscene array of gaslights lit up the Stygian gloom as they approached the newly built Dominion House. Fogue flaunted his wealth, secure that no one in Old Nickol would oppose him.

'Well,' mused Darian. 'I'm not a cowed local, I'm from Mayfair and about to give you the fright of your life.'

With the steam coach's dogged and unwavering approach towards Fogue's home, a gang of punishers ran out, opening fire with elephant guns. These were seriously powerful weapons which were no match for the carriage and her reinforced metal sides.

'This is going to get messy from now on,' shouted Darian above the hail of bullets ricocheting off the *Brigantia*'s exterior. 'Time for you to do your demonic best, Belial.'

Deliberately to provoke fury from the other men in the team, the demon kissed Darian farewell on the forehead before disappearing from the coach. Hardwick and Cambion had seen it all before but it never got any easier and that the alchemist did not object added to their discomfort. 'Nothing more to see, concentrate now,' Darian pretended to scold. 'I think it is time to let them know we mean business.'

'Break out yer barkers!' shouted Fogue to his punishers. 'All the 'eavy stuff!' As his henchmen raced to get their weapons, Fogue cursed his people's lack of vigilance. This gammy steam coach bit back at its attackers and bit back hard. Had to be Crimm-Smyth, the mage's mind raced. The nightmare of a Mechman attack was something he dreaded and had planned for since his interest in the Technomicron had become common knowledge.

Something was agitating the breeth, no longer interested in circling and cursing her in many stolen human voices, they left her alone to scrabble and whine at the door demanding release. Normally if trapped, breeth could leave their host bodies and disperse through solid walls, but these appeared unable or unwilling to leave their shells of human flesh. The door opened and a burly villain ushered them out. 'Yer needed up above, the toff twist ain't going nowhere.'

Before he closed the door to leave her alone, the man gave Athena a lewd wink and gesture with his hands. 'Not long now me nug, I'm first in line to grind yer. No buttered bun for me. I reckon yer 'ave a good set of bubbies under there, you'll be a right rantipole once I break yer in!'

Athena hadn't a clue what he was talking about but suspected it wasn't good. She sighed in relief once finally left alone, with time to plan her escape. While under observation by the breeth, she had not struggled but did her best to stay relaxed, now it was time to work at loosening her bonds. A skill taught to her by a former maid called Lila who had starred in the Great Zarino's Three Ring Circus in her youth. The same maid had taught her to shoot, rope and ride feisty horses, unladylike behaviour but useful. Athena had long suspected Lila was not just a maid but had been hired by her father to teach her how to defend herself. Whatever the truth, she was grateful for what she had learned now.

Athena had been an apt pupil and with a little dextrous manipulating, her hands wriggled free from the rough hemp rope. Within seconds she had also untied the bindings around her ankles. Sore and stiff but liberated from her bondage, Athena scoured the room for anything she could use as a weapon. She considered breaking the chair against the wall, the legs were sturdy and would make a handy cudgel, but the noise might alert her captors even with the sounds of a battle raging outside. Explosions, gunfire and angry shouting: whoever Crimm-Smythe was, he was doing her a favour.

Frantically searching through a cabinet produced a curious dagger, intricately inlaid with Far Eastern occult symbols in silver and jade and bearing a long wavy blade. Perfect! She pulled out a long hairpin from her elaborate, though mussed-up coiffure, and began work unpicking the lock on the door.

'You could do it the hard way,' a deep, silken voice behind her said. Athena whirled, dagger at the ready only to discover Darian's demon slouching in the chair where she had been tied but minutes before. 'Or you could let me get you out of here.'

Affronted, Athena turned back to the lock. 'I am perfectly

capable of looking after myself, fiend, especially with some individual called Crimm-Smythe providing a convenient if somewhat violent diversion.'

Reluctant to keep her back turned against the handsome monster for too long, she continued in the same reckless vein. 'I have no need of your help, so fly back to your degenerate, Godless master forthwith.'

Belial laughed, the warmth in the tone hardly disguising the hollow echo of the Abyss from which he came. 'My dear Miss Dedman, I have no master and it is not Crimm-Smythe but the degenerate who has come to rescue you, along with your father and your love-struck swain.'

Shuddering, Athena stepped away from the door. 'Please tell me you are not referring to that odious little man: the shapeshifter?'

Belial chose not to answer. It was more amusing to let her think the wrong thing. 'I suggest in view of all these people putting their mortal lives on the line for you, that you shut the hell up and allow me to escort you out of danger.'

The demon ignored her blanching at such crude and forthright language. Like Darian, he found the priggish manners of so called ladies and gentlemen ridiculous.

'Though if it wasn't for Darian, I would have left you to it. Your father came to us for help and the pair of you have done nothing but whinge and complain in your frightful self-righteous manner ever since.'

A tremor of unease shivered through the demon's illusion of humanity. Something glinting in the woman's hand drew his gaze, to his horror, he saw she was holding a Malaysian demon-slayer. As a Fallen Prince, he was immortal, indestructible and as a human the dagger was too weak in power to kill him but it could still wound and hurt. Did she know what it was? He gambled that she didn't.

'We were misled, demon. My father and I are devout God-fearing Christian folk. We were told Cyrus Darian was a seasoned adventurer with the knowledge and courage to defeat demons, not that he indulged in unnatural congress with one.'

'Not that it matters but he doesn't,' Belial replied with a sigh of regret. 'But we have no time for this, the diversion can only last a finite time.'

With no time for finesse, Belial flashed his eyes and sent the woman into a trance followed by a swoon. He swept her up into his arms and over his shoulder and sought the best route out of the building. In their rush to join the battle, the breeth had left the door unlocked. One lucky break, he doubted there would be others.

17

Fogue's army fought back hard, but the heaviest artillery made no difference. His unknown enemies remained secure in their steam coach while the casualties among the mage's supporters rose. He yelled to his chief bludger, an ex-professional pugilist called Fancy Dan.

'That damn thing is built and armed like a bleedin' battleship. Let's see 'ow it likes a fire under its belly.'

The boxer nodded, uneasy at any prospect of getting closer to a machine that spat fire like a hellcat.

'And make it a well 'ot un, explosives and as much oil as yer can pack under the bastid.'

Left alone, Fogue decided to conjure up some supernatural help, the machine was already immune to breeth infestation: the creatures could not breach the metal exterior of the coach. He no longer suspected Crimm-Smythe as his attacker, this was someone with superior occult knowledge. It had to be that foreigner, Cyrus Darian, coming for the woman.

He strode to the temple built under his mansion, a basement room painted black with a white circle and pentacle of protection crudely rendered in paint on the floor. It had none of the sophisticated and knowledgeable safeguards of Darian's chamber of summoning. In fact it was downright dangerous given Fogue's lack of experience in the occult. He had gleaned all his knowledge about dealing with demons from a stolen grimoire written in archaic French, which had to be translated for Fogue who then laboriously memorised its contents as it was read to him, being unable to read himself. Up until now, he had only managed to conjure enough power to control breeth.

Desperate times demanded desperate measures, Fogue

wanted the Technomicron. Therefore the Persheeyan bastid had to be eliminated.

'This is not good, really not good at all,' a stressed Hardwick announced, stating the obvious as the underside of the *Brigantia* became dangerously hot, sitting above a blazing lake of burning oil. 'I have dumped as much water on it as I dare,' he continued, 'any more and we won't make it out of Old Nickol.'

'I'm not leaving without my daughter!' Dedman paced the unbearably hot interior of the steam coach. 'I have an AMF. I'm going in to get her.'

'You will last five minutes,' Darian replied evenly. 'Five seconds if you fire that thing with the equalizer switched off.'

He turned to Hardwick. 'We have to move her out, Miles, Belial will have Miss Dedman safe by now.'

Hardwick's face hardened, as it always did in his most stubborn of moods. Darian knew better to argue with him like this, the inventor would not move away from Old Nickol without Athena Dedman. The alchemist nodded to Hardwick, silently acknowledging that he would not leave until the woman was confirmed safe and free from Fogue's clutches.

'I have a reserve watertank midship, but it has to be manually operated – from the outside,' said Hardwick. He was relieved the alchemist had not argued with him, it was one of the advantages of knowing each other so well after sharing many life or death situations over the years.

Darian unslung his AMF and correctly primed it for action. 'Tell me where this water device is, how to use it and then let me out. I have no desire to be roasted alive by an unruly gang of Fogue's scoundrels.'

For once, Dedman was silent in respect for the man's suicidal courage but he did not volunteer to help him face Fogue's henchmen and the inferno surrounding the *Brigantia*. Unlike the demon, Darian was not fireproof, so how exactly was he going to survive?

The answer was contained within the canister Hardwick

threw to Darian. It contained promethetine, the result of another collaboration between inventor and alchemist. As a temporary fireproof coating for clothing and flesh, it was an unstable substance that Darian had counted as a total failure but would give him a few moments protection from the flames. He hoped that would be all he needed.

Pushing aside any understandable lingering doubt and fear, Fogue finished his makeshift safeguards by first lighting a white candle then pouring a thick line of salt around his protective circle followed by a sprinkling of holy water and a handful of hawthorn and oak leaves. He believed in covering all the bases, both Christian and pagan. He took in a deep breath, held it and steadied himself before beginning the ceremony of summoning. He had no idea what the sonorous phrases meant, only copying the weird cadences and sounds of the ancient words of power. Could he get the incantations right? Would it be enough to breach the portal? And could he control what might come through?

Over and over again, Fogue chanted, building up a cone of ever-increasing sonic energy around him, a vibration that could pierce through the dimension of this reality into another, darker realm. Interspatial cracks appeared as jagged rents in the air allowing the earthbound to pass through. With nothing to bind them in the room, they slipped unchallenged through the walls to join the world outside. Fogue had already opened a door he could not close.

Fogue's constant chanting increased in speed and loudness, increasingly he felt detached from his voice and from his body as if the words had a life and sentience of their own. The dark walls flitted with darker shadows and an oppressive feeling of dread fell like a leaden pall. Angry tremors in the ground beneath his feet grew to convulsions as if the very earth was protesting at what he had set in motion. And could not undo. Never had the circle and pentacle felt such precarious protection but stepping beyond it would make him instantly prey to unknown horrors.

The ground's spasms spread to the walls and ceiling, shaken by a silent earthquake yet still Fogue chanted on, he doubted if he could stop now however much he wanted to. He was possessed by the words. He was nothing but a vessel of vulnerable flesh for them to pass through and reach out to that which waited with infinite patience and unspeakable malevolence beyond.

A vortex opened up above him, a jagged scar in actuality, a swirl of charnel house hues and foul odours. He could hear the rasping roar of something approaching from a great distance and at phenomenal speed. His resolve faltered then shattered to nothing, he was terrified. Fogue's throat constricted with primal fear and he ceased chanting, dropping to the floor and hugging the ground within his small and vulnerable paint and salt circle. No longer a powerful mage but a helpless, frightened fool.

Fogue's sudden silence did not break the spell of summoning, indeed the vortex widened and the entity sped up as it approached from a dimension beyond human comprehension. Fogue began to whimper in terror, tears rolled down his fleshy cheeks. How could he dream of controlling this … this thing? What had he summoned? A primordial elemental? A devourer of worlds?

18

Flames leapt and surged against his legs as Darian jumped from the coach. He held his breath, unwilling to breathe in the super-heated air, smoke and soot that would kill him as assuredly as the blaze. He sprinted the distance along the *Brigantia*'s burning hot sides and, praying that his promethetine-coated gloves would protect the vulnerable flesh of is hands, began to turn the wheel to release the water from the inner tank that could buy them some precious time. Where in Hades was the demon? Doubt crept into Darian's mind. Had he been arrogant in his assumption that Fogue was too inept to be able to harm Belial? Could he have the power to vanquish a prince in the demonic hierarchy of Hell?

A gunshot rang out, and the bullet clipped his shoulder, missing the flesh but ruining a perfectly good coat. Darian spun and took aim with the AMF. His sharp eyes scoured through the flames and smoke for sight of his assailant. Another shot sounded, this time, the bullet thudded into the *Brigantia* less than an inch from his head. Too close, the next shot would be on target. Hating the lack of finesse, the flames forced Darian to send AMF shock waves over a wide area, pulsing through the inferno, the deadly Accelerated Momentium Fragmentiser beams left no prisoners in their wake.

His success, measured by the sudden silence, meant Darian was able to carry on his mission with the flames and smoke as his only enemies. The heat and fumes around him rose and he felt the sting of flames as the promethetine began to fail. Darian concentrated on turning the wheel. It was painfully hot and partly buckled by the heat, so it resisted at first. Grateful for the last few seconds of protection from the fireproof coating on his gloves, Darian used all his strength to wrestle with the wheel and was rewarded by a sudden deluge of fire-quenching water from the tank.

Weeping in terror, kneeling in a pool of his own urine, Fogue watched something from beyond slowly insinuating itself around the edge of the vortex. As he watched, a chitinous multi-jointed limb extended through thin air and planted itself on the floor beside him. It was not the vast roaring entity approaching through infinity, but a slow, measured infestation, and the sight of it spurred Fogue into action. For an insane second, he considered leaping clear of the circle and fleeing from the room, as if closing the door to his chamber would seal the vortex and shut out the creature attempting to crawl through.

Then survival kicked in through his despair. If Fogue was strong enough to command a criminal empire, then he could stop this! He began to chant the words of dismissal and closure. Words his panicking brain thought he had forgotten. Somehow he dragged them up from the recesses of his mind and tried to reverse the summoning. The vortex, once opened, violently resisted his attempt to close it. Once again the room endured the turmoil of silent earthquakes created by the battle between two dimensions. That something was happening, changing, spurred Fogue on. He rose to his feet and chanted louder, pouring his entire being into the words, giving them more power. Enough to send the insect-like being scuttling back to its own dimension.

The vortex found a voice, an ear-piercing scream of thwarted ambition joining with a now fading roar from the retreating vast entity from the void. Fogue did not stop, could not stop, not until the seal was complete and the chamber returned to normal. As he focused on the shrinking vortex, his eye caught but did not fully register a plume of oily brown smoke issuing through the rent in reality.

Fogue collapsed back onto the floor still within his protective circle, his body shuddering with exhaustion. The ripped portal collapsed in on itself leaving nothing remaining but solid ceiling and silence fell on the room like a blessing. He began to weep again, this time with relief but his joy did not last long. As he recovered he realised he was no longer alone in the room. Lit by the last candle to survive the tumult, a brown shadow encircled him, elongated and swift like a monstrous snake made of smoke. A lesser entity had invaded his world, one he must strive to control.

The mage plunged his hand into a deep pocket within his coat's lining, producing an amber crystal sphere. Made from one of the rarest elements in the universe, gold celestialene, it was nearly flawless but for one sliver of inclusion deep within its depths. No one owned a perfect Orb of Jhan. Yet.

Fogue held the sphere high and towards the near formless creature, stumbling over the words to make it obey him. The smoke snake coalesced into a more solid form. It rose unsteadily on two legs, a bizarre blend of demon and hydra at first, the many serpentine heads hissing and snapping and with a long, lashing tail. A myriad of fiery eyes glared with brute malice at its summoner and new master.

Fogue completed the spell of submission and obedience and the hell creature changed shape again. The many heads fused together to form a single nightmare fisage. Protuberances of slimy flesh stiffened to form horns and one central eye glowed with a baleful yellow luminosity, full of the purest form of hatred for Fogue, for all inhabitants of this world. Its body took on the appearance of a massive simian, powerful forearms trailed the ground, ending in claws tipped with sharp, curved talons. A powerful prehensile tail ended with a barbed tip. Long insect-like black hairs sprouted from its mottled pink/brown naked body. Within seconds, the creature's flesh had hardened to a stone like consistency, making it an even more formidable foe.

It remained still, as if waiting for its first command. Fogue felt his courage and confidence rise. He was used to barking orders at soulless, murderous minions.

'Can yer speak?'

The being hissed its contempt and reluctance but compelled

by the orb, it spoke with a cacophony of many voices merged into one. 'Only with one worthy to be addressed by a Megoleth. You are not he.'

Now Fogue knew what he was dealing with. A Megoleth was a creature of Hell formed by a fusion of many damned human souls, a blend of those too weak to survive the afterlife with their individuality intact. A minor player in the legions of Chaos but still dangerous. Megoleth were known for their lies, treacherous ways and physical strength.

'Well, sunshine, that person is neivver 'ere or in possession of the Orb of Jhan, so yer must accept yer're totally under my command.'

The Megoleth answered Fogue with a fearsome hiss but had no choice but to comply. It bowed its head and waited for its instructions.

'I want yer to find Cyrus Darian and bring 'im to me. Dead or alive, I'm not bovvered as long as I 'ave 'is 'ead. Do yer understand?'

Belial met with no human opposition as he ran through Fogue's mansion. The occasional free-flying breeth rushing by bowed in deference and let him pass. The demon correctly surmised that all of Fogue's cronies would be fully occupied fighting off the *Brigantia*. With Athena still in a trance, he was able to make several spatial leaps to save time, but as he neared the front hall of the mansion, something with the all too recognisable stench of the damned blocked his way.

It was a Megoleth.

Putting the woman down, Belial approached the creature. It seemed Stanley Fogue had been busy while his men bled and died outside defending his miserable life.

The creature hadn't expected to encounter a Prince of the Inferno, and recognising Belial despite his human form, it froze in its tracks, crouching low in snivelling obeisance.

'It would be no use commanding you to return to the Abyss, I suspect,' drawled Belial wearily. Dispatching Hell's lower servants was a bore and somewhat unseemly. He only did it when Darian's life was in danger.

'My Prince, some primate scum has me in thrall to an Orb of Jhan.'

'How vexing. What did this parasite command you to do?'

'To bring him the head of Cyrus Darian.'

What a surprise, thought Belial as his mind searched for a solution, these humans playing at being evil were never very imaginative in their demands. He could seek out Fogue, kill him and try to smash the Orb. But by the time he did that, Cyrus would be dead and there was no guarantee the demon could break a substance forged in the heart of the universe's first-born sun. Furthermore Belial would need to return to his Fallen form to fight and kill the Megoleth which he was loathe to do. He was not yet ready to return to Hell – and suspected he never would be.

The Megoleth growled, it was compelled to fulfil its task and attempted to pass Belial who stood directly in its way, arms folded. Tormented by conflicting loyalties, the creature shook its head, inadvertently hooking Belial on one of its many horns and hurled him sprawling into a far wall. Belial swore as blood poured from a gash in his side.

Overcome with guilt at harming a Fallen prince, the Megoleth's answer was to cover up his mistake by finishing the job. Head down, the creature charged, ready to crush and gore the demon against the wall.

Belial was able to leap out of the way but he knew the monstrous thing would not stop until it killed his human form. This was going to get messy. Very messy.

He considered reviving Athena Dedman, persuade her to plunge the Mayalsian demon-killing dagger deep into the Megoleth's head, all without both of them being bludgeoned or gored to death. And then hope the woman didn't turn the knife on him. Belial himself could not hold the dagger, it would not kill him but the hilt would burn right through the human flesh of his hand. Feeling pain was a downside to living in this weak form, though the pleasures more than compensated.

Thwarted, the lumbering monstrosity pounded the walls in fury, reducing them to rubble and dust. There was no time to plan.

Belial picked up Athena's body and, holding her hand in his, used it to pick up the dagger. Then as the Megoleth began another charge, he made Athena plunge it deep into the creature's head.

Despite having a hide as tough as granite, the dagger slipped through with ease. Belial left it embedded in the beast and, protecting the woman with his body, waited for the inevitable aftermath.

Screeching in agony, the Megoleth threw itself around the room clawing at its head as the dagger dissolved into ancient elements, all poison to its Hell-born metabolism. Its form became less solid, heaved and thrashed for a few violent seconds before dissipating to smoke, and then to nothing.

Belial picked up the still slumbering female and spatial jumped to outside the mansion.

'Well done, my girl,' he laughed to the unconscious woman, 'you have slain your first Hell beast!'

'What kept you?'

Openly impatient, Darian sighed with relief as the demon appeared outside the *Brigantia* holding the rescued damsel in distress. Once inside the steam coach, Athena revived quickly, her only injury being a badly bruised right hand. Far from simpering and complaining, the team were relieved at her feisty recovery. It seemed that she thrived on danger.

'We met some resistance ... some otherworldly opposition,' said Belial. 'Fogue is punching well out of his league. The idiot conjured up a Megoleth.'

'He has an Orb of Jhan? Did you get it? Did you kill Fogue?' questioned an agitated Darian as the demon slouched in a chair, eyes closed as if preparing to sleep.

'Sorry, Cyrus, I was a little preoccupied preventing a Hell beast made of stoneflesh from crushing the delicate flower that is Athena and also from decapitating you as a trophy for Fogue's wall.'

Darian's hands trembled with frustration, Fogue was a loose cannon, an inept dabbler in terrifying forces beyond his limited comprehension. There was now another thing the alchemist just had to possess, his hunt was not just for the illusive Technomicron, now the Orb of Jhan called out to him.

As Hardwick guided the *Brigantia* out of the chaos of a burning Old Nickol, Darian's agitation grew. He wanted to go back, defeat Fogue and take the Orb. Belial signalled the valet to fetch a cognac for himself and his friend before gripping Darian by the shoulders.

'Relax, Cyrus, my human magpie. We have won a victory but the war is not over, but at least Fogue will be too busy rebuilding his army and his shattered reputation in Old Nickol to concern us now. We can always go back and obtain that glittering bauble for your collection another day.'

Blood of a vibrant ruby hue seeped through Belial's shirt and pooled on the *Brigantia*'s floor. All thoughts of Orbs fell from Darian's mind. 'God damn it, Belial, why didn't you say you were hurt?'

The others shrunk back, nervous about the reaction of a demon to injuries to his weaker human form. If Belial were to lash out in pain, he could easily accidently crush their skulls or snap their spines. Darian stooped down beside him and examined the long gash in the demon's side.

'It's nothing a tight bandage and a good night's rest won't fix.' Belial made light of the deep gouge. 'Though I suspect if I were fully human, I'd be a goner, right?'

'Right,' Darian confirmed, tearing makeshift bandages from his shirt and binding the demon's side. 'But it has still made a mess of you. Keep still, damn you, this is difficult enough. You are going to get blood all over my clothes. Again.'

19

Ever vain, Darian checked his Bohemian style apparel in a full length mirror. He was sporting a long burgundy velvet frock coat, an extravagant cream silk shirt worn open at the neck with no cravat, and a richly embroidered waistcoat of gold and copper hues. He checked his black lacquered iron pocket watch, one fashioned from an ancient Japanese amulet against vengeful ghosts, which was attached to a gold chain and fob set with a heavy stone of pure uncut ruby. A cut stone would have been far too gaudy and ostentatious. Something only a recently-rich northern coal baron would flash about.

Outrageously, Darian also wore no hat or gloves on his journey beyond the confines of his home. Something Hardwick would die before doing. Darian could not abide the stiff, starched collars and fussy accoutrements worn by the English upper and middle classes and saw no reason to mimic their attire. He wasn't one of them and never would be. He picked up his swordstick cane and headed for the front door, already late for a night-long supper with the delightful Li Mei.

'How can you contemplate going out alone after all we have been through?' asked Athena, voicing the views of all the others. The humans had returned from the battle with Fogue exhausted and shaking from their close brush with death. Belial had retreated to his quarters to be alone and recover after his bruising encounter with the Megoleth. Only Darian appeared untouched by the experience. He had bathed, dressed and was now ready for a night on the town.

'Your concern for my welfare is touching though puzzling in view of your antipathy for me,' Darian answered, 'but uncalled for. Crimm-Smythe thinks I am dead, dashed to my doom falling from his dirigible and Fogue will be fully occupied for some considerable time fending off the good people of Old

Nickol made homeless by the fire he started.'

Remembering the vengeful earth bound spirits Fogue had accidently released, Darian added, 'And not to forget the terror and fury of those whose victims have come back from beyond the grave to torment them. Who else is there to blame but Fogue and his clumsy, ignorant meddling?'

'There are still other enemies,' reminded Hardwick, pausing from fussing over the rescued damsel no longer in distress. In fact, Athena Dedman seemed the least disturbed from her traumatic kidnap and dramatic rescue. 'There are those religious zealots and the unknown sender of the Wraith to contend with.'

Hardwick was right of course, but Darian was once more feeling edgy and claustrophobic, his house, though spacious, felt overcrowded. He hated the sensation that unknown strangers dictated the direction of his life. He needed a rebellion, a little show of independence and where better to find sanctuary than in the gentle embrace of a woman who loved him.

He saluted them with an impudent gesture with his cane, strode out of his home and headed back to Madam Xiu's establishment.

'How long have you known?'

Darian shifted onto his side so that he could gaze directly into Li Mei's exquisite dark eyes. 'Always, *xingan*, from the very first time we kissed.'

Darian lied with a gentle smile, while behind his forced composure his heart pounded with shock. That night, he had dined with, and then bedded his beautiful Chinese paramour. Had fallen asleep entwined in her silken embrace, fragrant with jasmine perfume. He had slumbered, sated and serene, feeling safe in the small bedroom above Madam Xiu's opium den.

Her room was a poignant reminder of her homeland: family heirloom silk robes and fans hid the ugly brick walls; and scented incense sticks smouldered before a small red statue of the Buddha, the thin sticks of smoking sandalwood doing little to mask the stinging smell of opium rising from below. A pet songbird rustled, hidden by a turquoise silk cover over its cage for the night. Darian's eyes had become heavy, not helped by the heady incense that filled the room.

'*Ni hen wumei,*' he murmured, 'you are very lovely,' before succumbing to contented sleep.

Darian woke in the same room, in the same bed, in the same arms, but in another country. The shock of fresh, clean air in the bedroom made him giddy, blown in by a wind off snow-capped mountains, and whispering through a bamboo grove. More sensory overload came from downstairs as someone bustled about, singing in lilting Mandarin as they prepared a breakfast of hot sweetened rice. He knew those smells, those sounds. He was in China!

The Lady remained in the form of Li Mei and snuggled her petite body closer to his. Darian caressed her silken body and ran his fingers through her long raven hair. He refused to give her the satisfaction of revealing his distress. He did not love Li Mei but he had cared for her and trusted her. A trust, he now realized, based on illusion, on a lie. Li Mei did not exist and never had.

'You looked like you needed rescuing last night, *xiou long.*' The Lady spoke in Li Mei's soft voice. 'You arrived in my bed stinking of burnt flesh and fuel.'

'Nonsense,' Darian replied, affronted, he had bathed scrupulously before leaving his home.

'Not your body, your soul,' she said. 'Spend some time here in the Wuyi Mountains, recover and make love to me. It is very beautiful here in the Fujian Province, a mystical land of necromancers and other seekers of spiritual truth. Best of all, *qin ai de,* it is so far away from your many enemies.'

'And from the Technomicron,' Darian replied with a smile that did not reach his eyes. She could so easily strand him here, penniless and needing more than a slow boat from China to get home.

'Ah, yes, that,' she replied, her voice hardening, 'so many fools chasing that which will destroy them.'

'Including me.'

'You can never be a fool, Cyrus, but you can be blinded by your arrogance and avarice.'

'I love you too.'

The Lady laughed, disconcertingly in the Chinese girl's silver tones.

'The only person who should find this terrible book must be the one who destroys it and that could never be you, my darling. To possess it is your obsessive goal, to discover and harness its power for yourself. The Technomicron has the capacity to obliterate all of existence but that knowledge would not stop you trying. It is your nature.'

'And yours, my sweet,' Darian replied. 'You will seek it too. For a client?'

The Lady did not answer but rolled back on the bed, remaining as Li Mei, and knowing of Darian's long term trust and affection for the Chinese girl.

'Whatever he/she/it has offered you, I will treble,' Darian declared, hoping that appealing to her sense of commerce would get him back to London. 'Quadruple.'

'There is no price I would accept for your life,' she answered, her face solemn, her eyes imploring.

Darian wished that was true. The last scrap of stability in his life had faded into nothing with the loss of Li Mei. He would never trust again. For the first time he felt anger towards the Lady but it would do no good to show it. He was trapped in the Emporium just as certainly as if she had chained him in a dungeon.

20

Floating like the bloated bladders of giants, dirigibles belonging to many rich and powerful individuals jostled each other above the Department of Industry and Improvements building. They waited, their engines silent, straining against their anchor chains eager for the sky.

Three floors down, six men and one woman were seated around an impressive polished walnut table. Despite their eminence they were unattended with all servants and aides waiting well out of earshot. All those in the meeting had enormous influence over the fate of the country and their clandestine gatherings were always conducted in secret.

'Before you is the missive from the Palace stating the personal views of Her Majesty.'

The speaker was a tall man with impressive patrician features framed by well-trimmed silver sideburns, a mustache and a commanding manner. He was Sir Edgar Quibbe, the British prime minister.

'As you will see,' he continued, 'the Queen is most insistent that the building of the turbines must be continued with considerable alacrity. She will not tolerate the continued poisoning of her subjects' air with the resultant suffering and loss of life.'

This forthright endorsement from their sovereign brought smiles and sighs of relief from the others. Particularly from Charlotte Meridian, Duchess of Limington, a wealthy landowner who owned the site for the turbines. Astringent of features, thin and as stiffly upright as a new poker, Lady Charlotte was said to have been a great beauty when she ensnared the elderly and now sadly deceased Duke of Limington. It required a considerable imagination and a beneficent nature to believe that now.

Edward de Lacey, the government's choice of chief engineer who would head the ambitious project also had a great deal to be pleased about. For him a future full of wealthy patrons and a knighthood beckoned. Chief shareholder and financier Peregrine Gillette had reason to rejoice, as had Eustace Brinks who owned the Ephesysium Gas Works. His company bore the brunt of the public's wrath about the poisonous fogs, though they did not complain when his gases lit and warmed their homes.

Another investor was industrialist Sir Vivian Crimm-Smythe who had financed this project in order to present himself as a philanthropist and win favour with Her Majesty, which in turn would help him gain influence throughout the expanding Empire.

The final figure at the table was a man known only as Villance. A shadowy, silent presence who the Prime Minister always deferred to. The other members of the party therefore never questioned the mystery of his attendance at their meetings.

Quibbe continued: 'The last objectors to our project have been silenced and now we have the Queen's official endorsement. I intend to allow no obstructions from Parliament or any other source. The foundations are nearly finished and soon London can cease to be a festering sore and become our great pride again.'

The thought of a future with clean air over London was attractive but not as alluring as the financial gain all would gain from the project as the only shareholders of the newly formed Pneumaeris Company. The meeting continued for many hours with in-depth discussions over ways to speed up the project.

As they dispersed, Quibbe asked for the industrialist to remain behind.

Reluctantly Crimm-Smythe complied, though he resented being ordered about by some jumped up civil servant elected by fools. Alarmed by the continued presence of the sinister Villance, a man who dressed in black and always wore black leather gloves, he sat back down and waited to hear what the

Prime Minister had to say.

'I hear you have been a little careless towards a certain mixed race rapscallion.'

Crimm-Smythe did not answer, his gaze was drawn to the brooding form of Villance, now standing in front of the door, arms folded. His rough-hewn features as inscrutable as an Easter Island stone head. This was an openly threatening gesture, an outrage towards a respected and influential member of upper class society. This man needed an intimate encounter with one of his Mechmen one dark night.

Quibbe continued: 'Our official position over Mr Darian has not changed. He may continue to be an exotic thorn in the side of this country's establishment but until he perfects a stable form of Infernion, he is not to be harassed or harmed in any way. Do I make myself clear?'

Blanching, Crimm-Smythe fought to remain in control. It seemed that they had not found or identified the alchemist's body, or rather what was left of it after falling from a dirigible high above the city.

'Of course,' he replied forcing his features into the approximation of a smile. 'Though Mr Darian makes new enemies on a daily basis. Are you going to warn off all of them?'

'If we have to. I do not need to tell you the value to this country, to our Empire, of securing our own source of unlimited energy.'

'Of course not, Prime Minister.'

Quibbe stood up and without another word left the room followed by Villance, leaving the industrialist alone and breaking into a cold sweat. There would be no forgiveness for the killer of Infernion's creator. He was doomed unless he was able to offer the government something else ... something better.

And that was where the elusive and mysterious Technomicron came in. An informant in the supernatural underworld had told him about this object: an energy source of unlimited and eternal power.

With the wretched meddler Darian permanently out of the

picture, Crimm-Smythe was one step closer to gaining its fabled power for himself. Then let that jumped up civil servant and his glowering henchman grovel at his feet for favours like the crumbs off his table. How he would enjoy having them ejected bodily from his mansion by his Mechmen and dooming them to a life of penury and humiliation.

With this thought, Crimm-Smythe rose and headed back to his own transport. The day of his triumph was approaching. He could feel it.

21

Back in Mayfair, the gash in Belial's side healed quickly. Thankfully the Megoleth had no deadly hellish venom coating its horns: many underworld monsters did, making them dangerous to both human and supernatural beings alike. With Darian away seeking solace with his beautiful Chinese paramour, the demon sought to make himself useful.

Darian needed information and the demon had the means to find it. Belial checked his bandages. No more blood seeped from the wound though the healing was not complete. His body was immune from the dangers of infection but the smell of fresh blood would be a hindrance where he planned to go. Some creatures became unreasonable and irrational when their senses were inflamed by bloodlust.

Belial dressed and masked the blood scent with some ghastly cologne stolen from Hardwick's room. The man had taken to wearing it in his primitive courtship ritual of the Dedman female, and curiously she was responding, despite the cologne. Perhaps the lure of a title robbed human women of their sense of smell as well as their discernment. The demon wondered how long this fledgling alliance would last once the Dedmans discovered that Hardwick was penniless.

Slipping out of the servants' entrance, Belial began the journey to his destination, made easy by his swiftness and the occasional spatial leap. It was impossible for him not to make an impression as he passed. Animals were the most perceptive. Carriage horses shied away or reared, and even the oldest and most overworked nags managed to throw up their heads and snort in fear, Belial's angry glare at their drivers sparing the poor beasts a lashing. Feral dogs ran towards him, hackles raised, their teeth bared in frightened snarls. Those on leads embarrassed their owners by lunging at the passing demon:

friendly mutts and lapdogs turned into growling furies by his presence on the streets. Some tried to apologise for their wayward canines but on seeing Belial's eyes, hurried away, hauling their pets with them.

The skies above his head grew dark with circling birds: timid pigeons that kept to the skies and bolder crows who dared to mob him. Belial flash-fried a few as a warning to the others to leave him alone. It worked.

Before long, leaving a trail of shudders and bad dreams in his wake, the demon arrived in Islington. The area – recently swallowed by the ever-growing sprawl of London – did its best to retain the pleasant atmosphere of a small village, once surrounded by green fields and woodland. But judging from the overcrowded state of Upper and High Street, its main thoroughfares, the good citizens of Islington had already lost the battle.

Belial strolled past a drinking fountain topped with an imposing new statue of some old Elizabethan worthy. He read the inscription to find it was a certain Sir Hugh Myddleton who stared down on him with an expression of stony superiority. One flash of the demon's eyes and the statue was minus its nose. There had to be some compensation for losing his princely powers even if it was just some occasional frivolous mischief.

He arrived at his destination, an innocuous looking Tudor inn in Hobb's Place called The Serpent of Eden, built with a thatched roof and half-timbered overhang. He entered through a low, narrow oak door and strode past a handful of early lunchtime drinkers leaning over the bar deep in conversation which did not stop at the demon's arrival. What he sought was in an even older part of the inn, down beneath the cellars, a labyrinth of caverns whose stone slab walls had stood since before the arrival of Christianity.

Belial pondered over whether any of the current denizens of Islington knew about the ancient satanic pact sealed by their ancestors in the Sixteenth Century, a time of religious turmoil and savagery. With so many lives lost to this clash of fundamentalist beliefs, the people decided that both sides were wrong and chose to pledge their allegiance to the Devil instead.

That there wasn't actually such an entity could have been problematic had it not been for Fallen Prince Sammael stepping in to fill the expectations of the would be worshippers. Now no trace of the old pact remained beyond the name of the street and the existence of the Serpent Inn. Their loss, Belial thought. The locals may have won a recent doomed battle to prevent their large village green from being enclosed and built over, but some residual memory must linger. The drinkers up above had kept their backs to Belial despite his being a stranger and Belial had found the entrance to the cellar and labyrinth beneath it unopposed.

At first, the chambers were unlit and though he could see in the dark, Belial set pitch torches in the walls alight with his eyes. He was not alone, sheltering in this refuge of the damned were many demonic life forms, half-humans, fae and shapeshifters waiting until nightfall to emerge and spend time above ground. His arrival caused great excitement and all fell to their knees in obeisance to Hellish royalty. The caverns were spacious, well appointed and comfortable with fine furniture and gilded wall hangings, display cabinets lined the walls, full of treasures stolen from humans over the centuries.

He allowed the creatures to fuss over him, fetching him a jewel-encrusted throne and a large gold goblet of finest wine. It was good to be appreciated for a change. To be given the due reverence as a Fallen Prince. He also began to attract female attention. A sinuous succubus in her most tempting form curled at his feet, lasciviously stroking his legs. One of the fae risked a venomous bite from the jealous she-devil by sensuously caressing Belial's long hair, her deceptively ethereal body glistening with silver fairy dust. The attention was understandable: he was beautiful and perfectly capable of pleasuring all of them. Belial raised one hand and everything in the room froze in fear and anticipation.

'If someone can truthfully answer me one question, my mission here is over and I can get on with enjoying myself with so much delightful company.'

Belial got his answer within seconds from an angry and bitter full demon summoned by an inept human mage and not returned to Hell. One that hated the human world and punished it at every opportunity.

With his mission accomplished and with a grin of anticipation, Belial allowed himself to be taken away to the succubus' bedchamber along with the red headed fae and a charming pigeon-pair of half-human, silver skinned twins with knowing twinkles in their obsidian eyes.

Loving Darian did not stop Belial delighting in carnal pleasures. He looked forward to an exhilarating night of continuous steamy tumbling of lithe limbs, long probing tongues, lashing tails and the stimulation of erogenous zones unknown to humans.

The next morning, Belial left his completely exhausted bed companions slumbering and returned to Mayfair with a jaunty gait.

22

Although trapped in China, at least Darian could eat breakfast.

He was famished and couldn't remember the last time he'd eaten anything. He'd imbibed a considerable amount of alcohol but nothing solid and nutritious. He sat on a padded mat on the floor and gratefully accepted a bowl of steaming *congee* and *yu za kuei* from an elderly woman. He had no idea if she was one of the Lady's illusions or a genuine local woman but the rice gruel and deep fried dough were real and delicious.

With no sign of the Lady, he yearned to walk outside and breathe in the untainted air of the mountains. He wanted to walk on grass that was not yellow and withered, to hear bird song, and watch a flight of white cranes across the valley, to see trees full of green life and not stunted and dying. Even so, Darian was loathe to leave the Emporium, even for a few moments. That is all it would take for the shop to disappear, abandoning him in this beautiful but remote region as a penniless outsider in a land closed to foreigners.

Revived by the meal, Darian's agile mind raced to find a solution to his dilemma. He doubted any amount of pleading, coercing or threatening would change the Lady's mind. He was far too great a threat to her success in acquiring the Technomicron.

The old lady put down a pot of tea, refilled his rice bowl and placed newly cooked 'deep fried devils' on the plate beside it.

Darian smiled, and nodded in gratitude. 'Thank you,' he said. 'Forgive my foreign bad manners. I do not even know your name.'

The old lady's wrinkle-seamed and weathered face broke into a gap toothed smile. 'Nor I, young master. It has been so long since anyone addressed me by my own name.'

Her head turned to the outside world. 'You could wander in

the valley if you wish, the Emporium will wait for you.'

Darian sighed, another of the Lady's tricks?

'I will remain within these walls, wise mother.'

The old lady rose to her feet and began to walk away, her feet unbroken and unbound, proclaiming her status as a peasant working the land.

'This place is not always under the control of the Lady,' she said. 'The Emporium has a beating heart and sometimes it seeks its own destination and that of those it loves.'

With that she stepped towards the nearest wall, her body becoming fainter like a fading dream before she disappeared into the fabric of the Emporium. Before he could deliberate over her words, with a shudder and a shimmer of many bright lights, the Emporium became the lacquered splendour of an audience chamber in an Emperor's Palace. The humble kitchen became a glory of painted silk screens, intricately carved wood dragons and gilding.

The Lady appeared, no longer in the form of Li Mei but in the formal, heavy and elaborate garb of a Chinese princess, austere and untouchable in her red, gold and flower embroidered silks. Her hair hidden beneath an intricate red and gold headdress of silk and precious metal, hung with long strings of pearls and vivid pink silk tassels. Clearly she was in no mood for lovemaking but for negotiation with her holding all the winning cards.

'So, Princess, what do I have to do to get back to London?'

Darian could see no point in being anything but direct with her in this uncompromising mood.

'Let me have the Technomicron.'

'Is that all?' Cyrus replied with a nonchalant shrug. 'It's yours.'

Her face and voice hardened. 'Too easy, *sai gwai lo*, if you are going to lie at least make it more convincing.'

Beyond the chamber walls, Darian could hear the sound of someone sharpening a weapon, a sword. There was nothing subtle about the implied threat.

'We have a stalemate then,' Darian continued. 'How are we

going to break it?'

The Princess gave a haughty, dismissive gesture with her extravagant long lacquered fingernails, a symbol of an indulged and worshipped woman who would never need to lift a finger in life.

'We don't. You are to remain in China until the book is safely in the hands of my client.'

'What if I were to acquire it for you? You have already said it is too dangerous to be left in my reckless hands. In return all I want is your help to gain a perfect Orb of Jhan. A spectral rainbow one with no flaws or inclusions.'

'Such a sphere does not exist.'

'Doesn't it?' replied Darian, delighted at the hint of uncertainty in her voice. 'Are you so sure?'

Desire sparkled in her near-black eyes. Reluctantly she conceded that to acquire both esoteric treasures would require Darian's assistance. She could imagine holding something as exquisite as a rainbow Orb in her hands, to feel its great and as yet unknown power pulsing through her. She had to have it! Not for any client – however wealthy – but for herself. It was a need too great to consider that Cyrus Darian might be lying again. The Emporium began to change appearance once more.

'I will take you back to London, my precious one, but not before we enjoy each others company to celebrate our accord.'

Darian walked out into a familiar world of London obscured by a denser than usual London Particular, it was noon but the smog made it as dark as early evening and his lungs, now used to the clean air of the Wuyi Mountains, now filled up with the putrid smoke and gas fumes of London. The situation with the air quality had worsened and with it, the power of anyone offering a solution. The sound of blaring foghorns drew his attention to the Thames, once a river now a noxious liquid thoroughfare. He had never seen so many heavily laden steam barges heading upstream to the Great Turbine scheme building site. The directors of the Pneumaeris Company must be rubbing their already wealthy hands in triumph.

Shaking his head sadly, Darian made his way home, all the time considering how he might obtain either the Technomicron or the Orb of Jhan. At this point, both seemed as unobtainable as the other ... but there had to be a way ... there had to.

23

Darian remained in his laboratory. He told the others that it was to work on something vital to the mission, but in truth it was to shut himself away from the clamour. Four wild, dangerous days had passed and he was no nearer tracking the Technomicron, he was beginning to question its existence. Was it another fraud like the Scroll of Thebus? Would he not be better employed seeking a perfect rainbow Orb of Jhan which actually might exist? Something of cosmic beauty that he could use for his benefit.

Darian liked being alone with his jars of rare earths, phials of mercury, sulphur and more mysterious contents, precious stones of power and obscure minerals. The ornate platinum-lined chests containing glysander seeds, tannis leaves and whole mandrake roots gave him comfort. He was able to relax in a world that was familiar, where in theory he was in control of his destiny.

Alchemy was an esoteric mixture of the spiritual, the philosophical and the use of the five elements of water, earth, fire, air and spirit. It was Darian's first calling in life, and the continued investigation and research led him to his second: adventure – the means to an end to bring him what he needed to progress. This in turn had led him down paths dark and dangerous … the pursuit of the knowledge of necromancy.

Modern day chemistry had no interest for Darian. He found it limited in aspiration and frankly far too tame for his adventurous spirit. No chemist would be searching for the Elixir of Immortal Life or a stone that could transmute base metal into gold. He needed the adventure to go with it. The spirit of discovery … something he was in danger of losing in this frustrating hunt for a wretchedly elusive book.

Was the Technomicron really worth it? Was it worth tearing open his heart and letting unbearable pain flood in by contacting his beloved: his peerless and beautiful Nafrini, his wife?

Darian was not ready to answer this question but as weariness overcame him, he lay on a *chaise longue* and prepared to seek solace by chasing the dragon. He laid out the means: a hookah, a box of matches and prepared opium paste. Then, with Misha curled protectively at his side, Darian entered oblivion.

He felt warm sand move beneath his feet and recognised a familiar smell: a blend of eons old silt, fresh flowing water and lush green reeds. The scent would rise in the midday heat from the nearby Nile. Darian knew if he turned and looked behind him, he would see an ochre and red brick building decorated with multi-coloured tiles in patterns of birds and palms. It would be surrounded by tall palms and a carefully tended fragrant garden irrigated by a series of dancing fountains. Darian knew this was only a dream. A cruel temptation … how easy it would be to give in to the illusion and walk towards that building, stroll through the garden, where he once watched the planting of every bloom, helped tend each growing shoot …

Would it be so very wrong to let the dream engulf him? Let him spend time in the mirage of a place and time forever forbidden to him?

A hot kiss on his forehead awoke Darian, groggy from his opium dreams. He struggled to rise, pushing the grinning demon away.

'This had better be good, Belial. Something better then floating adrift in Paradise.'

'A fool's Paradise, built on poison,' snapped Belial, who hated Darian indulging in this weakening human vice. Not any other human of course, anything that made men more corruptible was fine by him. 'While you were wasting your life in a self-pitying stupor, I have been busy.'

Darian arose and, filling a bowl of cold water, splashed his face trying to clear the bitter opium fog from inside his head. He could smell the lingering taint of succubus venom and saw telltale traces of fairy dust on Belial. He had been very busy.

'All healed? Silly question. Good. Now go on then, tell me what you have discovered.'

'Not until I have your full attention,' Belial replied with a wicked grin and emptied the entire pitcher of water over the alchemist's head.

'Thank you. I am fully awake now,' Darian muttered with ill grace, his hair and clothes now soaking and cold.

'I have called back some favours in the capital's Underworld and discovered who created the missing grimoire which is supposed to be part of the Technomicron. It was a powerful magus called Ostanes.'

'That damn Persian,' muttered Darian with a disappointed groan. 'He was supposed to have aided both Xerxes and Alexander the Great which took some doing as there was a century separating them. Doubt if he is still available to have a cosy little chat to.'

'You would have a great deal to talk about, Cyrus. The man was an authority on alchemy, necromancy, divination, and on the mystical properties of plants and stones. Revered by all those dabbling in the mysterious arts for centuries,' said the demon.

'And by my parents!' Darian countered with a sharp release of old bitterness. 'I was born and raised in the shadow of the wretched man. Nearly got named after him.'

Darian began to collect himself, ready to join the rest of his team but Belial halted him with a hand on his shoulder. 'You cannot leave it like that! I need to hear the whole story now.'

Well used to the demon's curiosity about his life, Darian knew it was quicker to comply.

'Ostanes was a great hero of my father. From a tiny child, my bedtime stories were the legends surrounding the magician's mysterious life. My father made me study the books supposedly containing his wisdom. Even said I was a direct descendant of the man. My mother said I was born an old soul, perhaps Ostanes reincarnated.'

'Families!' laughed Belial. 'Nothing to be envious about there.'

'Never mind that my achievements were down to my own brilliance!' Darian continued, reopening old hurt. 'It all had to be down to some long dust old Persian! I vowed to be a far greater alchemist than Ostanes.'

'Well, it is time to make your acquaintance with your nemesis and countryman,' Belial said. 'Prove that you are a better sorcerer than him and conjure up his ghost.'

Darian returned with Belial to the others. He needed distraction. His mind was racing at the implications of what the demon had proposed. There were doors best kept closed. One to the afterlife and an encounter with a man once able to live for centuries was such a door. Releasing a restless, clever spirit who may be eager for another chance of mortal life was fraught with peril to the man who raised it. His own life could be forfeit, his body commandeered, his own spirit sent to the afterlife in its place.

It would be down to who was the best necromancer. Long dead Ostanes or vibrantly alive Darian?

If the others were aware of Darian's mood, they did not show it. Dinner was prepared and eaten but he did not join in their conversation or eat anything but remained quiet and contemplative in what may be his last hours alive.

The alchemist had to be alone: the danger to himself and the living was too great. He also needed to be in a remote area with no buildings close by that could act as a temporary sanctuary to the bidden soul. Darian could at least find reassurance in the company of Belial who was immune to any peril caused by calling up the dead. They took a fast locomotive to the Thames Estuary town of Tilbury and from there by hired horse and trap to the wide, lonely expanse of wetlands that stretched to the North Sea.

Sheltering the horse in an abandoned boathouse, they finished the journey with a mile-long walk on foot. A bitter east wind cut through their clothes, chilling them to the bone, causing even Belial in his human form to shiver. The bleak, dramatic landscape of wide pewter sky sullen with low clouds, open grey sea and seeming endless mudflats spread around them. As if sensing something other worldly was about to happen, the teeming birdlife of the marshes was silent, even the arrival of the waves onto the pebble strewn shore seemed subdued.

Wrapped in a thick wool coat, with a turned up fur collar, Darian stood quietly, focusing on becoming serene and in complete control of his mind and body. With Belial's assistance, he burnt several protective large circles with ancient Egyptian pitch taken from the Pyramid of Khufu. In between the circles he created many ancient symbols in carefully poured salt, reinforced by talismans of binding and protection. Around the inner circle, he scattered a dried mixture of henbane, mandrake, aloe wood, hemlock, aconite and opium.

Satisfied he had done all he could, Darian stood in the centre of the circles and removed a wand from his coat.

This was a simple rod made of old oak unadorned with symbols or stones, and infused with deep, old earth magicke. Ignoring the strengthening, bitter wind, he removed all his clothes and handed them to Belial. Then he spent some more time meditating and gathering his inner power before setting the herb ring ablaze.

As the heady, bitter scent of the smoke rose into the gloom-laden sky, Darian began complex incantations of summoning, a mixture of many languages: Sumerian; Chaldean; Latin and Greek; and other words of languages so ancient their origins were long lost. Getting any of the words wrong or spoken in an incorrect order could be fatal to the necromancer, such was the might of the dark forces he was evoking.

As Darian's voice rose in strength and power, the already chill air became glacial, and indistinct shapes formed and dissolved beyond the outer circle: the inevitable gathering of earthbound spirits. Darian dismissed them with a violent Chaldean oath and a powerful gesture with the oak wand. He then switched to an ancient form of Farsi, the language of his ancestors, the language of Ostanes, and the summoning became personal.

Unlike the drama of summoning demons, calling on the long dead Ostanes to appear in spirit form created no whirling vortex or rents in the fabric of reality. The force of Darian's will

CYRUS DARIAN AND THE TECHNOMICRON

reached out and connected with the never ceasing essence of all
things ever created, seeking and finding the immortal soul of
the Magus. Darian connected with Ostanes and called him
forth.

Darian had little time to speak to the spectral figure standing
outside the circles: the Magus brought with him the dread cold
of the void that separated the worlds of the living and the dead.
He could make out the man's features: a strong, handsome face,
authorative and confident. Even in their spectral form, his eyes
blazed with power and knowledge. And, Darian felt, a hint of
possible insanity.

'Spirit, I command you to answer my questions.' Darian
dredged up some sense of certainty and conviction while
shutting out the doubt and fear that this presence evoked.

'Who are you to summon one such as I? A mere child
playing with forces beyond your comprehension and control.'

Ostanes attempted to step forward and breach the protective
circle, his eyes gleaming with need. He wanted to live again. He
wanted Darian's body.

'Stay where you are spirit!' Darian shouted, holding out the
oak wand towards Ostanes like a sword. 'You made six
grimoires, one is missing. I need to know where it is.'

'You think you know the art of necromancy, boy? That any
spirit you summon from beyond the void must obey you? I am
not any spirit, I am the greatest sorcerer ever born. I am the
immortal Ostanes.'

'You are still a life form made of ethereal matter subject to
the laws of the universe,' Ostanes turned sharply as the demon
approached, 'so be a good little ghost and answer the nice
gentleman.'

Shocked by the unexpected presence of a prince of Hell, who
had the power to make his afterlife very unpleasant, Ostanes
backed away, subdued, his opportunity to return to life dashed.

'I see you have friends in high – or should it be low – places,
young man. You clearly are worthy to call yourself a
necromancer. Not surprising: you are of ancient Persian blood.
The grimoire you seek is kept safe in a castle in what you call

Northumberland. Protected by occult forces and the ingenuity of your age. That is all I know.'

'Is is true it is bound in human skin?' Darian asked, more in curiosity then need.

'Indeed!' Ostanes' spirit form grew stronger, the shape of his body and clothing becoming more distinct as Darian's strength began to fade, energy drained from the encounter and the fearsome cold. 'It is bound in my own skin!'

The spirit moved closer, his eyes blazing with a fierce intensity. 'Let me touch your hand, let me bind you to the grimoire, it will call out for you and only you. Only you could possess it, control it.'

Ostanes was getting ambitious, it was time to dismiss the spectre and send it back to the afterlife.

'I dismiss you by evoking the might of all the gods and goddesses of Earth. In the name of Isis, Osiris, Danu, Astarte …'

Ostanes grew agitated, his spirit resisting the invisible bindings that pulled him back from the world of the living.

'Fool! Base-born son of a dog, I am offering you unimaginable power!' Ostanes snarled as his form began to fluctuate and fade. Only his eyes remained, glowering with power. 'Nothing ever came from that fly-blown village of Darian except thieves and whores. In my time as in yours.'

'In the name of Odin, Amaterasu, Atua Fafine, Podaga, Brahma …'

Darian grew weaker, exhausted and freezing cold yet he could still see Ostanes' spirit as it refused to leave, Belial could threaten him but it was down to the necromancer to send the spirit back or perish in the attempt.

'I curse you, beggar boy, worthless son of a cur and a whore. Curse you never to possess the book, never to enjoy another day or night of your miserable existence.'

'I have been cursed by better than you, Ostanes,' laughed Darian before glancing at Belial. 'Is that all he can do? What a pathetic old bag of wind!'

Turning his attention back to the outraged spirit, Darian continued his incantation.

'I dismiss you in the name of An, Ra, Lei Kun …' Darian focused all his last dregs of energy into one last name, the Persian god of infinite time, space and destiny, of light and darkness. 'In the name of Zurvan!'

The power of this name was enough. Ostanes shrank back, eyes flashing with contempt then he appeared to bow in defeat and vanished.

Darian collapsed heavily onto the ground like a marionette with its strings cut.

Belial's eyes flashed and set a pile of driftwood alight, desperate to get Darian warm. The alchemist's skin was blue, coated with frost, his body shutting down in a crisis beyond hypothermia. His soul had touched that of the Magus and had nearly lost to the man's will and the void between all worlds and dimensions. Darian had fought and won a battle and gained vital knowledge but nearly at the cost of far more than his life.

Belial held him tightly, transferring as much of his demonic body heat as Darian's body could safely take, urging him to wake up, cajoling and demanding, every thing but praying. Even a demon had principles.

Before Belial could make any progress reviving him, the darkening sky thundered with the sound of a fast approaching large dirigible. Hardwick? Leaving Darian close to the fire, the demon stood up and prepared to welcome or fight the approaching visitors.

An airman accurately shot a harpoon anchor from the gondola. It dug in and dragged along the deep, wet sand before stopping the braking dirigible close to Belial's fire. Ladders fell and a squad of dark-clad men, scrambled down, all heavily armed with Cusack Traction Repeaters. Powerful weapons usually only used by the British military. So these clearly were not Mechmen or Fogue's punishers. The demon held his wrath in check until he knew their intent.

A hatchet-faced man, unarmed, and by his manner, their leader, stepped forward. 'I know how much damage you can do to my men, demon, but it only takes one well aimed shot to kill Darian.'

'I take it you are not here to go wildfowling,' Belial sneered, contemplating whether he could take them all out without endangering the stricken alchemist.

'We are here to have a private talk with Mr Darian.'

'Best of luck with that,' returned Belial feigning nonchalance but desperate to get back to Darian before he lost him forever. 'He is not receiving visitors at the moment.'

Ignoring the threat of their gunfire, Belial returned to cradle the alchemist, trying to warm him back to life, willing him to live with all the tortured burnt cinder of his once angelic heart.

'He needs urgent medical help,' insisted the leader, 'we will ensure he gets it.'

'Not without me,' Belial snarled, his eyes flashing with hellfire., 'Who are you and what do you want with Cyrus Darian?'

'My name is not important, but Mr Darian is. His work is highly regarded by the highest authorities in the land. He has however been under threat recently, at least more than is usual for a man of his nature and occupation. My remit is to take him to a place of safety, a refuge. You are most welcome to accompany him as a gesture of our goodwill and beneficent intent.'

Belial was torn. Should he attempt to fight a whole squad of armed men and risk harm to Darian, or comply and let them take him to an unknown fate. He put his hand over Darian's heart and struggled to find a beat. He had no actual choice after all.

'I'll carry him up to the dirigible and stay with him but I hope that bag of hot air is swift. We are losing him.'

As the demon ascended to the airship, Villance walked back to where they had found the stricken alchemist. He gazed with grim satisfaction at the complex of strange symbols burnt into the ground. So, the intelligence from his agents had been right,

Cyrus Darian did more than mess about with weird potions and rare metals. He was also a skilled necromancer. There was no doubt in Villance's mind he had found the right man to get him the book.

24

Mirhennis Gates. So, they had thought of nearly everything, Belial mused as he rushed the fading form of the alchemist through the Tower of London under the guard of the men in black. The historic Tower was a place of security and the last forlorn hopes of the condemned: a thousand years of tears and screams still resonated from the pale stone walls. Belial was not surprised they had brought him to the old royal fortress. Trust the English to be traditional in their choices of confinement.

The still nameless leader indicated a set of rooms down a corridor. There was nothing unusual to the human eye but the entrance was booby-trapped to prevent anything supernatural stepping across the threshold, the power hidden deep within the stones. Belial had thought that this had been too easy, their captors' ready compliance far too quickly given. Now he knew why. The Mirhennis Gates could destroy breeth and blaggers, hell minions, wraith and most minor demons. They had expected their supernatural ward to deter and repel higher entities but Belial had stepped through without hindrance. They had not planned for a prince of the Fallen!

Enjoying their shocked expressions, the demon entered a bedroom where several men waited. They were senior physicians by their equipment and demeanour. Belial stepped back and allowed the doctors to do what they could for Darian, which seemed to involve a great deal of examining, puzzled head shaking and numerous calls for more blankets.

He turned to Hatchet Face, the man's confident air badly shaken by Belial's scornful dismissal of the Mirhennis Gates. 'Why have you brought him here? Cyrus is no traitor.'

'Nor is he a British citizen, we have the death penalty for foreign spies but be not concerned demon. Mr Darian is here to be protected from his enemies in the national interest.'

The demon didn't bother to mention that Cyrus would not accept any form of confinement however well intentioned. That they could discover for themselves if he recovered. When he recovered.

'His heart has stopped,' called one of the physicians. 'Bring in the amberite resusciton galvaniser! Now!'

Unable to do anything to help, Belial paced the floor. The curse of losing the healing powers of angels to the destructive nature of demons had never felt so crushing.

The medical team rushed a large machine into the room. It was supported by solid wood pillars on heavy casters. The medics placed the centre of the machine above Darian's chest and a damp cloth pad above his heart, and with no time to lose threw a series of switches to set it in motion. The whirring noise of the internal generator filled the room. Friction against a line of amber rods set within the machine built up a charge. The air became ionised and painful static sparks prickled around metal objects and the living as an electric charge built up inside the galvaniser. With a command for everyone to stand well clear of the bed, one doctor, protected by rubberised clothing, remained to operate the machine.

The medic pulled down a lever and a miniature flash of lightning hit Darian's heart, his body arched and spasmed then fell back on the bed, juddering from every nerve ending. Another medic quickly checked for a heartbeat and shook his head. Hatchet Face commanded them to shock him again, and one senior physician tried to argue with him.

'Villance,' he said, 'there is no point, this is a dead man.'

Conflicted, Belial wanted them to stop. It looked so cruel, like some sort of sadistic torture, but he didn't want Darian to die. 'Do it again,' he commanded, his eyes giving a warning fiery flash. 'If he is already dead, then what have you got to lose?'

He stood by the bed and took Darian's face in his hands. 'Come on my friend,' he urged in Farsi. 'You have succubus venom in your bloodstream, you are tough and resilient and you can pull through this. Live damn you! Live!'

'Shock him again!' Belial snarled at the physicians who looked to Villance for guidance.

'Do as the creature says,' Villance replied, grim faced. Losing the alchemist would be a personal disaster for him and his ambitions of power.

The one in protective clothing primed the galvaniser again, urging Belial to stand well clear once the charge had built to a critical point.

'Let it stay,' Villance ordered. 'Miniature lightning cannot harm it.'

Once again Darian's body arched and flailed as the charge hit his heart, but once again he fell back on the bed lifeless.

'This is madness,' the chief physician protested. 'Let him go, in the name of God.'

'Leave *Him* out of this,' Belial's voice was cold, insistent. 'Use the machine again. Do it as many times as it takes to bring him back.'

Two more futile shocks from the galvaniser and the physicians' protests grew more strident, urging Villance and the demon to stop.

'The man is dead,' the senior doctor declared. 'Stop this insanity – no amount of lightening coursing through a corpse will resurrect it.'

Another remonstrated: 'This is the real world, Villance, not *Modern Prometheus*. The lurid fiction of a deranged mind.'

Belial's eyes flashed with fury, scorching a deep hole in a stone wall opposite him. 'You stop when I tell you!'

Too terrified to argue, the physicians set up the galvaniser one more time. The power built, the charge discharged, and this time they were rewarded when Darian's heart started an unsteady rhythm before stabilising into a regular strong beat.

'A miracle!' shouted one of the physicians.

'Much overrated,' replied an overjoyed Belial. 'Always trust your knowledge and well oiled machines over miracles.'

As the physicians, watched over by Villance, set about

ensuring that Darian was indeed alive, and checking him for all other signs of health or otherwise, so Belial took his leave of them.

The demon could see that these unknown but well-connected men needed the alchemist safe and alive, and so he was in the best hands at this moment. However Hardwick and Cambion would want to know where Darian was, and Belial needed to check that the Dedmans were well on their way back to the colonies.

Belial sighed to himself. A demon's work was never done.

25

Athena Dedman had no intention of becoming the swooning victim of the next attempt on her life and that of her father.

As soon as she was able, she stripped off the frivolous ruffles of her extravagant bustle skirts and chose from the wardrobe instead a smart brown riding habit. This would be both decent and practical for any misadventure that may befall her. Beneath it, she wore a pair of boy's trousers so that her modesty would never be compromised. That scoundrel Darian had so enjoyed translating what Fogue's henchman had said to her. The memory of how deeply she had blushed as he defined the meaning of 'rantipole', 'grinding' and 'buttered bun' was horribly etched in her mind as were the lewd and loathsome acts he described with such unseemly relish.

Cyrus Darian was no gentleman, a total decadent cad like the wild bohemian artists he befriended and went carousing with. His was a reckless world of overindulgence, with an impudent disregard for the strictures of polite society and the unchaperoned company of their 'stunners': the artists' models and other girls with loose morals. At least she was under the protection of her father: a real gentleman.

As no true lady went anywhere in public without hat, gloves and a parasol, Anthea frowned as the surveyed the selection available. She passed over hats that were light-hearted riots of feathers and lace and chose instead a stoutly made riding bowler. A pair of leather gloves were perfect and more practical than mittens of embroidered silk. The parasol, however, was more problematical.

Athena frowned at her reflection in the mirror. Ah well, if she had no parasol then so be it. She brushed down the riding habit and left the room to join the others.

Later that day, Athena sat for afternoon tea with her father in Darian's parlour.

Nobody was too concerned over the whereabouts of the alchemist in the aftermath of the siege of Old Nickol. Darian had become withdrawn and silent for a few days but as he was on a research mission at the old museum archives with the demon, the others did not appear to worry about his safety.

The parlour door opened, and she welcomed the enthusiastic arrival of Sir Miles Hardwick, his face plastered with a smile that somehow combined boyish awkwardness and pride. He carried a long parcel wrapped in brown paper beneath his arm and addressed Athena with a rush of enthusiasm.

'My dear Miss Dedman, I have been heartened by your fortitude since the regrettable incident with those blaggards. May I be so presumptuous to offer you a small token, a gift which I hope you find both practical and efficacious.'

Athena hesitated, aware of the inventor's growing puppy-like adoration for her.

Her father gave her hand a gentle squeeze and smiled. 'My dear child, anything this gentleman brings you as a gift will not be unseemly or improper.'

Suspecting a conspiracy between the two men, she agreed to accept the gift, allowing Hardwick to open the large and awkwardly shaped parcel. He produced what appeared to be a neat silk parasol, the colour perfectly matching her brown habit. Athena broke into a wide smile of delight at the thoughtfulness and reached out to take it from him.

'Not so fast, dear lady,' Hardwick replied with a wink, 'this is no ordinary parasol. Please, may I ask the indulgence of yourself and Mr Dedman to accompany me to the garden?

'The London Particular has chosen not to grace us with its foul presence,' he added, 'the afternoon air is almost tolerable.'

They strolled out into the small, unattended overgrown mess that had formerly been Darian's garden. Unfortunately virtually nothing grew in London now beyond sickly looking nettles and brambles. With a flourish, Hardwick demonstrated that the pretty ivory carved handle in the shape of an elegant greyhound's head was in fact the handgrip of a hidden pistol that could be detached and fired separately or used to trigger the release of a dart disguised in the tip of the parasol. He aimed it at the trunk of a dead plane tree, greatly satisfied by the squeal of astonishment and delight from Athena as a dart sped from the parasol ending up deeply embedded in the wood.

'Amazing!' declared Zachariah Dedman. 'Truly wonderful. And look, my dear, another dart has automatically moved to take its place!'

'And there is more, with your permission …'

Hardwick opened the parasol and pressing a switch hidden in the handle released a series of vicious looking blades at the end of each tine. He gave the parasol a fast twirl to show the extent of how lethal it had become.

'This may look like silk, but do not be deceived. It is a revolutionary new fabric developed by myself and Cyrus: bullet resistant and as strong as steel.'

Bowing he handed the parasol to Athena.

Dedman senior clapped him on the back., 'How can I thank you, sir. I will sleep easier knowing my beloved daughter can fend off any scoundrels with this fantastical invention.'

'It is one of a kind, Mr Dedman,' added the inventor, 'so any potential assailants will not be suspecting a harmless lady's parasol.'

'Please, call me Zachariah, my dear boy,' an avuncular Dedman announced as he watched his daughter practice with the weapon. This man was an English Lord, no doubt with a fortune, a fine family mansion and huge country estate, unmarried and with an obvious attraction for his daughter. Fate worked in the most fortuitous ways. He decided to forgo his plan to leave Darian's home and flee back to America with Athena. This was a newborn romance needing a little cultivation.

'Then you both must call me Miles. We are after all partners in this struggle against adversity.'

Both men applauded as Athena accurately fired a bolt to

land within a whisker's breadth of the other in the tree trunk.

Without turning her face towards Hardwick, she addressed him sternly. 'I am still Miss Dedman to you, sir. Adversity is not a cause for a breakdown in morals and the standards of decent society.'

Hardwick bowed in silent assent, her strong, stalwart manner only fuelling his growing adoration.

As they returned to the house, Cambion was back from feeding the dragoncat down in the cellars. He kept his head low, unable to look directly at the woman without displaying his unease at her proximity.

'I don't suppose any of you know why Darian and the demon are not back yet? They do seem to have been at the museum for an awfully long time.'

'Not long enough in my opinion,' sniffed Athena as she removed her coat. 'Mr Cambion, you are a quiet-living educated man, Lord Hardwick, you are an English aristocrat, why you tolerate the company of this man and his demon is beyond all comprehension.'

'Beyond ours too,' admitted Cambion, still keeping his head down. 'He has this way of making you believe black is white. You know it is not true, yet something about Cyrus Darian makes you go along with the lie.'

Hardwick had no simple explanation. That the alchemist occasionally supported him financially was something he could never admit to any one, ever. He was poor but he had the tattered remnants of his pride to protect. The Hardwicks were an old, respected family with a noble heritage. It was deeply shameful to be the first black sheep, the one who had squandered centuries of land and wealth. The collaboration between him and Darian in scientific discoveries was at least something he was proud of and said so to the American woman.

'That I can understand,' Athena said, settling in the drawing room, 'but the other matters: the search for occult artefacts and the great danger he puts you in. That I cannot understand.'

'Yet, meaning you no disrespect, Miss Dedman, but isn't

your father in the same business, as a collector of the curious and bizarre?' Hardwick replied, the need to justify his alliance with Darian to this woman had become increasingly important to him.

Dedman senior, alarmed at his daughter's manner toward her potential future husband, tried to intervene. 'Athena, please, there is no need for this.'

Flustered, but unwilling to discontinue, Athena fiddled with her delicately worked silver pendant watch. 'No, not the same business at all. My father is interested in ancient art, in history – not the accoutrements of the supernatural. Of evil.'

'Talking of which,' a familiar silken voice made them turn around, 'the Prince of Darkness has returned.'

Belial.

'And before you all ask, Cyrus is alright. Though in a bit of an awkward spot, so nothing new there.'

26

Darian was not aware of much beyond being comfortable and well cared for. He drifted in and out of consciousness from a dreamless state to one where a sweet smelling female soothed his brow and offered him sips of water and a light chicken broth. He was in no state to care, too weak to lift his head let alone explore his surroundings. He was blind but for a vague awareness of blurred shapes. One thing was certain, he was no longer in the Tower. At some point while unconscious, his captors or even the Lady had moved him elsewhere. The Tower smelled of the ages, its walls held the shades of past miseries. Here in this room the stone walls held nothing beyond the shock of being ripped from their sleeping place in the earth.

As time merged into a continuum of darkness and gentle light, his senses gradually began to sharpen up. He made out voices, mainly female and none hostile, all appeared concerned about his wellbeing and recovery. Deciding they had nothing to do with the Lady and were there as nurses, he started to recognise individuals: an older, brisk woman clearly in authority, and two younger girls, one with a genteel London accent and one with a distinct Kerry lilt. He waited until the Kerry girl was caring for him and whispered to her in Irish, 'Where am I, *mo stor,* what is happening to me?'

Taken aback at first at the surprising sound of her native tongue, the girl paused as if making sure no one could overhear their conversation and replied, 'My Lord, you have nothing to worry about. You have been very ill, but you are in safe hands and recovering.'

'Whose hands?'

'Why, Her Majesty's Government of course! You are a personage of great importance, we were told we must do everything to make you comfortable and facilitate your swift recovery.'

'Where am I?'

Again the girl appeared flustered but could see no reason not to tell him the truth. 'You are at Cramburgh Castle.'

Northumberland. Whoever they really were, how did they know to take him to a castle in Northumberland?

'*Caoimhe,* there are twenty guineas in my coat and another twenty waiting for you when I am back on my feet if you can send word to Sir Miles Hardwick of Hyde Park Gardens that I am here in Cramburgh. But the message must come from you and not from one of the staff at the castle. As you can see by all this protection, I am a man with many enemies.'

It was an extravagant amount, enough to buy the loyalty of all but the most fanatically incorrupt of this world. A small fortune to pass on such a harmless message. He was confident the dark eyed colleen would oblige. He had seen a flush on her cheeks and an appreciative twinkle in her eye at his enthusiastic response when she bathed him.

Villance waited outside the bedroom door and took the Irish nurse to one side. 'What has he asked you to do?'

The young woman told him, sparing no details. Villance smiled with some satisfaction, he chose his people most carefully. He patted her on the shoulder in encouragement. 'Then my dear, you must hurry along and get the message sent straight away.'

Darian recovered enough to finally meet his benefactor/captor. Villance arrived at his chambers and introduced himself as a representative of the Government but at the sight of the man's escort of black clad henchmen, the alchemist gave a shudder of recognition. He recognised one of the men, Poole, from the night at the Steam Citadel, possibly the murderer of the Amazing Bizarro and Fanny. The perception of being under the benign protection of the Government evaporated, Darian knew he was a prisoner. Why was yet to be openly established but he suspected that the Technomicron lay at the heart of his abduction.

Wrapped in several blankets and his face white as a marble sepulchre, Darian sat as close as possible to a well-banked fire and did his best to ignore Villance and his interrogation over the alchemist's progress with the new fuel. Tension laced every word between them as if they both knew this was not the true reason Villance and his men had brought Darian here.

'Villance, whoever you are, tell your master or mistress, that infernion is by nature unstable and I need more time and to be left in peace to attempt to stabilise it.'

'And yet the *Brigantia* is fuelled by your creation.'

Darian sighed, bored by this persistent man, his black eyes seeming unable to blink, staring with an oddly fanatical intensity at the alchemist's face.

'Sir Miles Hardwick, flawed human specimen though he is, happens to be Great Britain's greatest engineering genius. No one else could handle the substance without blowing half of London to Hades.'

He had enough and overcome with exhaustion, head lolling, he dozed off. At least that is what Villance saw. Darian was in fact still sharply alert, his strength returning swiftly. Not for the first time did he thank his near fatal tussle with the succubus Bruxa and her unwitting gift of venom.

So convincing was his ruse, Darian was able to eavesdrop a brief, tense conversation between Villance and his second in command.

'We have succeeded in convincing Her Majesty's Government that we alone can protect this *didikko* beggar to safeguard the future of infernion. Now we have to convince the scoundrel to obtain the book for us. I saw what he'd been up to on the estuary sands. If he succeeded, Darian knows not only that it is here in the castle but more importantly where the book is hidden.'

'Like hell I will,' Darian thought to himself. Was Villance yet another player in the scramble to get the book? Or one who had shown his hand already? And why did he seem so strangely familiar?

27

While the humans and the almost human fussed about their travel preparations, the furious demon paced the floor, dangerously impatient to be *en route* to Northumberland and Darian. He should never have left him alone with those black-clad men. They had duped him with the phoney imprisonment in the Tower. Belial could not feel guilt but he could experience rage and right now this was directed at the Dedmans ... and Hardwick ... and Cambion. Damn them all to an infernal prison!

Athena Dedman made the mistake of entering the drawing room looking for an errant scarf, believing travel in a dirigible would play havoc with her coiffeur and hat. Her heart missed a beat at the sight of the deceptively beautiful demonic youth standing in the middle of the room, fists clenched, amber gold eyes narrowing with contempt. The temperature in the room dropped suddenly but Athena, unaccustomed to the ways of demons, assumed it was from a cold draught and not a warning sign of Belial's fury.

'I beg your pardon, Prince Belial, I was not expecting to find you still in the house.' She made no attempt to hide her disapproval. 'I believed you were helping Sir Miles prepare the airship for our journey. I will grab my head scarf and be out of your way.'

'I do *not* labour,' he managed to growl, struggling to rein in his urge to rip off her head.

'I understand you are eager to be leaving but surely another pair of strong hands would speed things up?' The woman scolded, oblivious to the danger she was creating for herself. 'Sir Miles is an English aristocrat but he is not too proud to get his hands dirty.'

A flame flickered in his eyes, but Athena pressed on, adding that this long and perilous journey would be unnecessary had

Belial not left the alchemist alone with the Government agents at the Tower and had he stayed, perhaps the alchemist may still have been there.

She had seen those fiery eyes in action but was in no doubt the demon would honour their fragile alliance and not kill her. She could not have been more wrong. Belial was close to eliminating her from his and Darian's life without a flicker of hesitation or remorse.

Belial began his pacing again, wondering if he could conjure enough power in this weakening human form to make this irritating woman simply disappear. A pile of steaming, oily human ash was hard to explain away but no body, no blame?

'I am at a loss why we are taking you and your father with us, you are not and never will be part of Cyrus's team, you weaken us and slow us down with your infuriating presence.'

The door burst open and Hardwick stormed in. He was alarmed that Athena was alone with the capricious and deadly being, especially with him in such an obviously foul mood.

'It is my express wish that Miss Dedman remains with us for her continued safety and her father of course is needed as chaperone,' he said. 'Without us they would be alone in London and at the mercy of our mutual foes.'

Hardwick stood between Athena and the demon. She had no real concept of just how dangerous Belial was, expecting him to have emotions and understand social niceties to match his human appearance. What could a Fallen know about humanity beyond how to spread misery and despair?

'Now, we must not tarry,' said Hardwick. 'The wind is in our favour, let's go.'

Belial stormed out of the room and strode to the waiting dirigible, determined to stay in a foul mood until he was certain Darian was safe and back in his company.

Loaded and with all the passengers on board, the machine rose above the city, with Belial sitting in a huddle on his own in the gondola. His mind went back to the first time he had seen the human who had such a hold over his life. Belial had been in human form, summoned by an inept Albanian Satanist cult hoping to evoke a female demon, a beautiful succubus or Lilith. After slaughtering them, Belial had decided to remain on Earth for a while, causing mischief, and after a couple of centuries, he had wandered into the teeming Persian city of Tehran.

Curious about an exhibition of the Shah's esoteric treasures, the demon became fascinated by an unusually blue-eyed street urchin: a ragged, scrawny boy who ducked blows and kicks, slipping past the city's wealthy citizens like an agile shadow. In human form, Belial had used his limited powers to help the lad, amused by his courage and determination. Why was he here? There were many easy pockets to pick but the lad ignored them all. Belial followed him as the boy wandered towards the heavily guarded glass exhibition cases, the gleaming treasures lit by flickering torches.

The boy's eyes grew large at the beauty and glittering gems but pausing to admire them, drew the attention of the guards who moved to intercept him. Belial stepped beside the boy, putting his arms around his shoulders. 'Beloved nephew, which is your favourite item in this fine collection?'

The guards paused, a well-dressed young foreign gentleman with an eerie aura of great power had taken command of the street child. It was no longer their business and they had backed off.

The lad had grinned, grateful for the reprieve. 'Dearest uncle, the Dagger of Osiris is the most beautiful. So many fine rubies and wonderfully worked gold filigree.'

'Then you shall have it,' Belial had replied before creating bloody mayhem and forging a friendship that defied every convention of Heaven, Hell and Earth. Summoned back to the Inferno by Prince Sammael, the demon vowed to return one day, fascinated by the child who was now the proud possessor of the Osiris Dagger. He sensed that the child knew this was not just a fine weapon encrusted with priceless gems, but a powerful athame for working dark magic. This child was destined to become a remarkable man.

28

Feigning the weakness expected of him by his captors, Darian began to quietly explore his surroundings. Always accompanied by one of the nurses, he began to suspect they were not the innocents he'd once thought. To his face, the women were sweetness and light, full of concern for his wellbeing, but could not hide the hardening of their eyes and manner when they thought he was not looking.

The castle was a recent reconstruction, the original reduced to ruins centuries before but repaired with many of the old stones painstakingly recovered from nearby walls and peasant's cottages. Clearly demolishing people's homes had presented no hindrance to the project.

Under the guise of needing some support and rest, Darian sometimes paused and lent against the stone walls as he made his daily short walk through the corridors. For as long as he could without raising suspicion, his left hand touched the rough-hewn granite to feel the vibrations of centuries trapped in the stones. Wave after giddying wave of emotions surged through him, mostly mundane and fleeting, the occasional echo of some tragedy, the confusion and pain of old, long forgotten wars. He stepped away, disappointed. If the Technomicron was here, its presence would dominate all the trapped echoes, reducing them to what they really were, no more than a background of emotional history recorded in the stones. It would thrum above them all in a malevolent heartbeat, calling out for some greedy fool to find it and release its power. But there was no sense of it.

Usually in the evening, the nurses brought him a light supper on a tray to eat by the fire. Though he was ravenous, Darian ate sparingly like an invalid, picking at the food and leaving most of it, pushing his knife and fork away with a weary sigh.

That night he was brought a change of clothes: a sensible and smart black evening suit including a shirt with an irritatingly high starched collar that couldn't have been more unsuitable for a man with his flamboyant tastes.

'Mr Villance is back from the city and has arranged for you to have supper with him in the Duke Gregory Suite,' he was informed as the formal outfit was laid before him.

'How delightful,' Darian replied weakly. 'I hope I can muster enough appetite to do the cook's hard work justice.'

Helped along with a nurse at each side of his elbow, he made slow, hesitant progress along new blood red carpets to a well-appointed pleasant yet formal small dining room. Warm light from pine logs in a well-built hearth danced off oak panelled walls and gleamed on gilded tableware and candlesticks. The wonders of gaslight had not reached this region. Steaming tureens sat on a crisply starched white linen tablecloth and Darian's senses reeled at the aroma of roast pheasant, fresh vegetables swimming in butter, bacon and stuffing. His body screamed at him to devour the lot. Villance arrived, also formally attired and bowed stiffly to his guest. For once, black clad enforcers did not flank him, though Darian could see four of them waiting beyond the door.

'This is most edifying to see, Mr Darian. Our physicians had quite a battle on their hands bringing you back to the land of the living.'

'I am most grateful, but still puzzled at the reason for such continued and lavish beneficence. And so far from my home. Anyone would think I was your prisoner.'

Villance shook his head as he bid the alchemist to sit down at the dining table. 'Perish the thought, Mr Darian. You are an honoured guest of the Empire, your welfare is our concern. You may go home as soon as your are able to endure the hardships of the journey.'

Darian waited as the man poured him a glass of full-bodied red wine. Darian took a sip before continuing. 'So why choose this remote location? Could I not have recovered just as easily in the Tower?'

Villance held up his own cut crystal glass to the candlelight and slowly swirled the liquid before replacing it on the table untouched. 'Your safety became dangerously compromised the moment your demon disappeared from your side. My agents are not the only ones observing the comings and goings from a certain Mayfair address.'

The conversation ceased as one of Villance's men entered and served up the first course of a watery vegetable soup. Darian was bored to distraction with soup and only took a few polite sips, saving what he could of his supposed poor appetite for the roast pheasant.

'There is something very familiar about you, Villance,' the alchemist ventured as they paused between courses.

The man raised one quizzical eyebrow. 'I very much doubt it, Darian,' he replied coldly. 'I did not know of your existence until assigned to your case by the Prime Minister.'

'I remember you now!' Darian exclaimed. 'With different hair colour and twice the weight, you were Auguste Ville de Nance, also known as the Great Mesmero!'

Villance's eyes flared in temper, he raised a fist ready to strike the alchemist but instead found some reserve of self-control and attempted to make light of Darian's remark. 'Sadly sir, you are quite mistaken.'

'I'm right aren't I, you are good old Auguste? Worked at Bragginton's Supremo Circus. Had a great act after you changed your name from Frederick Squills. You came on after the Flying Milliband Brothers.'

'That is not who I am and you damn well know it, you gypsy scoundrel!'

Darian broke into an impudent smirk. It was worth risking a blow to see the outrage in Villance's face, his steely composure reduced to spluttering indignation. The man was straining to stay in control while Darian was useful to him. Darian had no doubt once he had located and recovered the Technomicron, Villance would kill him. Or at least attempt to. There was an uncomfortable moment of silence.

'I must apologise profusely for my ill-tempered outburst, Mr Darian, clearly you were having some jest at my expense.' Villance had to grit his teeth to force back his anger and get Darian back on his side.

Darian shrugged, unconcerned. 'Maybe I was wrong about the circus, but you are also wrong about my parentage. My mother was an Anglo-Irish countess and my father was a son of one of the Shah of Persia's lesser wives.'

'Of course they were,' Villance deferred unconvincingly. 'But let us return directly to our present business. Mr Darian, the importance of securing infernion for Her Majesty's Government cannot be underestimated but another matter has compromised your safety.'

'Indeed?' Darian focused his attention on a slice of rather fine fresh, poached sea trout. 'And what would the nature of that matter be?'

'We can play this game of dalliance and subterfuge all night but it is a pointless waste of time, Darian.' Villance's short fuse was beginning to smoulder again. 'In the mean time, our competitors, the Brethren of Satarel, the Lady, Fogue and Crimm-Smythe will be closing in on the Technomicron's whereabouts.'

'*Our* competitors?'

'Why not? Your well-informed search for the elusive object of our mutual quest has led us to this splendid historical edifice – my far from humble home. It is in both of our reciprocal interests to continue our endeavours together.'

'Mind you,' Darian interrupted, 'Freddie Squills was also always rather verbose.'

Ignoring Darian, Villance continued. 'So we both know it is here, but where? This castle is vast and complex and its owner had made many bizarre and dangerous alterations.'

'It would help if I knew this man or woman's name and where they are.'

'Tragically, Mr Aloysius Fortune met with an unfortunate accident.'

'By gad sir, how exceedingly vexing, and how frightfully inconvenient. It would have been so much easier to have asked him in person,' Darian murmured, mimicking Villance's upper class drawl.

He left the table and wandered over to a narrow slit window and gazed out as the nightfall light turned the calm sea a luscious shade of damson. Beautiful, but he was missing London and the familiarity of his surroundings. Aloysius Fortune, the name was all too familiar to Darian. Fortune was another wealthy amateur dabbler in the occult, driven by the same need to gain more power, more wealth and eternal youth. The mansions of England must breed them by the dozen.

Darian had encountered him in the past, a nervous, twitchy, whippet-thin man whose demeanour hid a voracious lust for magickal power. They had fought over a potion discovered from a Scythian burial in one of the Ukrainian Kurgans. Hollowed from a large piece of white jade, decorated in intricately worked gold, the well-sealed bottle contained one element reputed to be an ingredient for the fabled Elixir of Life. Fortune won – at least Darian allowed him to – as the bottle contained nothing but a few drops of two-thousand-year-old vinegar.

'Fortune was an easy victim of fraudsters. Last I heard of him, the man had lost his belief in the occult and had discovered a passion for new technology,' Darian remarked. 'We will need Sir Miles Hardwick on board. This place will no doubt have been engineered to be a death trap.'

'Then we are in luck,' Villance preened. Manoeuvring these over-eager young fools was too easy to be satisfying. 'It seems the gentleman has followed hard on your heels and is travelling towards Cramburgh in an airship.'

Darian's mind raced, Villance had played him like a game of poker and appeared to be holding the winning hand. Of course Hardwick was on his way, Villance and his Irish nurse spy had ensured it.

The sky glowed with a deep orange fire streaked with peach, pink and gold as the sun dropped low on the horizon. A glory no artist could accurately capture without fear of provoking scorn for over-embellishment and exaggeration.

Athena gasped as the sun set behind the dramatic outline of Cramburgh castle, she had never seen anything so starkly beautiful and so mysterious. Her travels in Britain so far confined to the filthy metropolis of the capital, had not prepared her for the majesty of Northumberland's landscape. The journey by Hardwick's spacious and luxurious dirigible had been swift and uneventful, for once the winds had been in their favour and the inventor's precision engineering at its best gave a smooth ride with half the noise of other airships. They also appreciated the reduction of soot and steam that always seemed to seep through into the gondolas.

Passing over England's green and chequered landscape, Athena had become aware for the first time of this little island's long history in a landscape shaped by thousands of years of continuous habitation. As the hours passed, Hardwick had delighted in pointing out to her the hill forts and pretty villages, magnificent cathedrals and impressive castles of this remote region of the British Isles.

As the dirigible lowered close to their destination, he explained that Cramburgh, originally an eleventh century ruin was rebuilt ten years before by an eccentric coal magnate to dramatic and evocative effect and at a huge cost. Kept faithfully to the original design, she could see that it rose in brutal warrior splendour from an offshore island in the North Sea, only reached by a narrow stone road submerged at every tide.

'It is said that the owner died in most curious circumstances before ever setting foot in his creation,' Hardwick continued, 'and the identity of the new master of Cramburgh remains a mystery.'

This statement made Athena shudder and the black outline of the castle against the darkening sky no longer looked so fascinating but seemed sinister in aspect. She had no doubt the new master of Cramburgh and the Technomicron were undoubtedly interlinked.

They received no opposition as the airship descended to a mooring point with other dirigibles already tethered. In fact the welcome was quite the opposite. A group of unarmed men dressed in black uniform ran out and helped get the airship safely moored and its passengers off onto the platform. They were taciturn in manner but respectful and not hostile. Following orders to be useful in facilitating the visitors' arrival.

'Something is telling me that we were expected,' Hardwick whispered to the others, whether this was a good thing was yet to be ascertained. Ushered through to a spacious and dramatic entrance hall, the attendants left them alone for an uncomfortable half an hour. Free to wander around the hall, Hardwick and the Dedmans gazed at an eclectic and priceless collection of artwork and antiquities. Cambion had no interest in the art. He found a seat and sat stock still in abject misery, recovering from the hours of close proximity with that forthright female. If she was typical of American women, Cambion vowed never to cross the Atlantic. At least well bred English women knew not to be too forward in the company of gentlemen.

Viewing the castle's art collection was not an uplifting experience. Whether gathered by its builder, Fortune, or the mysterious new owner, all the art on show had a morbid, macabre theme of death, mutilation and fear. None were occult in subject matter but were 'celebrations' of the worst of human nature over the centuries.

'Charming, utterly charming,' a grim-faced Hardwick muttered as he turned away from a graphic painting of a near naked Christian martyr in the throes of disembowelment. He grew concerned for Miss Dedman's sensibilities: this was not for the delicate eyes of a gentlewoman.

'The Martyrdom of Saint Erasmus, painted by Nicholas Poussin in sixteen hundred and twenty-eight.' Athena's voice was calm as she joined Hardwick beside the picture. 'He used such beautiful, bright colours for such a grim subject matter. Even the unfortunate saint's intestines are a dainty shade of pink. Curious.' She walked away to peruse another artwork leaving a delightfully startled Hardwick. Educated, fearless, there was no doubt this was the future Lady Hardwick. He was adamant: no other female could compete with her perfection.

'My dear guests, can you forgive this appalling display of bad manners?' All heads turned as a deep, commanding voice rang through the hall.

A tall man with distinctive sharp hewn features and a public school educated accent approached. 'My name is Villance. And you must be Mr Cyrus Darian's friends, come to visit him as he recuperates in my home. You are all most welcome. My staff will see you to your rooms.'

For staff substitute cold-eyed henchmen, all clad in the ubiquitous black livery, thought Hardwick. 'Is Mr Darian your prisoner? And by coming here, are we also captives?'

Villance laughed, a humourless, hollow sound, 'My goodness, no! Although the way your friend complained about the dearth of Gaston de Casteljac cognac in my wine cellars, you would think he was being tortured.'

'I call that conclusive proof. Cyrus is definitely here,' Belial added turning to the others with a wide grin of relief.

29

Darian relaxed in an armchair, allowing the demon to fuss over him.

'Vile-Ness is convinced the book is somewhere in this castle and that Fortune built many fiendish defences to protect it,' said Darian as Belial offered him another glass of fine brandy. It was a relief to have someone he could speak openly with. The irony of having Belial as a confidante never lost him, demons were supposed to be despised beings of lies and deceit yet he had never known anything but a refreshing honesty from the Prince of Hell. The arrival of his companions had led to the dismissal of the nurse, resulting in one less set of prying eyes and ears to avoid.

'The man is convinced we can overcome the traps Fortune set in place or at least die trying. All pointless, as the bloody thing is not here.'

Athena Dedman grimaced at the profanity then sipped some tea from a bone china cup, at least life in the castle was civilised. Villance had given her the use of two ladies maids and there was a well-run kitchen serving their needs. 'And how can you possibly know that?'

'The walls told me,' muttered an annoyed Darian.

'The walls?'

'Belial, old chap, why have you brought Dedman and this frightful woman here?'

The demon shrugged as he relit the dying fire with a flash from his eyes deliberately to unsettle the strident American woman. 'I suggest you question Miles when he returns from exploring the battlements with Dedman, all his idea I'm afraid, Cyrus.'

For once genuinely fatigued, Darian returned to the privacy of his bedroom. What had been a trap now felt like a haven. He adored women, in all their myriad shapes, ages and characters. Difficult women were his favourite as he enjoyed the challenge, loving to watch the fire and fight in their eyes melt to smouldering desire at his touch. He made one exception with Athena Dedman, who had about as much appeal to him as a plate of long-cold over-stewed cabbage. In fact he would rather devour the cabbage than touch her with any intimacy beyond a boot up her bustled rear end. Miles clearly had other ideas: why else would he drag her along to a mission laced with grave dangers?

He helped himself to a cup of coffee from a silver pot standing on a heated tray and sat by the fire. The weather outside had turned hostile with a deep storm system straight down from the arctic North bringing the threat of early snow. Low, dark grey clouds lumbered across the roiling pewter sea like a herd of angry rhinos, a piercing wind whined through the many castle turrets, whistling through the cracks to create cold draughts within its walls. A candle flickered and went out but Darian knew it was not by the north wind off the sea. He was not alone.

'Darian.'

He heard the voice clearly and distinctly. This was not his imagination but a visitation from beyond the grave. An earthbound spirit so troubled it did not wait to be summoned. Darian had a good idea who it was.

'Cyrus Darian – I must speak with you.'

'Of course you do, Fortune. I should imagine you are exceedingly displeased.'

An even colder draught than anything the outside wind could produce whirled around the room, knocking over ornaments and throwing cushions about the room. A powerful spirit, fuelled by great anger.

'Why are you inconveniencing me, old chap?' Darian continued, unbothered by the petulant display of ghostly wrath. 'It is Villance you should be spooking to, or are you still so vexed by the incident with the Scythian potion bottle?'

'Darian.'

'We have already established you know my name, get on with it man.'

His impatience was fuelled by the knowledge that no earthbound could sustain such a high level of physical energy for long periods of time.

'Let him have the book. You will find it housed in a chamber in the central core of the labyrinth.'

'I fully intend to,' Darian answered, 'as it is a fake. Something you must be quite an expert on. Your castle is full of them.'

Darian could swear the spectre was seething with regret and bitterness, though its mood was only illustrated by another wild whirl of spectral energy around the room. Most tiresome.

'And the real one? You might as well let me have it. It's no good to you now.'

'Never! No mortal should ever possess such insane power!'

Darian sighed. 'I was offering you the easy way. You know I am a highly skilled necromancer. I can summon you and charge you with complete obedience to my will.'

'One day perhaps, you double dealing rogue, but not now. That last effort to dredge up that old magician has cost you dear.'

Darian took another sip of his coffee with an appreciative sigh at the rich taste and heady aroma. 'A delightful blend from the African colonies. I'd offer to pour you a cup but it has more body than you do, old chap.'

He waited until the next furious display of ghostly anger calmed down. 'At least give me a clue to where this maze of yours is and how to survive it. Can't help you with Villance if one of your infernal tricks has mashed me up.'

The spirit responded with a mocking sneer in its fading voice. 'You are wily enough to last long enough to trick Villance and his black clad minions. After that you can join him in Hell for all I care.'

'What a bore. I cannot abide sore losers,' Darian remarked, aware that the irate spirit of Aloysius Fortune had left the room.

Night fell as the castle was battered by a howling onslaught of gale-driven hail and sleet. Drawn to their cosy bedrooms and well-stocked fires, the travellers, fatigued by their long aerial journey across the length of England, wanted to do nothing more than sleep. However with an invitation to dine with their host, Villance, they reluctantly bathed and dressed in formal eveningwear.

After a tension-laced and near silent supper, Villance ushered all of his guests into a large study, one unchanged since Fortune's short-lived ownership of Cramburgh. Evidence of the man's obsession with the occult littered the room with many bizarre and ugly totems and amulets. Books on the subject filled two tall bookcases. Athena shuddered but it was less intimidating than that Darian creature's spooky home.

Spread across a large table were several blueprints from the castle's restoration. Villance gestured for the others to examine them. 'Gentlemen, dear lady, may I beg your indulgence to peruse these plans. Somewhere within them is the clue to the whereabouts of the hidden book.'

'Damn it, you have to admire such optimism,' laughed Darian, ignoring a furious glare from the Dedman woman. She should hear his language when he really wanted to curse, especially the colourful and obscene demonic ones Belial had taught him.

At first there seemed nothing remarkable about the plans. There were the usual details of the layouts of bedchambers, kitchens and servants quarters written to a large scale. To Villance's annoyance, his guests, especially that Irish/Persian scoundrel, soon became bored with studying the blueprints and began to make small talk. Only Zachariah Dedman continued to examine them with great concentration.

Eventually he looked up at the others. 'Pardon my ignorance

as a mere visitor to these charming isles, but is it normal to build such a large structure with no foundations?' Everyone stopped talking as he continued: 'For according to these plans, Cramburgh rests on the island supported only by its weight with nowhere to hide the obviously needed pipes for water. I have seen no well, so it must be brought in from the mainland.'

'Which means, father?'

'Which means my dear Athena, there are no plans drawn here for beneath the castle. It must have cellars for food and wine storage, basement rooms for clutter, steam driven power generators perhaps to warm water for bathing.'

'And a hidden maze, a labyrinth, to foil those seeking the Technomicron?' ventured Darian, already knowing the answer.

Villance's face broke into a brief, uncontrolled grimace of impatience before returning to his mask of genial affability. 'I can assure you, we have searched most diligently in the basement area. As Mr Dedman so rightly pointed out, the castle does indeed have extensive storage cellars but nothing as exotic as a labyrinth.'

'Can we return home now?' A deeply uneasy Cambion inquired, dropping his head low as a bevy of maids entered with trays of post-prandial sweetmeats and coffee. 'You have a fine staff at your command, Mr Villance, if there was anything hidden, they would have found it by now.'

Villance did his best to overcome his distaste at addressing the furtive little shapeshifter. 'But Mr Cambion, they do not have the many talents of this assembly of ...'

'Misfits!' Belial interjected with a devilish grin. 'A fallen angel, rat boy over there, a cog and steam obsessed titled dilettante and of course Cyrus himself, the man with kaleidoscope eyes.'

Relieved not to be on the demon's list, Athena spoke up. 'Let us be realistic, gentlemen, and Mr Darian, and under no illusions. No one will be leaving until we find the Technomicron. Am I right, Mr Villance?'

The man bowed in grave assent.

30

The expected snow had not arrived. The ice storm had blown itself out overnight and any settling hail had melted by morning. Darian professed to wanting some exercise in the fresh air and so, flanked by Belial and Hardwick and shadowed by Villance's agents, he made slow, hesitant progress around the castle grounds. Appearing to admire the washed out blue sky scattered with gliding sea birds and the glistening sands laid bare by the retreating tide, Darian was actually looking for the site of an entrance to an underground maze.

'We could take these clowns out and make a run for the airship,' Belial suggested in Farsi. 'Cambion could become a gull and catch up with us.'

'I had considered it,' Darian replied, 'especially as the book isn't here. But how can we persuade our love-lorn swain to leave the latest object of his affection? We cannot operate that thing without him.'

'Pack that in, you two. I hate it when you do that!' Hardwick grumbled, knowing no language but his native English and a few scraps of schoolboy Latin. 'And if you think you can operate that dirigible without me, forget it.'

'Are we that transparent?' Darian replied with a grin.

'As glass, my friends.'

A heap of broken stones caught Darian's attention. They did not match the castle's granite and were unlikely therefore to be left-over building material. More likely a ruin. He made his way straight to the debris with his entourage in tow. As they neared it, Darian's hunch was proved right. Framed by a tall wind-twisted ancient yew stood the remains of a chapel. Time had not destroyed it, nor a religious war, this was recent.

Encouraged by Darian, the group picked their way through the piles of shattered stone, mortar and stained glass.

Hardwick also quickly spotted the recent nature of the destruction. 'It looks haphazard but there is careful planning about this arrangement.'

'Agreed,' replied Darian, deep in thought, 'but for what reason?'

'Hiding in plain sight,' Hardwick replied. 'The focus is all on the castle and its splendour and mystery. Not on a pile of old stones.'

'Time to get Villance and his men out of that comfortable castle and get their hands dirty moving this debris,' Darian announced. 'I suspect you are right, Miles, that wily old reprobate Fortune built the entrance to his labyrinth beneath the chapel.'

Within an hour, a work party toiled among the ruins, clearing the stones and glass from the floor of the former chapel. As the official invalid, Darian stood to one side and observed, as did Belial: a Prince of Hell did not labour. He had an endless supply of the damned down below to employ. The others caught up in the excitement of discovery became more involved. Even Athena stepped elegantly through the broken stones, carefully examining the shards of broken stained glass.

'A crime, an absolute disgrace. This chapel was very old, possibly eleventh century, from the images on this glass,' she announced. 'What sort of barbarian would destroy something so precious, so sacred?'

'One who has lost faith in everything but the power of human evil?' Villance replied calmly, his hopes rising with every lump of masonry removed from the chapel floor. 'Including his own.'

As morning blended into an afternoon lit by the pale autumn sun, Hardwick called Darian over. There were no tell-tale symbols or obscure puzzles to solve. Just flagstones with fresher mortar than the rest. Darian clapped the inventor on the back. A subtle clue that many would not notice.

Villance ordered his men to remove the stones, and within

minutes they were frantically digging out the mortar with picks and levering up the flagstones. Darian discreetly urged caution to his own people. They were expecting traps in Fortune's labyrinth, why not at the entrance itself? The last of the stones and the light covering of earth underneath was removed and the entrance to the maze was revealed as a brass and steel hatchway with a flywheel to open it.

Darian's unease grew.

Ordering one of his men to turn the wheel, Villance also stood well back.

The flywheel eventually yielded with two of the henchmen hauling on it, releasing the hatch with the loud hiss of a monstrous snake. Belial gestured to Darian and Hardwick to listen. Deep beneath them they heard the deep rumbling of vast machinery churning into life. Not good. Not good at all.

Peering in, Villance and his men could see below them a circular wood-panelled chamber just over six feet high with a set of simple controls on one side. There was a button with a down arrow on, and one with an up arrow. A brass ladder led down to the highly polished metal floor. Villance beckoned the inventor over. 'Explain this.'

Wisely unwilling to climb down, Hardwick took his time to study the curious narrow chamber. 'It is clearly a reverse ascentor device. A descentor so to speak. The size of the chamber would suggest it can carry no more than two people at a time.'

'I have no patience with that nonsense, it is clearly a sturdy construct. Brown, Banks and Robinson, take this thing down to the first level and send it back up.'

The men obeyed in disciplined silence, climbing down the ladder and waiting as Brown pressed the descend button. The speed of the machine was as shocking as the outcome. The metal floor beneath their feet shot to one side, sending the men tumbling helplessly from the chamber, their screams echoing for what seemed an eternity until they were silenced.

The floor returned to its original position and waited for its next passenger. Blanching with shock and anger, Villance pulled out a pistol and grabbed Zachariah Dedman. 'You are of the least use to me, get down there and operate the device.'

'Under no circumstances!' Dedman blustered. 'This is your search, I have no interest in what lies down there!'

Before the American could protest further, Villance trained the gun on Athena. 'Boys, hold the lady, it seems our guest needs a little extra persuasion.'

Holding up his hands, Darian stepped forward. 'There is no need for all this hostility. Hardwick warned you not to overload the descentor. One man could operate and travel in it with no danger.'

Villance's eyes narrowed. 'That one man will not be you, Darian, I will need you in the labyrinth. I will also need Hardwick and I cannot order a demon to do anything. But all the others are expendable.'

Before the situation escalated, ignoring Villance's furious command to stop, Darian clambered down and pressed the control button, travelling down with no difficulty. His gamble that Fortune would be alone when visiting his hidden treasures had paid off. He also wanted to show Villance up in front of his men as a coward, only too ready to sacrifice them in pursuit of his goal.

As the descentor reached its destination, it triggered flint sparks to light a row of gaslights illuminating a narrow corridor, bizarrely luxurious with a thick maroon carpet, highly polished wood-panelled walls and gleaming brass sconces for the gaslights.

Darian stepped to one side into the corridor, and pressed the 'ascend' button, watching as the device returned back up top once more.

One by one the group descended to the corridor, where they all waited, bunched together, until everyone was there.

No-one was willing to move along the seemingly innocuous corridor until Hardwick had examined it for hidden perils.

'Not exactly built to inspire fear and mystery,' Darian said, enjoying Miss Dedman's grimace of disdain. 'More like the lobby of a cheap bawdyhouse for hard up aristos and tradesmen.'

Again Villance's impatience pushed matters along. He grabbed Cambion by the back of his collar and forced him forward. 'Turn yourself into a bird or a rat – something that can scout ahead.'

The terrified shapeshifter looked to Darian and Hardwick for assistance but to his distress they appeared to agree with their host-turned-captor.

'You will be fine in bird form,' urged Hardwick, 'but stay as a bird until you return to this spot, just in case.'

Cambion hated metamorphosing in front of observers but, all too aware of these people's weaponry, he had no choice. He crouched down low to the ground, head tucked in, hugging his legs with his arms, a tight ball of human flesh that liquefied and reformed as a peregrine falcon. The raptor sped along the corridor, its super sharp eyesight and acute sense of danger scanned the walls, ceiling and floors for any tiny clue of aberration but saw nothing. In one superb aerial turn, the falcon returned to the others and morphed back into his human form. 'Nothing, just a seemingly endless, featureless corridor gradually spiralling downwards.'

'But why so ornate?' Dedman wondered aloud. 'And so repetitive, no portraits on the walls, no furniture – just the same thing stretching on and on. It's all so jo-fired strange.'

Keeping Darian and Hardwick to the back, Villance and his troops kept the rest of the visitors in front of them at gunpoint and began a slow journey along the corridor. After ten minutes of uneventful walking, Villance upped the pace, eager to make swift progress to his goal, the baleful treasure he was convinced lay almost within touching distance.

'*As you approach the fourth gaslight sconce to the left from now, hold back. All your people will be safe.*'

Darian glanced around, curious to see if any of the others had heard Fortune's ghost beside him. Belial ran his hand down his long silver-gold hair in a well-used signal that he had heard, but no-one else seemed to have done. The search party continued, already losing some of their earlier nervousness.

Could the lethal descentor be the only trap? That would make sense ... Fortune would want to walk through his own corridors in safety ...

A sound? Like a split second metallic scything of the air? All stood perturbed, unaware of the terrible consequences. The group glanced at each other looking for answers, all except two of Villance's men who remained stock still, a fixed expression on their faces. Athena Dedman cried out in horror as a thin red line of blood began to seep from one man's temple, spreading in a line downwards. Cut cleanly through vertically from ear to heel, one side of his body fell against the man's body next to him which in turn, like a hewn carcass at an abattoir, fell in sheared slabs to the ground with a drenching gush of hot blood and spilled and splitting organs.

Horrified at the sudden carnage, nobody could move or dared speak at first before Darian drawled what everyone but Villance wanted to hear. 'I would suggest it is time to make a strategic withdrawal.'

'No!' was inevitable response from Villance struggling to control his shaking hands. Games and Poole had been with him from the start of his covert agency, good men, difficult to replace. 'Only now Hardwick is on my expendable list, what use have you been up until now?'

'Do you know how this outrage was done? Are you likely to find out before the next surprise?' Hardwick demanded, both intrigued and horrified by the apparently invisible scythe which had cut the men down. An extraordinary piece of precision engineering surpassing his own. He wanted to shake the man's hand – before killing him. A rumbling beneath them announced that the infernal machines were engaging again. Cyrus took out his pocket watch, it was exactly half an hour since they entered the subterranean corridor and the machines had fallen silent. The noise signalled that the devices were cranking up for another set of traps. He turned to Hardwick. 'Spring-loaded?'

'At a mind boggling tension and power,' the inventor agreed. 'The speed and ferocity of whatever killed those men was phenomenal. If it took a half an hour to wind up the devices, we may be safe for now.'

'Do I have to remind you that the balance of power has shifted since the unfortunate demise of so many of your people?' Belial stepped forward to confront Villance. With the speed and sleight of hand of a master magician, Villance grabbed Athena's left wrist and attempted to slap a pair of handcuffs on her, he could not have predicted her reaction. She flipped his wrist around and had his arm pulled around and held tightly behind his back.

'You mess with a lady at your peril, Villance,' she remarked with a new calmness and authority.

The man's remaining four henchmen raised their weapons and pointed them at Athena's head.

'You tarnal son of a bitch!' Dedman's face became florid with anger, his hands curled into fists, he was a big man and his age no barrier to the damage he could do in such a rage.

'Five against four plus a demon and the formidable Miss Dedman,' an amused Darian remarked, 'who has a parasol and is not afraid to use it. That outnumbers you, Villance. By a considerable percentage.'

To emphasise their advantage, Belial's eyes flickered with hell fire and Cambion gave a rumbling wolf growl of warning.

'So I suggest that, as it would seem to be as dangerous to go back as it might be to continue, we carry on this search for your holy grail but without the threats and weapons,' Darian said calmly. 'Nobody should be forced forward to be used as a human sacrifice but we use all our expertise so that we stand a chance of getting out alive.'

This played well with Villance's men as Darian intended and they lowered their weapons. Outnumbered and with the desire to possess the Technomicron unabated, Villance nodded a surly assent.

'In theory, and only in theory, we have half an hour's grace to carry on. I suggest we make the most of it,' said Hardwick as he stood to one side allowing Athena to release her prisoner with a splendid flourish of ladylike contempt. What a fizzing woman!

They carried on, silent since the horrific deaths of Games and Poole. The corridor began to dip down more steeply, narrowing and becoming more winding. They were in a spiral tightening up to its conclusion. Darian received no more warnings from the ghostly form of the labyrinth's creator and suspected he had already fulfilled his usefulness to the vengeful haunt.

The corridor's steepness increased and the group soon found keeping their balance problematical with no helpful rail or banister to grip. The frequency of the gaslights lessened and if continued to do so, would soon leave them in darkness. The unpleasant sensation of being lured into a closing trap grew with only the dogged Villance seeming immune.

Two of his men began to whisper to each other in a swift, furtive dialogue, clearly they had more than enough of Villance and his obsession. Darian stoked up their mutiny with a few quiet well-chosen words of his own. The countdown to the next sprung trap had begun but this seemed forgotten in their eagerness to leave Villance's increasingly short termed employ. The two men held further and further back from the others, preparing for their opportunity to desert.

Hardwick's luxite chronometer flared white light in warning. Something fiendish was going to happen at any second. The group froze – holding their breath listening for the infernal whirring of the hidden workings of Fortune's mechanisms. Eyes scanning for anything wrong, any clue to the next attack. It was too much for one of the mutineers who panicked and ran back up the corridor, only to become shredded lumps of flesh caught between two large intermeshing razor sharp cogs which emerged from the walls. The spinning hell was so rapid the man had no time to scream.

'I doubt if it is over yet,' Darian's voice was little more than a whisper, the only one, other than the demon, whose eyes were not transfixed in horror by the gore dripping from the walls that seconds before had been a man. Belial felt a coolness rushing towards them. 'On the floor. Now!'

Already poised, ready for a quick reaction to more danger,

everyone obeyed though Hardwick had to grab a hesitant Athena and threw her to ground as a spring-loaded scythe swept past at head height.

There were no casualties. They waited, still lying on the ground not knowing if the monstrous blade had finished its grim toll.

31

Nervously, one by one, they shuffled hesitantly to their feet. Ten minutes had passed and with no sign of any more whirring cogs or scything blades, they prepared to move on.

'Proprieties can be abandoned in times of great peril, Lord Hardwick,' Athena announced as she wriggled free from his grip, 'but must be re-asserted at the earliest opportunity.'

Dedman senior was genuinely concerned for his daughter's safety but also unwilling to let such a moment of useful intimacy pass in his plan to make her Lady Athena Hardwick.

'I have had more than I can take of this. Contact Fortune, bring him before me to be questioned,' Villance ordered the alchemist through tension-clenched jaws. His plans to obtain the Technomicron with relative ease had collapsed. The vast whirring cogs and chains of Fortune's diabolical machines ran red with his men's blood but the book was not in his hands to justify their unwilling sacrifice. There was only one thing left to try. Necromancy. 'You raised the spirit of a three thousand year old magus from the depths of the afterlife. How hard can it be to summon that of a recently deceased coal merchant?'

Darian folded his arms, playing for time, his mind racing for a believable answer. Fortune was an earthbound spirit, currently haunting the labyrinth. Summoning him would be easy but most likely pointless. Fortune did not want anyone to possess the book. Darian also wanted to save any direct communication with the ghost for later, to compel it to get them safely out of the corridors. 'I cannot, Villance, not so soon after raising the magus.'

'You can and you will,' Villance's face was taut with frustration and fury. Good men lost to Fortune's nightmare machines and not one of Darian's people harmed. It was as if the rogue had planned it from beyond the grave. 'I doubt if your companions will survive this labyrinth unless you do.'

'If your agents were better informed, you would know I really don't care,' Darian replied with an impressive display of believable nonchalance. 'My past track record with accomplices is somewhat littered with casualties.' He glanced across to the others, looking them squarely in the eye. 'A few more will not make any difference.'

'Go to blazes, Darian and rot there for eternity,' Athena's words were bitter with loathing and disappointment.

'Oh, Miss Dedman, it won't be me rotting in hell,' he replied with a grin. 'It helps to keep in good favour with the demonic aristocracy, eh Prince Belial?'

He turned to an apoplectic Villance. 'But that doesn't apply to everyone *en route* to that final destination. Sorry, old chap.'

'When I am in possession of the Technomicron, all the realms of Earth, Heaven and Hell will bow down before me,' Villance returned. 'Being a devil's molly will be no protection, Darian.'

'Fine,' an insouciant Darian remarked. 'I am sure your heart's desire is further down this interminable corridor. I no longer give a damn.' And with that he sat back down on the floor, leant against the wood panelling, folded his arms and closed his eyes. He did not need to see the frustration and anger in Villance's face. Another little nudge would make the man reckless with impatience and provoke a fatal mistake. The biggest dilemma was going to be how to get out of this paean to Fortune's paranoia.

All heads snapped around to look back up the corridor as a low rumbling like subterranean thunder approached them at great speed. Darian abandoned his show of rebellion and leapt to his feet. Whatever was heading their way was bound to be Fortune's *tour de force*. His *grande finale*? No time to linger as the rumbling became deafening.

'Run!' yelled Hardwick needlessly as they all fled away from the sound in a headlong scramble down towards the darkness below them. It could be a trap, a dead end with no escape other than in death, but they had no choice but to keep going, there was nowhere else to go.

There was no time for any of them to admire the feat of

engineering tumbling towards them, filling the corridor with a whirling, slashing maelstrom of lethal devices. The huge clockwork killing-machine was spherical at its core, bristling with appendages: spinning blades, pounding hammers and whip-thin metal flails. Armed only with rifles and a demon in human form with limited incendiary powers, it could not be fought or stopped – only fled from. Unless … Darian's mind whirled as fast as the machine, it was clockwork with a mechanism that could be jammed. He snatched Athena Dedman's parasol from her and threw it to Belial, the one with the fastest reflexes and strength. 'Small gap above the mace … Now!'

The demon's golden eyes narrowed with concentration as he drew his arm back and sent the unlikely missile speeding to its target. The strengthened narrow tip of the parasol penetrated the tight gap in the metal hide of the clockwork beast and jammed between two inner cogs. The sphere continued on for several yards before grinding to a noisy, stuttering halt, pieces breaking and flying off in a scream of tortured metal as the machine's weapons turned on itself.

'Jolly good shot, well done that demon!' cried a delighted Hardwick, clapping him on the back in relief.

And pride, Belial may have thrown it but it was his invention that had brought down Fortune's killing machine.

He turned to Anthea. 'Miss Dedman, I beg you not to be concerned at the loss of your property, I will have another made for you once we get back to London.'

'*If* you get back to London,' Villance sneered. 'That was a lucky throw. You have nothing left to defend yourselves against Fortune's fiendish contraptions with now.'

'Nobody is getting out, now you are all trapped,' Cambion's melancholy voice cut through the relief and jubilation. The monstrous sphere blocked the corridor with barely an inch between it and the walls. He didn't need to be tactless and point out that he alone could shape shift into something small enough to get past the immovable blockage.

'Then it is a good thing we have reached our journey's end,' Darian said. He had carried on walking while the others had stopped to stare at the stricken machine and was now at the entrance to a featureless circular grey stone chamber with three doors leading off it. There was nowhere else to go but through the portals. Did one lead to freedom? Darian doubted it. Everyone clustered around the entrance to the chamber, not daring to step in for fear of another trap.

'There is no way of telling which one leads to the book.' Darian looked to Villance, assessing how much the man would risk. 'Even from here I can see no markings, no clues on the doors.'

'Hardwick, Cambion, Dedman – open a door each!' Villance spat out his command with an air of desperation.

'You may think you are the biggest toad in the puddle,' replied the American calmly. 'But from what I can see, there ain't nothing in tarnation you can do to make us!'

'Odds are one in three.' Hardwick added, 'Are you a gambling man, Villance?'

Finally faced with the reality that he had no choice, Villance stepped into the centre of the chamber, the ground felt solid beneath his feet and continued to do so as he walked from door to door. His fingers brushed against the stone surfaces searching for any indentation, carvings, symbols – anything that could lead to an informed decision rather than a potentially lethal guess. There was nothing. He needed the demon. Belial's sharper senses could make all the difference. He needed the necromancer to summon and command Fortune's spirit to tell the truth. But he had no way of compelling them. His only chance was to find the book and command its power to destroy these noisome wastrels. Obliterate them so completely, that even their ancestors would perish in a wave of annihilation so powerful it would reach back through the centuries.

He flung open the first door but would not step over the threshold. Inside was blackness beyond all comprehension, a void where no light had or could penetrate. Villance stepped back, now he needed the co-operation of the shapeshifter, transformed into a bat that could use echoes to navigate the darkness. He knew co-operation would not be forthcoming. On some deep instinctive level, from a sense that had no name, everyone accepted that this was a threshold not to be crossed. Nothing emanated from the darkness, no tangible threat or feeling of dread, just the knowing to back away and stay away.

The second wooden door yielded after some difficulty revealing an inner one of heavy steel, apparently opened by a series of three stout wheels. This was more promising. This could actually lead somewhere. The third door opened to the disappointment of discovering a rather prosaic bricked up wall. Villance wondered if it was an illusion, a Fortune mind game where the most impenetrable barrier was the easiest to overcome. Cautiously he touched the wall but felt only the rough, cold texture of bricks and gritty mortar. He pushed against it gently at first then firmly but was met with the stolid resistance of a real wall. Not for the first time Villance wondered at what had gone on in Fortune's twisted mind. Here was a man who had had access to the Technomicron but did nothing with its great power.

Villance returned to the metal door and, taking time to compose himself, decided to turn the wheels and gain entry. He had nothing to lose, already trapped in Fortune's labyrinth with the prospect of dying slowly of starvation ... no ... not that. He suspected the debauched bastard Darian would feed him to the ravenous demon to keep his lover's human form alive.

With a shudder, Villance turned the three wheels and the inner chamber finally gave up its secret, slowly opening with an impressive, dramatic groan and grinding of massive hidden cogs. Villance sighed deeply in relief and satisfaction.

The walls on the inner, circular chamber were lined in shining metal sheets, possibly of highly polished platinum and etched in gold with intricate cabalistic symbols. In the centre of the chamber was an elevated plinth of pure black marble, all the more impressive for its featureless sides. Set centrally within the plinth was a book stand made of black starite crystal, an emperor's ransom worth of the rare precious stone that sparkled with its own inner light as if carved from a portion of the universe itself.

And on the stand was a book. No. *The* book. The

Technomicron.

The book itself was surprisingly small, no more than twelve by ten inches and the cover was a dull brown colour, bearing no gemstones, no gilding or ornately carved leather bindings. It looked like an ordinary working notebook, perhaps with parchment pages primed for discoveries or spells. Something of a disappointment but for the elaborate housing.

'*Fanacht,*' muttered a stern Darian in Irish, a command to remain still which all of his people understood. Hardwick held Athena back and signalled to her father to do the same with his eyes. None of this registered with Villance, his whole being shivering with the thrill of being within touching distance of the Technomicron at last. That old bastard Fortune had done his best to keep him away from his destiny but now Villance was master of Cramburgh and with this book, master of the world.

He stepped into the room, his heavy footfall triggering silent alarms deep within the chamber floor. As Darian yelled for his companions to run for their lives, huge steel panels slammed down in front of the metal sides of the chamber. Villance turned in horror. That old bastard Fortune had left one last trap. Villance still had seconds to flee but he was not going without the book. He hurried to the centre of the chamber, reached out, and grabbed it in both hands as a final metal panel descended over the doorway, trapping him inside.

'Darian! Yer filthy coward! Get me 'out of 'ere!'

All the upper class accent was lost in his terror. Villance glared at the book, hope returning. A locked room would be no barrier to the holder of the fabled Technomicron. Rifling frantically through its yellowed pages, Villance discovered that it was a locomotive timetable for Alnwick to London. An out-of-date timetable at that.

Villance's face fell as he realised that Fortune had had the last laugh.

'I was right you know, that was Freddie Squills.'

Appalled, Athena grabbed Darian's arm, 'Cyrus Darian, are

you really going to leave that wretched man trapped in there – alive?'

Darian shook her off. 'He won't be for long.'

That left two more doors.

Villance's last remaining henchman, now released from his master's employ, had one thought on his mind: a swift escape from the hellish labyrinth. Trapped in a chamber with enemies including a demon and a shapeshifter, the only other door blocked by a solid brick wall, he decided to take his chances in the darkness revealed by the first door. Bravely he stepped through into a blackness so dense it appeared solid. The very air pressed in on him, trapping him in complete silence, absorbing him with infinite slowness, atom by atom by atom.

Even without hearing a scream, the others knew something truly terrible had happened to the man and would to them should they follow him through the door.

'Hello?' called Athena into the darkness, but her voice was soaked up and muffled.

There was no reply.

Darian walked across to the remaining doorway, aware that a further half an hour was nearly up since the infernal unseen workings of the labyrinth had rewound. His slender hands ran across the bricks which blocked it, looking for flaws. What, if anything, was behind it?

'Sorry to inconvenience your delicate sensibilities my friends, but the only way this brute of a wall will yield its secrets is for all of us to do some hard manual labour.' He glanced across to Athena, her face pale from the shock of the henchman's fate and the pitiful, ignored sounds of Villance's desperate pleas for mercy. 'And I do mean all of us.'

'As long as this is never mentioned in any of my clubs,' Hardwick announced with a grin and a wink, removing his coat and rolling up his sleeves.

With only the merest suggestion of mutterings of dismay, the men in the group returned to the stricken sphere and using Belial's eyes as a blowtorch removed some of the spikes and blades from the metal carcass. With no space to transform into a useful African rhino or buffalo, Cambion alongside Athena, had the task of piling up the rubble that the others hewed from the brick wall. Within seconds of breaching the wall, a waft of sweet, fresh air rewarded their toil. The final bricks tumbled revealing a plain shaft, earth lined and set with a simple, stout wooden ladder up to the surface, a small circle of hope above them illuminated by a sprinkling of stars.

The damp air coming down to them smelled of simplicity, of a natural world without the workings of mankind's ingenuity. It also smelled of safety and freedom.

32

Puttering along at dawn high above a countryside slumbering beneath a cover of autumn mist, Hardwick's dirigible carried mainly silent passengers, lost in their thoughts after the too close brush with the Reaper in Northumberland.

The pitiful, beseeching cries of the trapped Villance still haunted Athena, perhaps for the rest of her life. He was an evil, murderous man without doubt but the lack of mercy shown by her companions towards his plight, shocked Athena to her soul. She blamed Darian, his influence over the others, including her father, was powerful and to her, inexplicable. What possible hold did he have over these otherwise intelligent men? Even over a Prince of Hell?

Darian was a compulsive liar, devoid of a conscience, had the morals of an alley cat and was as trustworthy as a renegade jackal. The man mocked every bastion and moral code of decent society. He was utterly contemptible. Somehow aware of her thoughts towards him, Darian raised his head from a light slumber and gave an impudent grin. Furious with herself for blushing Athena looked away sharply. The man was despicable.

Her respect for Lord Hardwick had diminished during this last adventure; a true gentleman was chivalrous even towards mortal enemies. He should have attempted to rescue Villance from entrapment and a slow, horrible death. *Time to go home*, Athena's yearning for her Virginia mansion and servants returned. The awakened spirit of adventure was still there within her heart but not with this unseemly gathering of reprobates. Darian's corruption had tainted them all, he was an immoral, amoral man who consorted with demons; this was not the company for a God fearing woman of good conscience.

As the airship dipped lower to traverse the busy sky lanes above the city, the clear, bright air of the English countryside gave way to an almost solid wall of London's polluted fog. The capital had not rested during their brief absence. A convoy of vast barges moved up the Thames laden with building material for the new project: the turbines designed to clear the air above London. Hardwick took a dim view of this development. Partly through vanity because he was not involved, which he perceived as a monstrous slight to him as the country's leading engineer and also because he could not envisage the turbines succeeding in their role. It was pie-in-the-sky engineering at its over optimistic worse, fraught with problems yet to be addressed.

As they neared Mayfair, Hardwick slowed the dirigible and picked up an adjustable portable visualiser, similar to an everyday telescope but with the added advantage of sound. Training it on Darian's home, his suspicions were confirmed, news had spread that celebrations over Darian's demise had been somewhat premature. He could see from the glint on their metal casings that Crimm-Smythe had a squadron of Mechmen waiting close by for their return. He steered the airship away from Mayfair. It was too big and easy a target for a sharp shooting Mechman sniper, so instead he flew it to a safe house in nearby Knightsbridge and tethered it low in the grounds.

'I can keep the airship at Johnny Featherstone's. We have an arrangement but I cannot stay with him along with the rest of you. Fearful snob, I'm afraid.'

'Don't worry, Miles old chap,' Darian replied. 'We are within a short walk from the Demeter Hotel, a first class establishment that asks no questions and will not answer any either.'

With everyone exhausted and many demoralised, a pitched battle with Crimm-Smythe's metal-clad henchmen was not the return to London they needed. With Darian agreeing to pick up the bill, they booked into the Demeter under false names; it was a discreet and luxurious hotel where comfort and privacy was celebrated to the highest standards. The prospect of hot baths, fine cuisine and spacious eiderdown beds raised everyone's spirits.

'We will stay here for as long as we need to recover and be safe,' announced Darian. 'But let us pray to our various deities for a monsoon's worth of rain. Let the buggers rust while waiting to ambush us!'

For once Athena did not baulk at the man's profanity.

Darian prepared to indulge himself with a breakfast worthy of a hungry king and risking a few minutes of breathing disgusting air, sat by an open window. He did not have to wait long, a flourish of leathery wings announced Misha had found him. He rewarded the creature with a generous portion of bacon from his plate and let her find her favourite spot curled around his shoulders where she sat with a curious sound of contentment partway between growl and purr. With no announcement, the demon arrived carrying the morning newspapers under his arm. He sat opposite Darian, helping himself to breakfast.

'Our American friend is in serious trouble,' Belial announced folding down a paper and handing it to the alchemist. 'From all accounts, he has been financially ruined.'

Darian read the article with growing unease, something wasn't right – this wasn't a run of the mill business disaster. This stank of dirty dealings from an influential and unnamed source, perhaps a punishment for Dedman's apparent allegiance to him? The prospect of the American and his dreadful daughter leaving dimmed again, damn it. They could end up stranded and penniless in London, embittered and expecting some redress.

'Does he know yet?'

Belial nodded. 'He made a bee line for Miles, The fool probably thinks his lordship is loaded. No wonder Dedman is throwing the charming Athena at him.' The demon loaded his plate up again. He enjoyed the physical pleasures of his human form knowing excesses would not harm him. 'He's backing the wrong horse there, you are the one as rich as Croesus.' He gave a deep, rueful sigh, 'And the one blessed with the devastating good looks unlike our poor, pallid Miles.'

'With emphasis on the poor,' returned Darian with a wicked grin designed to make Belial's burnt cinder of a heart spark with a flash of emotion. A dangerous game but a necessary one to stay one step ahead of the game. No other human adventurer had a bond so close with any demon let alone a Princely one. Darian's insurance policy in this world – and the next.

'Divide and rule,' Darian mused. 'I suspect that is the tactic of this particular player in the game. Split us up then destroy us. Sounds too clever for any of the known suspects and not clever enough for the Lady.'

'Had you better warn Cambion and Miles?'

Darian poured himself more coffee into a bone china cup and sat back in his chair. 'Would you mind, old chap? The trials and tribulations of that last adventure have taken a fearsome toll.'

Fearful tears ran down Athena's face as she lay in a hot scented bath, all pleasure in the luxury, in anything, had dissipated the minute she read about her father's misfortunes. He had always been a risk taker, a man who had become wealthy by speculating and never choosing an easy route through life but he was scrupulously honest in his business deals and did not deserve this calamity. Did she have a home to return to? Were they utterly ruined?

That morning her father had risked breaking cover and gone with Lord Hardwick to investigate what had happened, leaving her alone in a hotel with strangers and that … that man. Everything in her life had spiralled downhill since Cyrus Darian entered their world. Corruption and despair followed in his wake as if he was the very Devil incarnate. Perhaps he was indeed Lucifer! It would explain how he could pass through life unharmed and unaging, how he held normally sane men in his thrall, why Belial worshiped the ground he walked on. And why women found him so inexplicably irresistible. She would never find a man so cynical, louche and so foreign-looking, attractive. Never!

She stepped out of the bath and wrapped in a cloud-soft cotton robe wandered into her suite where maids had lain out her clothes and left a light breakfast. Athena's fingers ran along a dark peacock silk day gown, trimmed with delicate tracery of pale grey Nottingham lace, garb discreetly chosen for her and delivered to the hotel by one of Darian's many female admirers. The gown was beautiful and tasteful. A high born lady thankfully! Athena shuddered at what she would have done had he arranged for one of his brothel strumpets to find her clothes.

Surrounded by such luxury and good service was the only life she knew, an existence under threat now. Even the stay at the Demeter was down to the reluctant generosity of an ill-bred rogue.

She sat at the table and glanced down at the lightly buttered toast and poached egg she had ordered, pushing the plate away with a sigh. The news had stolen her appetite. She took a few sips of elderflower cordial, the rich sweetness and unusual warmth slipped down her throat unnoticed.

A few minutes later, a sensation spread through her body, becoming more and more concentrated in the core of her belly and womanhood. Waves of pleasure and an aching need threatened to overwhelm her. Flustered and embarrassed despite being alone in the suite, Athena paced the room. As if they had a life of their own, her hands began to caress her own body, her mind imagining a man's strong, elegant and skilled fingers. What was happening to her? She was behaving like a wanton. A disgraceful wagtail! A flush of warmth flared at her throat and she drained her glass of cordial, then finished the rest to wash away the unseemly sensations.

This was a disastrous decision, this time a shocked Athena became aware of the effect of the liquid, not as a harmless infusion of wild spring blossom but some form of poison coursing through her veins. The craving, the raging heat within her became unbearable. She ran back into the bathroom and throwing off her robe, climbed back into the bath but the cooling water did nothing to extinguish the need so great.

She began to whimper for fulfilment. Intense erotic images of intertwining limbs, of lips seeking hers, images of the man she loathed, polluted her mind. A man her body wanted as much as her mind denied him. She dried herself and dressed hurriedly, the elderflower infusion strengthening its hold over her, she had to find Cyrus, had to have him. Had to.

33

A man of decency and honour would have immediately realised Athena Dedman was not herself but the unfortunate victim of some hex. From the moment, she appeared unchaperoned at a man's hotel room door, her hair wet and loose, her eyes wild, a gentleman would have sought discreet female aid to protect her reputation and not returned with her to her suite. He would not have allowed Athena to fling her arms around his neck, nor let her kiss him with such passion and heat she could have made a sainted eunuch hard.

Cyrus Darian was not that man of decency and honour, unless giving the lady what she demanded was considered an act of chivalry. He did not resist as she hauled him towards her bed clawing at his clothes, hungrily kissing and licking every inch of his flesh as soon it became exposed. Her language was explicit, her voice low, earthy with desire, where on earth did Athena learn such ribald terms? Darian found this change in her amusing, irresistible, her starchy, prim manner replaced with voluptuous, wanton abandon.

Darian threw her on the bed and pulled up her dress, her need was too all devouring for time wasting finesse and foreplay. Underneath the gown, Athena was naked, still warm and wet from her morning bath, her legs parting eagerly for him, her hands grabbed his hips, pulling him closer towards her yearning womanhood. Darian groaned with his own need, fired up by her shameless behaviour. He suspected she was a virgin, but she didn't want a gentle first encounter. Darian gasped in pain and surprise as she grabbed hold of his manhood, doing her best to force it in her.

What else could he do? Surely to back away now would be cruel. Better a seasoned expert introduced her to the delights of sexual pleasure and not the inept flaccid prodding of a repressed English aristo. All thoughts of preserving her honour, of remembering Miles Hardwick's adoration for her was lost in the heat as he entered Athena in one strong lunge, rewarded by her cry of joy, arched back and shuddering hips.

Whatever was fuelling Athena Dedman's erotic mania was powerful and long lasting. Her voracious demands drained Darian as he fulfilled her needs by using a lifetime's experience of bedroom skills during a tumultuous, sweat-drenched tumble of limbs, thrusting hips and eager tongues. As his face pulled back from deep between her thighs, he was relieved to see she had finally fallen into a light sleep. Would she remember this torrid encounter when she woke up? Part of him hoped she would, the shame sending her fleeing back to America. His vanity wanted her to remember his conquest of her haughty disdain, albeit fuelled by some heinous action, perhaps from the same source that ruined her father? The easiest and best solution would be a merciful amnesia or the fleeting, fading memories of an erotic dream. Anyway, he reasoned, at least he had spared Athena of the curse of not knowing a man's touch and succumbing to green sickness and melancholia and other afflictions of old maids.

As for Miles? This was not the first time Darian had taken advantage of one of his crushes, Miles always forgave him. Why would this time be any different?

Darian washed, dressed and threw the counterpane over the slumbering form and deciding for once that discretion was the better part of valour, left her alone to recover. But not before sniffing the glass on her breakfast tray. He had his explanation. Fervoris root, as rare as blue platinum and the most powerful aphrodisiac known to humanity. He held up the glass and saw tell tale slivers of pale root floating in the dregs, similar in colour to the elderflower cordial, it was tasteless and harmless apart from the dramatic boost to the user's libido and reduction of their inhibitions. Darian fished out the remaining slivers and wrapped them in a handkerchief; fervoris was far too valuable to waste. So, the charming Athena was not under a hex after all and her lust for him was from a deeply repressed and genuine desire set free by the cordial.

He smiled as he left her chamber. 'Sorry, my lovely but that will be the first and last time you will have the delight of my company in bed. The first encounter should always be memorable but there is no need to thank me. It was my pleasure to oblige a lady.'

RAVEN DANE

34

Athena woke slowly, her mind full of disturbing, fading dreams. Her body ached with a pleasurable fatigue, every nerve end feeling tingly in a good way. Her hand strayed down her body with a will of its own right down to the pulsing centre of the delightful sensation, her fingers touched wetness. She forced herself fully awake, gave a yelp of disgust and dismay at the wreckage of her gown and the unspeakable bodily fluids despoiling it and her body. This was no dream. For the third time that morning, Athena immersed herself in the scented bath, too shamed to call the maids to draw her a fresh one. The now icy water cleansed her body but it could not purge the despoliation, she was ruined! Was this a further cruel punishment by her father's enemies, had she been drugged and violated? What other conclusion could there be?

So why did it feel so good? Climbing from the bath, she examined herself in a full-length mirror. No bruises, no sign of a struggle. In fact she had never felt so alive, so vibrant. A tiny voice within her mind reminded her that she had enjoyed herself and with who. She thrust the wretched unwanted voice into a dark, forgotten recess of her memory and locked it in.

Some unknown cad had stolen her maidenhead and in a drugged state she had enjoyed it like some bawdyhouse wanton. Athena broke down sobbing; she was undone, destitute and friendless. Ruined. Grabbing the blue dress, she bundled it up and threw it on the fire, wishing she could cleanse her body with purifying flame. Unable to tolerate the suite and its lingering musky odour of human degradation, Athena dressed back in her riding habit and fled from the rooms.

In the hotel lobby, she ran and tripped awkwardly into Sir Miles Hardwick whose quick reaction kept her from falling. His

197

concern and no doubt curiosity for her distress was the last thing in the world she wanted now, all hopes of a mutual understanding leading to a formal engagement lost forever. Knowing he would pursue her out of chivalry, Athena bolted like a spooked horse, ducking down the nearest alley, a narrow, mean thoroughfare with filthy cobbles strewn with the city's detritus. Not knowing or caring where it led, Athena ran blindly until forced to halt to catch her breath, taking in deep gulps of the thick, tainted air.

As she recovered from her flight, the warm glow of candles caught her attention, unusual in a city lit by gaslight. It came from a small Georgian townhouse, the walls a light pink sandstone, the black filigree metalwork of its railings adding grace and charm to the building. Above the door, a small placard announced it to be 'The Shelter of St Agnes, a place of succour for all distressed gentlewomen'.

Athena shuddered, had it come to this? Was she reduced to throwing herself onto the charity of strangers? It was unthinkable and she turned to walk away.

The door opened and a middle-aged blonde woman stepped out, beckoning for Athena to follow her inside. The compassion and understanding in the matronly woman's gentle grey eyes and the uncanny resemblance to her long dead mother was too much for Athena to bear. With the prospect of a day roaming the streets or facing the others ahead of her, she gave in and reluctantly obeyed the summons through an obscuring veil of tears.

Fortified by a shot of brandy in his morning coffee, Darian recovered from his efforts to satisfy the Dedman woman and concentrated on reading through his notes, trying to piece together the conflicting strands that might lead to the Technomicron. All the while he still doubted the book's existence. He did not look up as Hardwick stormed into his suite and slammed his cane and gloves down on the table in front of the alchemist.

'Miss Dedman is in a fearful state. Distracted and confused.'

'Of course she is,' Darian replied without looking up from his notes, 'it is not everyday an over-indulged American princess discovers she is a pauper.'

Hardwick ignored the alchemist's dismissive tone. 'We have to go out and find her. She ran past me out into the street unchaperoned. She could be in the most terrible danger.'

'Or simply enjoying a beverage and cake at a nearby respectable tea garden, somewhere ladies can relax without a chaperone or loss of their honour,' Darian replied, showing no inclination to chase after the wretched woman. It wasn't that long ago, she was naked, on her knees and begging him for more. He suppressed a knowing smirk at the lascivious memory. Poor Miles did not deserve the pain of the truth about Athena's secret desires.

'Cyrus, please, I implore you. We are in hiding from our enemies in this hotel. Anything could happen to Athena, I mean Miss Dedman. Her father is in no state to help us. The poor man is close to breaking point.'

Darian sighed, 'He is certainly poor.'

Another interruption caused by these unwanted Americans, when in Hades were they going home? He stood up and taking his time, fetched his coat and cane. He never wore a hat, like his clean-shaven face and long hair, another sign among decent society of his lowbred, foreign degeneracy.

'Why me, old chap? Where are Belial and Cambion? The shapeshifter in the form of a bloodhound can easily track her down. And the demon is already bored enough to do a good deed. Now that is seriously bored! All this fussing over these Americans is all so bloody tedious.'

A worm of suspicion began to gnaw into Hardwick's mind, why was Darian being so evasive and unhelpful? This was more than his usual laconic indolence. The man was hiding something. Suspicion burrowed even deeper into Hardwick's thoughts and what it whispered made his blood run cold. No – not with Athena! He forced the vile image away. Athena was

a young woman of impeccable morals and high standards.
 'Come on Cyrus, before anything dreadful happens.'

The streets around the Demeter were busy, milling with people, the streets clattering with horse-drawn carriages and wheezing and puffing with overhead steam trams. The fog level was exceptionally light, little more than a dirty yellow mist at knee height and the sky above, seen between the tram rails, was a cloudless bright blue. It was a day when the presence of unearthly forces lurking in the city's shadows seemed no more than tales to frighten children into behaving. Darian's hidden eyes did not miss a thing; he knew that even the most innocuous looking passerby could bear dark secrets in his soul. Or that the slender young woman with the large, vivid green eyes and riot of red gold hair had fae blood way back in her ancestry.

In Darian's world, nothing was ever as it seemed.

Joined by a bemused Belial and an awkward Cambion, they hastily tried to work out how to search for the errant Athena. A row broke out immediately. Despite a bloodhound being the most efficient way to track down the woman, Cambion refused to shapeshift. The concept of being held on a leash by anyone was abhorrent to him.

'I will not be demeaned in that way,' he fumed, adding to Hardwick's frustration and Darian's amusement. Cambion looked and sounded like a vexed shrew when angry and was just as effective.

With no other effective plan, they split up and wandered the streets searching for the wayward ex-heiress with instructions to meet back at the Demeter as soon as anyone found her. The shapeshifter reluctantly agreed to be the go between, taking the form of a beady-eyed crow.

Striding alone, Belial's sharp senses searched for clues, such as the glimmer of sunlight on Athena Dedman's red brown hair, her height making his task easier, she was taller than most of the male passersby. Or the waft of her scent, the delicate perfume of violets she always wore. Made exclusively for her back in Virginia, it was distinctive from any other violet fragrance. As he passed an alley entrance, the demon was certain he could trace the perfume still lingering in the air. He paused, wondering whether to wait until the crow flew over then decided there was nothing he couldn't deal with alone and sauntered down the alley way.

Immediately wrongness surrounded him, the alley became more illusion than reality. Walls lost their solidity and became fluid ghosts of their original form. The cobbled street beneath Belial's feet rippled and lost cohesion forcing him to crouch low to avoid losing balance. His eyes flared with angry flames, what was happening? He glanced back to the main street and life carried on as normal, unaware of the aberration of the alley.

The air around him became increasingly hot, soon too hot to be bearable by an ordinary human. If this rise continued, it would affect his enhanced human form. He would have to revert to being Fallen again to survive. Who was forcing him to change against his will? He was a Prince of Hell, who dared perpetrate this outrage? Belial turned and tried to leave the alley but the shifting ground became more unstable, now pitching and bucking like a wild horse. Snarling in frustration and fury, he commanded this interruption of reality to stop, threatening all manner of diabolical and unending tortures on his unseen assailant.

This only increased the heat and agitation. Belial's anger rose to breaking point, flame bolts flashed from his eyes with no target, deflecting off the warping surroundings without damaging anything. This was an outrage! He was a Fallen Prince, worshipped as a god by many ancient peoples. This helpless state insulted his dignity but so did being forced to change by some unknown assailant.

'Prince Belial.'

A voice addressed him through the chaos, flat, cold, sexless. If a machine could speak, this would be the sound. The demon spun around but could not see anybody in the alley which still lurched and wavered like a drunkard.

'Prince Belial, you can stop this. Instantly. Return to the magnificent Fallen Angel you are meant to be. Break free from this humiliating tomb of decaying flesh. How can you demean yourself by living in the form of a miserable lowly beast?'

The demon forced his unbalanced body to stand and despite the bucking increasing in violence, somehow managed to stand tall and proud. 'I am what I choose to be. Whatever you are, faceless coward, you have no power over me.'

'But I will, my Prince. I will soon have dominion over all the living and the dead. Mastery of the Technomicron will give me total rule of the souls of the humanity's dear departed, all that were and all that will be. Souls whose spectral energy I can direct to obey my every whim.'

The mechanical voice began a curious grunting sound which Belial took to be laughing, 'Angels and Fallen alike will have no purpose. No souls to protect or corrupt. For I will empty Heaven and Hell to create a new dominion. One under my complete rule.'

The tremors reached their peak and did not increase, whoever was distorting time and space had reached the limit of their power and could do no more to threaten Belial. He heard a long drawn out snarl of thwarted ambition and frustration and the narrow alley and crowded row of houses became solid brick and slate again.

The implications of the unknown assailant's threats sank in. The Technomicron was infinitely more dangerous than any of the team could possibly imagine. It must not get into the hands of any mortal or supernatural being. Himself included. Sorry, Cyrus, he thought, especially not you. The book must be obliterated from existence.

Belial dusted off his clothing and as he prepared to return to the main street, heard footsteps approaching from down the alley. He turned to discover a familiar form walking towards him. With head held high and with bold, confident steps approached an unharmed Athena Dedman.

35

That night, as the refugees from the Mechmen army sat together in the hotel's dining room for an early light supper. Athena arrived on her father's arms; her head held high, she looked proud and resplendent in a new dove grey formal gown. No trace of her earlier shame flushed her cheeks or humbled her gaze. After her visit to the sanctuary, she now knew what had happened but strengthened by her short stay, she refused to be broken by the incident. An unknown enemy had drugged her with Fervoris not the wretched cowardly bastard who took advantage of her uncontrolled state. She was not to blame. Athena knew now she had a choice, to be victim or victor. She chose the second option.

Athena sat down and raised her wine glass to Cyrus Darian, meeting his hidden eyes with a direct, challenging glare of superiority. He could not break her, but by all that was holy, one day she would destroy him. She turned away with a sneer of disdain to concentrate on caring for her father. The man seemed physically diminished by his distressing news, his broad frame hollow, his strong features sunken in as if he had aged several decades. He refused all food and his daughter had to coax him to sip a light chicken soup.

'This is not charity or an admission of any culpability,' Darian spoke quietly as the mood around the table grew in tension, 'but we as a group are under direct attack and London is no longer safe.' He reached into his coat and produced an envelope and handed it to Hardwick. 'These are the directions to Wildewish House plus my instructions to the staff. My private home in the Cotswolds is yours. For all of you, including your father Cambion. I have never mentioned this place to anyone, even to you, Belial. Sorry, old chap.'

The demon bowed his head in acceptance of the apology as

Darian continued, 'It will be safe and tranquil. I sent Maksat up a week ago but there are other horses for my guests to enjoy. No one must ride my Akhal Teke stallion – for your own safety.'

Darian took a long sip of wine as the others thought this offer through before adding, 'To ensure this house remains a secure haven, I will remain in London.'

Athena put down her glass firmly and replied, 'Mr Darian, we have already intruded enough on your hospitality, my father and I will return to Virginia on the next available crossing.'

'Steerage gets a bit crowded this time of year,' Darian replied with brutal honesty, 'and it's a bad place for contracting nasty infectious ailments.'

This was too much for Hardwick who slammed down his fist spilling a rather fine Ausone Bordeaux across the white table linen.

'Meet me at my club, the Rochester, at dawn.'

'Don't be ridiculous Miles,' the alchemist replied, righting Hardwick's glass and refilling it. He realised his friend suspected something had happened with the Dedman woman and was using euphemisms to call him out on a duel of honour. Only Darian was not a gentleman and did not give a tinker's cuss for honour. Nor had he any intention of fighting with an ally and friend.

This had happened before. Hardwick had always been murderously furious at first, before eventually thanking him in the past for his dalliances with the inventor's amours. It exposed them as shallow trollops, not worthy of carrying the Hardwick name. There was a new look in Hardwick's eyes now, heartbreak. What was the matter with these English men? He could still marry the wretched woman if he wanted. Hardwick as an enthusiastic supporter of high-class brothels when he could afford them, was no saint after all.

'Lord Hardwick. Mr Darian. If I may crave your full attention.' The unexpected interruption by Athena cut through the tension like a knife, 'Whatever the cause of your quarrel, gentlemen, I suspect it is of no great importance. Something is playing unpleasant games with our lives and tearing at each other's throats is exactly what they want.'

A light returned to Hardwick's eyes, Miss Dedman was back to her old indomitable form. Surely she was innocent of any improper behaviour with that scoundrel. He had to believe that, shut out all doubts. He bowed his head towards her, 'Of course, my dear Miss Dedman, you are most observant and wise. '

'Not that wise.' Zachariah Dedman spoke for the first time, his voice small, wavering. 'I didn't raise my daughter to be a darn fool. Of course we will leave this hellhole and stay at Wildewish. What choice do we have, Athena?'

'I'd rather starve.'

'I think you will find, my dear,' her father replied with a weary sigh, 'that an empty stomach is a great cure for pride.'

He turned to Darian, 'Sir, we will be happy and grateful to accept your kind offer.'

'As will my father and I,' added Cambion. He did not relish more time under the same roof as the American woman, but there was plenty of space in the Cotswolds to keep out of her way. The thought of fresh air and beautiful countryside was appealing enough but also he craved an escape from danger. He had more than enough of adventure already and this one had a nightmarish quality beyond anything he had ever shared with Darian.

'Then it is settled,' Darian sighed with relief, he did not relish another minute of responsibility for other people's lives. 'I think it would be best for you to leave tonight under the cover of darkness and before we outstay our welcome in this hotel.' He turned to the tight-lipped Hardwick, 'Miles, does your large dirigible still have the ability to fly at night?'

'Of course,' the inventor snapped back, 'it is fitted with a first rate vespertilian noctis-reverbatron.'

'Excellent,' returned Darian, 'then the journey can be made safely while our mutual enemies slumber in their beds.'

As the party dispersed to prepare for the flight, Hardwick managed to catch Darian alone, pinning him hard up against the nearest wall. The alchemist had never seen such fire and anger in Hardwick's eyes, the fool had fallen for that wretched American harridan in a big way.

'I would die to protect a high class woman's honour,' Hardwick seethed, 'but you! You would do all you could to ruin it just for the sport.'

'I hold many things dear to me,' Darian replied, 'but nothing so easily bought and lost. Or of so little real importance.'

Hardwick's face twisted with deep old contempt, his aristocratic upbringing rising unbidden pushing aside the years of friendship and shared endeavours. Cyrus Darian did not fit in, he was forever set apart from the established strata of civilised society, a gypsy, a rogue.

'I know in my heart something untoward happened between you and Miss Dedman. You cannot stop yourself can you? You have to ruin anything good I have in this life. It was too much of a challenge to resist, corrupting a woman with such staunch morality, such virtue.'

Darian pushed him away and smoothed down his velvet frock coat, 'I think you will find, my dear Miles, that virtue is a much overrated quality.'

He began to walk away but paused to add, 'And I have never taken anything from a lady that wasn't willingly offered.' Darian was glad the Englishman did not possess Belial's flame throwing eyes, for he could feel the heat of Hardwick's anger boring into his back. He was unconcerned, like all the other times, this would pass.

36

Unknown to Darian, the dirigible took off for the Cotswolds with Cambion's aged but still spry father gratefully on board but without the shapeshifter himself. Only Belial remained behind with him at the Demeter hotel. They retired to Darian's room for a late night cognac by a crackling fire, a celebration of freedom from the restrictive company of the Dedmans, and Hardwick's simmering ire.

Darian swirled the aromatic liquid around the cut crystal balloon, watched the dancing reflections of the flames through the amber glow. 'Right my demonic friend, I do not care to be barred from my own home a minute longer, any ideas?'

Belial shrugged, he had the power to cause a firestorm and turn the Mechmen into shapeless lumps of molten metal, charred flesh and ash but this was frowned on in the centre of a busy London thoroughfare. It was also difficult to tackle them individually; they were lurking in groups and had vibrophon communicators linking them. 'I suppose conjuring up that rust-inducing monsoon would be out of the question?'

'I'm an alchemist, not a witch,' Darian replied, laughing at the prospect of him dancing sky clad beneath the moon. For one thing, the fog was too thick to see the moon, its beauty and many phases lost on the inhabitants of the capital. Anyway, witches and cunning men were a rural phenomenon. Herbal healers, midwives and guardians of the Old Religion, popular with country folk, kept a low profile from the established church. Darian could not call on a witch's help deep in this urban sprawl. Yet their jesting conversation ignited a spark of inspiration. He reached into his jacket and produced a notebook, scribbled a list and tearing it out with a flourish presented it to Belial.

'You are going to be busy tonight, my friend. Can you use your speed and breaking and entering skills to gather these things by dawn?'

Belial stuffed the note into his coat without looking at it with a grin. 'One day you are going to push your luck with me too far, a Prince of Hell becoming an errand boy for a human? An outrage!'

'You could always say no, old chap.'

'Cyrus, does anyone say no to you?' Belial replied as he took his leave.

Never one to skulk in the shadows, Darian decided to risk a visit to a public lecture at the Royal Society while he waited for Belial's return. The great and the good of Britain's scientific establishment would be there as well as eminent politicians, churchmen and industrial magnates. The place was far too public for a move against him, other than the usual condescension and snubbing. He left the hotel using a staff entrance and walked for some time before hailing a steam cab to take him to Piccadilly.

The vehicle huffed and wheezed to a stop outside Burlington House, a grand, Palladian style mansion where The Royal Society had moved to the year before. As Darian alighted, he joined an eager crowd entering the imposing entrance hall to hear Professor Leonard Croviden's lecture on new discoveries on the gaseous state of matter, but before he could take his place in the auditorium, three liveried doormen halted his progress. Darian was expecting this; the Fellows of the Royal Society had no time for those on the renegade fringes of the scientific world. As an alchemist and a renowned Practioner of occult practises, Darian was right at the top of their list of undesirables.

'Mr Darian, I thought you would at least have the decency to spare yourself the embarrassment of being ejected from the premises.' The speaker was Percy Brangwell, eminent biologist, amateur philosopher and Fellow of the Royal Society. 'You are well aware that you and your kind are not welcome in these hallowed halls.'

'It is a public lecture,' Darian replied undaunted by the posturing of the small, barrel shaped, extravagantly bewhiskered man or the meek clerks in uniform who were supposed to be the building's security team. The alchemist attempted to move past them but the doormen stood firm.

'Now, now. What is this indecorous altercation about?'

Brangwell and the doormen blanched at the deep, commanding voice behind Darian who did not turn to investigate but folded his arms and stood his ground.

'Prime Minister, Sir …' Brangwell stuttered as the tall, imposing form of Sir Edgar Quibbe and his entourage approached. 'It's just that …'

'If you are barring the way of one our brightest and most ingenious scientific minds, well shame on you,' Continued Quibbe, patting Darian on the shoulder, 'I wish we had more young men so gifted to serve the Empire.'

Brangwell blanched and was grateful when several other Fellows arrived to support him. 'Sir, you do not understand, we have to take a firm stand against those who practise medieval quackery and dabble in the dark arts. This is a place of reason and enlightenment. We wish to banish superstition not promote it.'

'The Society champions the search for knowledge,' Quibbe interrupted, 'Mr Darian has already made more astounding discoveries in his short lifetime than you Brangwell. Or any of you for that matter. You would do well to remember your own motto, *Nullius in Verba*, take nobody's word for it.'

'Not by dangerous, amateur experimenting, this man refuses to go by proper scientific methods,' another outraged Fellow interrupted. 'He has not even studied at any respected university.'

'That's true,' Darian interjected, 'only at a disrespectful one.'

Quibbe took Darian by the shoulder and swept him past the outraged Fellows. 'By all means bar the man from being a Fellow but you cannot deny him entry to a public lecture. Come my young friend, you will sit with my party at the lecture.'

'But the dreadful questions he asks …' The peevish complaint spoken as their backs were turned, did not fall on deaf ears. Darian knew one of their greatest dislikes of him was not just that he was an alchemist or even a wretched foreigner but that he showed up the established scientists' lack of knowledge of the true nature of matter – and by Hades, how they hated that!

Once settled, the Prime Minister introduced him to the others in the party, powerful people, all staunch supporters of the anti-fog turbine project. For once, Darian put mischief aside and behaved himself. The temptation to point out the flaws and pitfalls of the grandiose plan was almost irresistible especially on a night where a sturdy south westerly wind had made the city almost tolerable but Quibbe had stood up for him and deserved some respect in return. For now at least.

To polite applause, the professor took centre stage and began his lecture and demonstration, Darian enjoyed the unease among the Fellows and many of their learned guests as Croviden expounded his theories, their sharp, nervous glances in his direction, as if waiting for an explosion of mocking laughter – well it had happened before, twice. As the evening progressed, Darian spent less time listening to the long-winded and flawed lecture on gases and more on surreptitiously studying Sir Edgar Quibbe and his companions. What was it about them that was so out of kilter? Quibbe himself had an aura of wrongness about him despite his pleasant manner.

By the end of the lecture, he was none the wiser and politely declining an invitation to dine with them, for which they were no doubt profoundly grateful, made his way back to the Demeter. It was late but the night was not yet over for Darian, not with some anti-Mechman disruption to engineer.

37

A survivor of the attack on Fogue's mansion, Fancy Dan flexed his newly enhanced muscles, still marvelling at his transformation from East End punisher to Mechman. Always burly and fit from his prize fighter days, the mechanical enhancements gave him strength beyond his dreams. He enjoyed smashing things, anything and everything he could, revelling in the wonderful moment a solid object yielded to his fist and crumpled to complete ruin. His enemy's skull would be easy to smash, perhaps too easy to be enjoyable but the satisfaction would be so much greater than any random pulverised marble statue or metal milk churn.

His memory of the night metal clad death came to Old Nickol burnt into the forefront of his mind, the horror of seeing his fellow punishers evaporate to nothing, destroyed by a toff bastard wielding a fiendish mechanical contraption. The toff bastard that was also a filthy foreigner – Cyrus Darian.

Leaving Fogue's service was no hardship. Fancy Dan could see the East End mage was a spent force, all respect from the locals lost as their already meagre homes burned to the ground. Accepted immediately as a recruit for the Mechmen, his seething hatred for Darian was something they could use.

Where was the bloody man? News of his death falling from Crimm-Smythe's dirigible turned first to celebration then fury when by some sorcery, Darian had survived. Fancy Dan was happy to volunteer to lay siege to the foreigner's home, there were no shortage of others willing to wait. No Mechman could tolerate the humiliation of defeat by some limp-wristed mandrake. Their fervour for revenge was steadily wilting with the tedium of the siege. Sitting, hidden in steam coaches parked around Darian's Mayfair home, the hours stretched out to endless boredom as time appeared frozen. Already his commander sent one Mechman back to the barracks in disgrace for driving the others crazy with noisy fidgeting and tuneless whistling.

At first Fancy Dan thought a child had rolled a bright coloured ball under the steam coach, quicker minds among his companions thought *bomb* and yelled for everyone to get out. They stood clear of the coach and waited for an explosion but all remained quiet but for the fearful murmurs of disquiet from the Mayfair passersby on foot and on horseback. The Mechmen were an unpopular phenomenon of the new technological age, a possible future threat to Her Majesty's Constabulary and armed forces.

With no detonation of the ball, Fancy Dan volunteered to pick it up from beneath the coach's armoured chassis. Tentatively, he knelt down and inched his fingers towards the gaudy bauble, swirling colours of blue and green like a child's large marble. He poked it and nothing happened. Getting bolder, he poked it harder using enhanced Mechman strength and still the ball was inert. Deciding it was harmless, he fished the thing out and held it up to the gaslight. A big marble. That was all it was.

Calling to his commander, Fancy Dan threw the bauble towards him but the idiot couldn't catch the pox in a brothel and dropped it onto the cobbles. Shocked, the Mechmen leapt back as the glass shattered into tiny fragments but still nothing untoward happened. Fancy Dan began to laugh,

'Look at us mates, all spooked over a kid's marble.'

The others looked angry at first with hurt pride then began to join in, releasing the days of tension with a belly laugh that even the dour commander joined in. They began to walk back to the coach when Fancy Dan noticed a discolouration on the armour of the Mechman in front of him. A reddish stain that seemed to be growing in size at an alarming rate. Holes appeared in the man's metal cladding, holes that spread and joined up leaving wide gaps in the plating and exposing his clothes beneath. Fancy Dan looked at his arm; the metal-eating contagion had spread to his own cladding, ruining the carefully manufactured armour, literally dissolving before his eyes.

'Back to base, lads!' the commander bellowed, his panic shared by all the Mechman troop. 'Now!'

Fancy Dan was the first to realise the steam coach also had the contagion, it was going to be a long, humiliating march back to the barracks. He had no doubt of the cause of his embarrassment as he strode through one of London's most refined areas clad only in a pair of grey flannel long johns long overdue darning particularly in the more sensitive regions where ladies were concerned. Cyrus Bloody Darian.

38

October merged into November in a seamless blend of fog and stinging rain that etched away more of the blurred features of saints and gargoyles on the capital's churches. Soon there would be no way of distinguishing the sacred from the profane. A strange peace descended on Darian and Belial as they re-occupied and re-fortified the Mayfair home. With no further clues to the whereabouts of the grimoire and no attacks by any rivals, Darian began to suspect the whole thing was an elaborate hoax.

At least he was safe from Mechman attacks for the foreseeable future. The lightning fast super rust formula was a spectacular deterrent but it was not the dreaded weapon against them that they suspected. The formula was unstable, fiendishly difficult to create and the ingredients did not always gel to create the desired effect. That night, Belial and the alchemist had got lucky, another time and the ball may have released harmless spores.

Darian also wondered how much influence the very public endorsement from the British prime minister had on his situation. Were there government agents warning his enemies off? This was a most likely scenario, one that might only last until he found a stable, commercial form of Infernion. Darian decided there was no need to rush his research.

Even the Lady had not reappeared into his life, a situation he was glad of, though knowing in his heart that if the Emporium found him, he would step through those enigmatic and ever changing doors like a sacrificial lamb. The Lady was as untrustworthy as a rattle snake, her kiss intoxicated him like opium, but he was just as bad as her, they were two sides of the same bad penny.

At least the Dedmans and Cambion's father had settled well

in the Cotswolds and were no longer a source of annoyance. No doubt Athena was recovering from the shock of her brief spell of destitution, Wildewish Hall was a large, gracious Jacobean country house set in a generous estate of five-thousand acres. It had a full staff despite the fact Darian rarely visited his country home, plenty of people to care for Ms Dedman's every whim. Hardwick returned to London occasionally but avoided all contact with Darian and the demon. Darian had to concede this was the longest sulk and grudge the inventor had ever held against him in their complicated history together but he still insisted a quick Fervoris-fuelled tumble with Hardwick's amour should be nothing between old friends.

The whereabouts of the shapeshifter was another mystery, unlike Hardwick he had not fallen out with Darian who had checked out all his usual haunts in vain. Curiosity led to an attempt at contacting him through necromancy but Darian soon discovered from an earthbound that Cambion was still in the land of the living. Cambion had also not visited his father at Wildewish which was a matter of considerable conjecture. The shapeshifter's love and loyalty for his adopted father was central to his life. He had the means to visit him easily and often in one of his avian guises but had not.

Darian had made a few visits to the Iblis club but did not turn up any clues to Cambion's fate, if the shapeshifter was being held hostage, then the beggars were taking a frightful long time in sending Darian a ransom note. A more worrying and likely prospect was that the shapeshifter had become a beast or bird and been killed in that form. An occupational hazard for such an entity. A pity, Cambion had been useful to him.

Though life for Darian and Belial was quiet and uneventful, their surroundings were not. London was in the grip of construction fever, once the Pneumaeris Company got the go ahead for the turbines, the huge project based on a high point of Hampstead Heath had moved ahead with speed unprecedented in human history. Unemployment disappeared and many more labourers poured into the already overcrowded city from all over Britain to man the vast workforce needed to build the tallest structures to rise above the capital. Indeed, they were the tallest structures in the world.

The turgid chemical brew also known as the Thames chocked up with vast purpose built barges ferrying the mind numbing quantities of lumber, metal and stone needed to create the turbines destined to be a new wonder of the world.

At first obscured by the fog the turbines, intended to be its nemesis, rose with extraordinary rapidity above the London skyline. For the first time, dirigibles were used to hoist building materials up the towering columns. With the whole of Hampstead Heath now forbidden to the public, the best view of the construction was from the overhead steam trams and business boomed as London swelled to bursting point with curious overseas visitors eager to see this new marvel of the modern age.

Perhaps the only sane living soul in London to be unimpressed by the scheme, Darian carried on life as if the search for the Technomicron had never happened. Of course, Hyde Park Corner spawned its fair share of wild-eyed ranters foaming at the mouth, declaring the turbine project to be a grievous insult against God as the fog was one of His creations. They insisted the towers were the new symbols of Sodom and Gomorrah and their construction would bring down God's fiery wrath for mankind's overbearing pride. Darian thought that if the deity had a sense of humour, He would be falling about laughing at the insanity of the project. One that was creating even more pollution than the fog it was meant to conquer.

By the time the last of a normal January in London's grey ice and yellow snow had thawed, Darian's thoughts were rarely with the book, already engrossed in rumours of a fabled Frahlian crystal that had the power to freeze and reverse time.

Darian celebrated the first evening of spring by a trip alone to his club, the first time to do nothing but relax since the madness over that damned and elusive book had disrupted his life. He slipped out of the house without waking a slumbering Belial, needing a break from the intensity of living with the demon.

Unlike anywhere else in the capital, the Iblis always warmly welcomed Darian, his occupation and mixed race heritage meant nothing to those who sought company and refuge within its walls. He nodded to familiar faces, the fellow adventurers, occultists, illusionists and minor demon hybrids that sat around together in conversation or alone quietly reading and took up his place in his favourite chair. The journals thoughtfully left on a table for him were full of the Great Project. He ignored this and sought any sign of anything more interesting and salacious.

Four men entered and sat on a table nearby, pretending to converse with each other but taking an uncomfortable interest in him, Darian knew all too well when too many sideward glances were sent in his direction to expect major trouble. Damn their eyes, he was enjoying his leisure time. The alchemist appeared to be deeply engrossed in his journals, but he positioned himself to take advantage of the special lenses on his spectacles, the ones that allowed him to see behind him. Now with his back turned from them, their focus on him was all too clear, the feeble attempt at small talk between them faltered out.

Darian searched their attire for clues to their identity and purpose with him. He could of course walk across and engage them in conversation but with their dull, badly fitted, shop bought clothing and no doubt boring conversation, he couldn't be bothered. They were clearly uncomfortable with what appeared to be brand new clothes; one by one they tugged at the tight starched collars revealing white skin etched raw with red weals. These were men used to wearing looser, less formal attire yet their hands were pale, soft not the calloused, dirt engrained of the working classes.

With no sign of the men leaving before he did, no doubt planning an ambush outside the Iblis, he decided to take evasive action and use his secret exit, one most of the club's regular and long term staff did not know about. He relaxed in his chair, took his time finishing a journal and sipping slowly on his generous measure of finest cognac as if he had no suspicion anything was amiss. Then, taking time to fold up the papers and smooth down his clothing, he strolled with an air of nonchalance towards the exit.

They were watching but did not follow him. No doubt they had colleagues waiting outside to spring the trap. He considered taking them on in a full on fight but again couldn't be bothered. This was the first time he'd worn this bespoke new suit complete with raw silk burgundy waistcoat, lightly embroidered with gold thread, one that had arrived only that morning from his tailors. Removing gore spatter was too tedious for words without household staff.

Darian chatted pleasantly to an old acquaintance and occasional colleague on adventures, the world famed illusionist, The Great Miraculus, aka Reggie Dumpe, and waited until the watching men's guard was down. There was no rush; Miraculus was pleasant company and a fount of genuinely interesting anecdotes and information. When a stout waiter blocked their view, Darian winked to his companion before slipping into the depths of the club's labyrinth of majorly discreet private rooms, ideal for entertaining lovers of opposite or same sex. Or escaping.

'You will show him mercy – if he repents?'

The speaker shuffled his feet on ice-glazed cobbles, he had waited for hours outside the Iblis and the first night of spring still had a cold bite from a reluctantly retreating winter.

'Calm yourself, my son,' his companion replied, 'should this creature so enmeshed in depravity seek the Lord's forgiveness, it will surely be given.'

Judged and forgiven in the next world, not by them, the man did not say out loud for fear of spooking the sensitive man beside him. Cyrus Darian would not be allowed to pollute the world with his degeneracy with a demon and myriad other crimes. By the time the next moon rose, he would be dead by the hand of the righteous.

39

Darian did his best to keep still. Any movement, even an involuntary twitch of his muscles cut the bindings further into his flesh. How had he ended up a prisoner, blindfolded, tied onto a chair with tight wire? Large splinters from the wooden chair were wrecking his trousers and digging into him. As the dizziness subsided, many heavy bruises gradually made their presence known. How long had he been unconscious? Who were the bastards that had done this? And how?

Without his sight, Darian needed to take in as much information about his surroundings as possible, however slim the chances of escape. He was struck first by the complete silence beyond his own ragged breathing and thumping beat of his heart. No dripping water or rattle of passing carriages and mercifully no scurrying rats or lurking breeth or blaggers. Wherever he was, it was dry, he smelt stone, clean with no damp. And something else, something that had seeped into the stone over centuries – incense.

A sudden cold draught announced he was not alone. He heard several footsteps closing in on him, surrounding him, all resolutely human. Darian's face snapped back from the force of a blow. His mouth filled with blood, his only comfort was he had not lost a tooth nor had his nose broken. Yet.

'I am glad you can join us, Mr Darian,' the man's voice was cultured, educated with the faint hint of a Scottish accent.

'I can assure you the feeling is not mutual. I do not mix in the company of cowards.'

He readied himself for another blow but nothing came. He doubted this reprieve would last.

'Nor do we pure, holy and exalted ones mix with accursed demons and their half bred bastards.'

Darian had his answer. He was a prisoner of the Brethren of

Satarel. He fought back the instinct to panic, that would only achieve more pain from his bindings and bring on another blow from his captors. They had him, had they also taken down Belial?

'Easily remedied. Just let me go.'

The unseen interrogator tut-tutted. 'And have you back looking for the Technomicron? What a frightful thought.' Darian heard him move away, 'The world needs protecting from the book and it also needs protecting from depraved, dissolute wastrels like you and your demonic cohorts.'

'It is time to remind our guest of his only value to us, Brother Jacob.'

'Yes, Brother Nathaniel.'

A knife cut across Darian's throat, deep enough to draw a thin line of blood. These people did not bluff and he felt the prospect of a long life rapidly diminishing by the second.

'Summon up your vile consort and we will not cut your throat.'

'What happened to "thou shalt not kill"?' Darian pointed out, not unreasonably. 'And which particular vile consort do you want? I have so many.'

He was relieved – at least they did not have Belial.

Brother Nathaniel spoke again, 'Do you know why we revere the glorious angel, Satarel?'

Darian had to imagine giving an impudent shrug, he was too tightly bound to do anything else. 'Er, because it is easy to spell?'

He paused before adding, 'Unlike Zgzagel or Tzadiqel.'

Another voice interrupted, 'Insolent cur! The angel grants us the grace of hidden knowledge.'

'Then there is no need for any of this,' Darian observed, 'you can ask your chum Satarel the questions.'

'Let us dispense with this time wasting banter, Darian. We know you will give up the demon to us because it is not in your nature to be noble and self sacrificing.'

'Nor is my nature to be stupid,' Darian replied calmly. 'Once you have what you want, there is no reason to keep me alive.'

Darian had become aware none of his interrogators had mentioned Belial by name. They could do little to summon or harm such a powerful denizen of Hell without knowing his name. A small but potent ray of hope.

'Anyway, hurt me again and he will boil your heads alive – slowly.'

That remark provoked another hard blow. Darian's head felt like a cross between a bruised peach and a punch bag but with added pain but again he drew some comfort his looks would not be permanently marred.

'An order of boiled heads all round then,' Darian muttered before falling into a merciful oblivion.

A shock of ice-cold water on his face and piercing shafts of light in his eyes snapped him into consciousness. Though the blindfold was gone, he was still bound by wire to the chair, only the location had changed. A chapel made of shining marble lit by a factory's supply of candles. The effect was dazzling, but Darian was convinced the over brightness stunk of fear. They believed that when you eliminate dark shadows, you destroy evil. But what of the dark shadows in their souls?

Slowly, his eyes adjusted to the glare, Darian could see the central figure above the altar was not Christ but a massive golden statue of an angel. A fanciful depiction with outspread gilded swan wings, flowing robes and strong features modelled on the classic statues of Grecian heroes. Nothing like the real thing.

'Brother Nathaniel, the Holy Water had no effect on him!'

'Yes it did. It has made me bloody wet!'

Darian turned to his right, a young monk held a stone pitcher in trembling hands, clearly terrified of the alchemist. Good.

'Maybe someone pissed in it for a lark?'

Not the cleverest quip he had ever given but Darian's sense of humour was at a low ebb. For the first time he could see their leader as the man approached, his jowly, florid face enthused with ruddy fury. Darian had imagined him tall, stick thin and gaunt. The reality was a stocky, square of a man with a humourless, self-important demeanour.

'Blasphemy! Is there no depth you will not descend to?'

'None whatsoever,' Darian replied without hesitation. 'In fact I have only begun my life long journey seeking the depths of depravity.'

'Such misplaced bravado. It ends here, with your life, cur. Though I am sure Satan will enjoy showing you the foul tortures of Hell.' Brother Nathaniel's relish over his prisoner's forthcoming demise was most unseemly in a man of God. His small eyes gleamed, spittle moistened his fleshy lips.

'Er, what version of your holy book have you read?' Darian queried with mock sincerity. 'All the "love your enemy", "forgive those who trespass" and "thou shalt not kill" sections missing from yours?'

'That is for humans, it doesn't cover demons,' the young monk chipped in, overcome by his own bravery in taunting a man bound by wires.

'But I am a hundred percent human,' Darian announced, looking at the man eye to eye, 'or hasn't Brother Nathaniel bothered to mention that?'

'With strange, eerie eyes like that?' the young monk stuttered pointing to the swirling violet curiosity of Darian's altered vision.

'Pretty aren't they? A war wound, the result of a battle with a succubus but I can assure you, the rest of me is all too human.' Darian looked across to Brother Nathaniel and added, 'Which makes what your leader plans for me downright cold-blooded murder.'

'Actually it does not.'

The familiarity of the voice startled Darian as was the incongruity of hearing it in this shining chapel to self-righteous insanity.

'It makes it an act of war, a necessity when the soul of humanity itself is at peril.'

Cambion!

'I thought you could help me, Cyrus, but I was wrong. You would never find a cure for me, not when I was of use to you or your nefarious schemes.' The shapeshifter circled Darian's chair, eyes streaming with tears, 'You use people, callously, with less thought and care than you lavish on that hell creature you keep as a pet.'

'And your point being?' Darian returned calmly, the man was not the first to betray him. Memories of how he ended up captured by the Brethren of Satarel began to seep back. Cambion must have been involved from the start.

'What aid are these madmen going to give you? They loathe demons and will destroy you.'

'Actually, we have offered this poor, blighted creature a safe haven for life,' Brother Nathaniel interrupted. He walked up to Cambion and put his arms around his shoulders in a protective gesture. 'This wretched half-breed rejects his demon father. He is a pious man who loves God. How could we turn him away?'

'You don't have any female monks in your cult have you?' Darian mocked. 'If so, you will have a problem.'

'Women are the weak vessels of the Devil's temptation!' roared Brother Nathaniel. Cambion's treachery and alliance with these lunatics began to make sense now. They could lock the shapeshifter in a cellar with bread, water and a bible for the rest of his life and the man would be deliriously happy. Now why hadn't he thought of that!

Hope drained away; the shapeshifter would give up Belial in a heartbeat. That left only Sir Miles Hardwick and his mechanical marvels to save him, a man whose loyalty was only bound by a shared love of adventure and the usefulness of Darian's alchemy discoveries. A man close to becoming a mortal enemy after Darian's wilful and reckless indiscretion with Hardwick's latest object of obsession. This was not looking good.

Beautiful and terrifying celestial light flooded the chapel, as if from every spectrum of the universe. Darian cursed, it meant the arrival of an angel. He had strayed too far from heavenly grace to expect any rescue from that source. He closed his eyes and bowed his head to avoid the brilliance that blazed into every corner, obliterating all shadows and making the humble stone and brick glow with crystalline beauty. The Brethren fell to the floor, weeping in ecstasy, mumbling prayers of joy and blessing. Their faith reward by the ultimate benediction, Satarel himself walked among them.

The angel did not have wings, but the intense energy around his chosen form gave the impression of magnificent wings of light. No human could comprehend an angel's true form. Darian risked opening his eyes and saw the angel was not alone. Another, lesser being of beauty and light appeared to walk beside him, the shape obscured by the streaming glory of Satarel's light.

Brother Nathaniel found the courage to raise his head and address the heavenly visitor, 'We are truly blessed among all men, our faith and fidelity rewarded by this wondrous visitation. All glory to Satarel!'

His words taken up by the others, 'Glory be to Satarel, Glory be to Satarel ...' in a chant rising in fervour and volume.

The angel made no reply but glided in silence through the chapel to stand on the raised altar. Darian could see the being that accompanied him was changing, becoming darker and more solid in form. A familiar form – Belial? What in heaven and hell was going on?

The Brethren climbed to their feet and ran to the altar, prostrating themselves before the angel, their bodies shaking as they wept and prayed in a manic, intense passion. It addressed them in a borrowed voice; angels existed on a dimensional plane beyond all human comprehension. They were beings created with the purest essence of love and light. Their song was that of the spheres, a harmony that bound all matter in the universe.

'What manner of blasphemy is this?' Satarel sounded disappointed rather than angry, a father discovering his children had been wilful and disobedient. 'My fallen brother came to me with a tale of humans turning their back on their Maker to worship the image of a mere servant of Paradise.'

Astonished, Darian could see Belial returning from angel to human form, mercifully spared the transition to charred and twisted demon as Satarel continued.

'These humans have tortured and killed in the name of a being of pure love. A desecration, an abhorrence to all that is Holy.'

The Brethren became silent, confused and frightened. Many turned and pleaded with their eyes to Brother Nathaniel, he was their leader. He must explain to the angel that their motives were pure. That they were soldiers fighting a war against evil but the man was almost catatonic with shock, all he believed in was falling to worthless dust.

'I have commanded my fallen brother to destroy this vile effigy but to spare your lives. There has been too much death, too much blood spilt in my name. Your punishment is to live on with the loss of the Creator's grace.'

Those wretches had got off bloody lightly, thought a furious Darian as the angel disappeared in a split second explosion of dazzling but painless light, leaving a triumphant Belial standing alone on the altar. Too shocked to move at first, the Brethren ran screaming from the chapel as the demon destroyed their statue with flashes of hellfire beaming from his eyes, his mocking laughter ringing in their ears. He stepped down from the altar and unbound Darian, slicing through the wire with his fingernails.

'You are letting the bastards get away!' Darian rounded on the demon, 'After all they did to me!'

Belial shrugged, unconcerned by the alchemist's pique. Of course he would have thoroughly enjoyed slaughtering the zealots, taking his time to relish each prolonged kill.

'I told them you would boil their heads if they harmed me!' Darian continued determined to be avenged. 'And that bloody weasel, rat, cockroach Cambion is with the lunatics, he betrayed me. Set me up to be tortured and killed by them!'

Belial silenced his friend with a tight embrace, lingering longer than Darian would normally tolerate, for all his slight form as a handsome youth, the demon was stronger than a normal human. Without meaning to, his friendly touch could hurt – a lot.

'Cyrus, it is not everyday in eternity that a fallen can make a deal with an Angel. If I wasn't a High Prince, it would not have happened at all. Keeping my side of the bargain can have rewards for both of us. Breaking it can have dire consequences. Trust me on this.'

Darian sulked in silence. Those religious madmen had earned some good old-fashioned demonic smiting. And they were still free to pursue the Technomicron.

'I agreed not to harm them in the chapel, Cyrus,' the demon grinned as if in anticipation of evil deeds to come. 'Once outside they are fair game.'

Relieved, Darian struggled to his feet, his body aching and stiff from the confinement, his injuries from knife and wire painful but already healing.

'As long as you leave the shapeshifter to me,' he murmured as he dusted off the non-existent grime from his clothing: the Brethren kept their cellars scrupulously clean.

The demon nodded assent before remarking, 'Oh, by the way, Satarel offered to purge your body of the succubus venom, a gift of heavenly healing love and all that.'

'I hope you said no,' Darian replied alarmed in case the angel returned. He liked the changes the she-devil had wrought in his body and would not relinquish them at any cost. His soul could only be damned once. Belial in a fit of mischief did not answer, but sauntered out of the chapel, setting fire to it with his eyes as he left. Darian ran after him in agitation, 'You did say no, didn't you? Belial!'

'Oh and another thing,' the demon continued, 'the Angel told me where we can find the Technomicron. Seems Heaven wants us to destroy it for them.'

'Seriously? I never realised angels were so naïve. A fallen prince and a degenerate unrepentant sinner? A *Persheeyan bastid*? Like hell we will!' Darian replied, laughing, as he caught up with Belial.

40

So there was an order from on high that Cyrus Darian was not to be harmed? Fancy Dan, though lowly in the ranks of the Mechmen troops, still had a sharp pair of ears. He overheard his lord and master Crimm-Smythe rage and rant in front of his commanders at the edict from the Prime Minister and by inference the Queen herself.

Well, Fancy Dan had no loyalty or respect for any toff and what had the Queen done for him? One little woman living in unimaginable luxury in loads of fancy castles, surrounded with flunkeys while he scrapped to survive among the sewage and rats of Old Nickol. Darian had humiliated him twice now. There would not be a third.

In an obsessive daydream that would not relent playing over and over in his mind, the Mechman imagined what he would do to the man. Not just crush his skull like an over ripe apple, Fancy Dan would not stop, hammering the body until it was a shapeless mass of flesh and broken bones, then he would continue to pulverise it until all trace of the existence of Cyrus Darian was obliterated. There would be nothing left to bury. Or for his topper trollops or demon mandrake to weep over.

When the opportunity to slip unnoticed from the Mechman barracks arose, Fancy Dan took off his cumbersome and conspicuous armour, leaving only one enhancing mechanism encasing his right arm and fist. That was all he needed. Disguising it under a voluminous cloak, he made his way to Darian's Mayfair home. Memories of the night that the alchemist had unleashed some hellish armour devouring rust made him shudder. But none of his fellow troops had been hurt that night. It made him realise he was not just doing this for personal revenge over the humiliation but to avenge all the punishers that had lost their lives defending their Old Nickol territory. Darian had had it coming for a long time.

Studying the alchemist's home for any weakness to help him invade it, Fancy Dan was unaware of someone approaching from the shadows. He did however catch a pungent whiff of something feral. An alley tomcat? He turned to see a small, meek looking man close by.

'He's not there,' the stranger remarked gazing up at the unlit townhouse, 'but I know where he is.'

Fancy Dan glanced around, agitated that this was some trick of Darian's but the man was alone. He grabbed him by the lapels and lifted him several feet off the pavement. 'Who the devil are you?'

Though stammering with fear, the stranger found his voice despite the threatening manhandling, 'My name does not matter. I am one whose whole life, hope and future Darian has destroyed. Someone who would celebrate if you could rid this world of the scoundrel.'

The pugilist stared deeply into the pinched face of this unlikely would be ally, for all the world like a timid clerk but for his underlying feral scent that betrayed a more unworldly secret. 'Are you one of 'is creatures?'

'In a manner of speaking,' the man continued, 'that is how the blaggard has perceived me in the past. But no more. If you want Darian at his most vulnerable away from all the gizmos, gadgets and occult traps he surrounds himself with over there …'

'I do.'

Fancy Dan eased him back to his feet and let go of the man's lapels.

The stranger reached into his coat and handed Fancy Dan a piece of paper inscribed with an address and a small leather pouch. 'Just Darian though, the others are innocents. I do not want them harmed.'

As Fancy Dan glanced at the paper and discovered gold guineas in the pouch, the little man had disappeared from sight at supernatural speed. There was no sound of footsteps on cobbles, just the scrattering departure of a large, filthy rat.

The bucolic air of the Cotswolds combined by the relaxed comfort of Wildewish had worked wonders on the spirit of Zachariah P Dedman. This was his first experience of an English spring and he was in love with it, the fragrant pastel flowers, first burgeoning of blossom and gambolling newborn lambs were charm personified. Should he regain his stolen fortune, he decided to make Darian an offer he could not possibly refuse on the manor. This was a place to live out his days, especially as his daughter could become an English titled Lady. There had been some progress to this happy conclusion. The inexplicable coolness between Athena and Sir Miles since fleeing to the countryside was beginning to thaw and Dedman senior still heard the happy jangle of cathedral wedding bells in his mind.

All these happy thoughts accompanied Dedman as he strolled along the bank of a tumbling brook that meandered through Wildewish's spacious grounds. Darian did not like formal landscaping and the estate's gardens had a carelessly romantic atmosphere with drifts of daffodils and narcissi and the first hint of bluebells peering from under the English greenwood trees. Dedman particularly admired a stand of blackthorn trees so laden with blossom they appeared covered with heavy snow.

Wafts of cooking bacon from the kitchens drew him back into the house and into the breakfast room. Already seated, Percival Platt, Cambion's father faced him but there was no habitual cheery greeting from the genial elderly gentleman who sat rigid, his face ashen. Dedman's heart skipped a beat, had the man died? Then Platt's eyes flickered a warning and the American froze.

'Sit down and keep yer trap shut.'

The gruff voice behind him brooked no argument and Dedman took the nearest seat, already despairing at what would happen to his daughter. What a time for Hardwick to be away. Dedman risked glancing up to see a tall, burly man with a Mechman enhanced arm and a handgun pointed at his head.

'Now ain't this nice and cosy,' the man sneered, helping himself to rashers of bacon and sausages laid out on the breakfast table, stabbing the meat with a fork, making the movement an ill-disguised threat.

'All we need now is the lady of the 'ouse, and its master of course.'

Dedman risked addressing the intruder. 'May I ask who you are, Sir. And what is the nature of your business in this house?'

'A Yank!' The man laughed, stabbing at another sausage. 'Always 'ated Yanks. Loud maffed show offs wiv more money than the brains they woz born wiv.'

'The feeling of antipathy is entirely mutual,' retorted Dedman grimly enjoying the look of the incomprehension on the brute's face.

'Be careful,' Platt spoke up with surprising calmness, 'our guest is feeling somewhat ill at ease. I am sure if he sat down to dine with us, any misunderstanding can be dealt with in a gentlemanly and civilised manner.'

'I am sure the staff can set another plate,' Dedman added to make sure the man knew his prisoners were not alone.

'Nah. They are too busy to serve us. Too busy being dead!'

The intruder thought this remark hilarious and he spluttered with laughter nearly choking on a mouthful of sausage.

Dedman tried to control his shaking hands but failed, this man was murderous as well as deranged. Again he feared for Athena, what horrors would she endure before this monster was finished with her? He had to act before she came down to breakfast. His gaze sped around the room for anything he could use as a weapon, anything, a knife, a fire iron …

'So where is the man of the 'ouse?'

'That is me, I am Zachariah P Dedman – Wildewish is mine.'

Dedman reeled from a blow to the head from the intruder's handgun, the pain momentarily blinding him. A wave of nausea overwhelmed him, the pain would follow behind it.

'Lying, Yank, will not best please me, keeping yerself alive is all abaht pleasing me.'

'Can I at least know your name?'

'Nah. No point. Tell me where that murderin', lyin' foreign bastid is.'

Darian, the blaggard wanted Darian. The chill of his own mortality shivered through Dedman's large frame. How would this lunatic react when he discovered the alchemist was not here? He did his best not to react when the intruder sat down and placed his mud-caked, hobnailed boots on the seventeenth century walnut table scratching gouges in the mirror-polished surface.

'I'll wait.'

'Then I am afraid, you will be wasting a great deal of your time, sir. Mr Darian is not here. And has not been for some time.'

Platt's admission caused the American to gasp, idiot!

The intruder aimed his gun and shot Platt between the eyes. Shock caused Dedman to jump to his feet, he had never experienced cold-blooded murder and his whole body reeled with revulsion. Swallowing back the bitter bile rising in his throat, he grabbed the side of the table for support. He prayed Athena, on hearing the gunshot, would be sensible and hide. But when was his feisty and courageous daughter ever that wise? This could not end well.

'You next Yank, unless you tell me where that foreign 'earnest' is hiding.'

'Then you had better shoot me now, you yellow-livered, no account varmint because all I can tell you is Cyrus Darian is not here.'

The next blow from the intruder's mechanical arm sent Dedman hurtling across the room, where he lay, still, mortally injured, a pool of blood and grey matter spreading from his shattered skull.

'I told you, I didn't like Yanks.'

'Here is another one you will not like.'

Fancy Dan span around to be confronted with a grim-faced young woman who stood with chilling calm, holding a brown parasol. Such an unexpected, frivolous-looking thing. It was the last image he saw on this earth before she raised and aimed the parasol and shot a bolt through his right eye.

Alone in a house full of corpses, Athena spent time to say her goodbyes to her father and did her best to make all the broken forms decent by throwing blankets over them. Good manners and respect still mattered even for the innocent dead. She left the intruder's corpse for the flies. Forcing aside her crippling grief and shock, she saddled a reliable horse from Darian's stables and galloped to the nearest town. There in flat, emotionless tones, she gave her report to the local constabulary and then booked into the nearest hotel suitable for gentlefolk, charging her account to the cause of all her sorrow – Cyrus Darian. She knew the next few days would pass in a blur of police inquiries, funeral arrangements and nightmares as the horror replayed over and over in her mind.

That Miles Hardwick did not arrive to help her added to the ghastliness for she was certain he too was either dead or in grave danger. The man was too gallant not to fly to her side. Unless – the thought that had haunted her for months came back to torment her at this, the lowest point in her life – Hardwick would come to her aide unless dead or a prisoner, or unless that utter cad Darian had told him about that night. Would any gentleman seek to give succour to a ruined woman, a harlot?

41

Like the stout legs of a monstrous metal titan, the two generator towers arose relentlessly above Boudicca's Mound on Hampstead Heath. All signs of the ancient tumulus where according to local legend, the Iceni queen were buried, obliterated by the granite foundations needed to support the weight of the colossus astride the hill.

Like every Londoner, Darian had observed the vast columns of bronze and steel rise to dominate the capital's skyline, the speed of their growth bordering on supernatural. Up close, the full scale of the project stunned the senses. It was the greatest engineering project in the world and in Darian's reckoning, one doomed to fail. What fool had positioned the turbines atop the columns to drive foul air from London's streets to the Thames estuary and out into the North Sea? In his opinion, they were set incorrectly and would only create an annoying gale far too high above the city and do nothing about the heavier industrial fug on the streets.

If they didn't blow themselves up first, for the first time Darian began to get suspicious about this project. If only that stubborn besotted Hardwick was here now, he would know exactly why the shape and design of the great blades felt wrong. Too much money and expertise had gone into the scheme and despite the extreme haste in its construction; Darian was convinced any flaws were deliberate. A conviction strengthened by the angel's assistance – the grimoire was beneath this hill. In Darian's mind there was no such thing as a coincidence.

He felt a hand on his shoulder, Belial silently urged him to step back deeper into the undergrowth as a company of well-armed Berkshire Guards began their regular patrol of the perimeter. Security was understandably tight; the havoc caused by a group of fanatic anarchists armed with bombs would be catastrophic. Or the damage caused by an alchemist and a demon.

'We need to find a way beneath the structure,' whispered Belial. 'That is where the angel said the Technomicron would be.'

'Will he come back, if we decide not to destroy it?'

'Most likely,' Belial replied. 'And this time he will be really angry.'

'Vexing an angel, that will be a new one for me.' Quipped Darian.

'Really? Some would say you do it on a daily basis.' For once, Belial's reply did not hide his hurt and disappointment. He may be fallen but was still an angelic being, one of the highest order in the celestial hierarchy.

Darian and the demon warily circled the wide perimeter several times. There was no sign of any weakness in the defences or of anything leading beneath the earth. This was not an area known for underground caves or tunnels.

'I think we must take our search wider – anything that could have carved a cavern or tunnel beneath the rocks,' suggested Belial.

Darian hit his forehead in exasperation. 'By Hades, I can be a clueless idiot sometimes.'

'Well, you don't say,' Belial sighed.

'A river!' Darian continued, ignoring the demon's pointedly sarcastic aside. 'An underground river and the Heath has good ones. The Fleet rises under here and legend says the old Abnoba still flows deep beneath the earth. That will be our best bet, the Fleet is still an early source but they say the Abnoba was big – big enough to turn those turbines! Old enough to carve an underground cave system.'

Darian rushed away into the woods, waving for Belial to follow. 'Help me find some willow or hazel to make a *virgula divina*, we are going dowsing!'

Abnoba, Belial mused, a river named after a Brythonic Goddess, one he had not yet encountered in person in the celestial dimension. And a goddess probably seething at seeing what had happened to her namesake, built over and forgotten by the teeming humans living above a once beautiful river. Could that be useful?

Within the hour, the curious sensitivity of the willow rods abruptly forced down Darian's long fingers. He fell to the ground and listened. Nothing. Time for the use of more acute senses.

'Forget your princely dignity and get your demonic backside down here, the willow twitching indicates a large source of water down below.'

Grumbling in foul-tongued ancient Chaldean, Belial reluctantly joined the alchemist on the cold, damp ground and with a long-suffering sigh, put his ear to the ground. There was no doubt a fast moving large body of water rushed beneath them and straight towards the turbines and like her sister river Fleet, was another sacrifice in mankind's headlong rush to industrial modernity. It would end in tears, it always did.

'Why did that little worm Cambion turn into a traitorous rat while we still need him?' Darian muttered. 'Or Hardwick go into the mother and father of all sulks over that irritating woman. I am certain he would have a device gathering dust in his workshops to help us.'

'You didn't? Really.'

'Didn't do what?' Darian answered the demon, swishing his cane through the brambles in agitation as if looking for a hidden entrance to the underground river.

'Violate that delicate prairie flower?'

'Of course.'

'We are talking about the same Athena Dedman? That upstanding example of tight laced professional virginity?'

'It would have been rude to turn down a lady,' Darian replied, giving the innocent brambles another hard swipe. 'She was begging me, old chap, the woman was stark naked, on her knees and pleading for my attention.' He gave an extravagant shrug and a wicked grin. 'I am only human after all, never could resist temptation.'

'Some enticement you always manage to resist with ease.'

Darian gave the demon's shoulder a gentle squeeze, 'There is nothing to lose from a tumble with a human female that I cannot fix with an elixir from my lab or a trust fund for any ensuing brat.'

He avoided Belial's pain-filled golden eyes. 'In our situation, old chap, there are tragic consequences too dire for both partners, a price too high to pay.'

Belial sighed to the depths of where his soul once resided and nodded agreement, as if he needed reminding.

Darian attacked the brambles again, this time with renewed savagery. People like Zachariah Dedman wondered why he had turned his back on their god; the alchemist had no time for sadistic tyrants however exalted. What else could you call a being that condemned his creations to an eternity of cruel punishment without mercy?

Any further musings on such matters ceased as Belial's Hell-attuned senses caught movement close by. Movement followed by a foul stench carried on the air, making the London Particular seem sweet and fragrant in comparison. An odious combination of brimstone and corruption reached Darian's nostrils.

'What in Hades is that?' whispered Darian. This was something new in the pantheon of unpleasant supernatural manifestations for him. He would not forget a smell like that.

'A way in,' Belial answered. 'A terramesh is a creature of the deep earth, one that has no business to be above ground. We must follow it.'

'Is it dangerous?'

'What isn't?' Belial replied, already moving in a swift, furtive run, keeping his profile low and urging Darian to do the same. 'Try to keep up. This may be our only chance.'

Easier said than done, thought Darian as he sprinted to keep up with the fleet footed demon who was making light of the tangle of tree roots and brambles in their path. Darian's gorge rose as the smell grew stronger – a mixture of all the foul, fetid odours of decay. At least they were getting closer to their prey. Belial raised a hand and stopped abruptly, crouching low behind a holly bush. Trust him to pick a prickly hiding place, thought Darian doing his best to avoid the tiny barbed leaves.

Ahead in a small clearing was their target, a heaving lump of misshapen flesh, like a large larva. The monstrosity was the colour of decaying human flesh, made even more horrific by its small, almost human head distorted by a thin, wide mouth sprouting a fearsome array of brown, needle-like teeth. The nightmare was busy, devouring an already unrecognisable body, one of the Turbine guards by the evidence of his shredded uniform.

Darian and the demon waited while the creature finished its meal, a thorough business, there was nothing left of the hapless trooper or his uniform by the time the terramesh had finished, it even licked the earth clean of spilt blood. Sluggish with its repast, the creature lumbered off towards a rise in the ground surrounded by densely growing hawthorn bushes. It struggled to get its cumbersome form through the sharp thorns, leaving behind dripping ichor from the many scratches on its body. *Helpful*, thought the alchemist, the filthy gloop allowing them to follow at a safer distance.

The trail led to the far side of the rise in the ground and cave entrance behind the hawthorns. Wisely waiting for the monstrous entity to force its way through the undergrowth and disappear with a grunt below the ground, Darian turned to his demonic companion. 'Are you ready for this, old chap?'

'More than you, my friend. There is nothing down there that can harm me.'

As if Darian wasn't aware of this from countless other escapades together. He stepped back and let the demon crawl down into the cavern first. As usual. Within seconds they were in darkness, clambering downwards. Both had excellent night vision but the stench of the terramesh somewhere in front of them and the sound of the fast rushing river aided their attempt at finding a way through the low, irregular tunnel. At first progress was slow, laborious and precarious. They found themselves walking along a narrow uneven ledge alongside the river, the wet earth crumbled beneath their feet and there were many gaps that they needed to jump. By the time the path widened, Darian was exhausted and bruised, his clothes sodden and filthy.

The tunnel became better defined as an unknown light source ahead of them glowed on the clay walls. The gamble had paid off: they had found the way under the Turbines. The easier going also meant they needed to progress with more caution, before long the bass heartbeat and drone of the vast subterranean engines grew stronger. Soon, they would not be alone. Within half an hour, they discovered their route blocked by a chasm – man made by its smooth, even sides. In a thunder of protest, the river plummeted over the edge, its wild nature tamed to power the turbines.

Darian growled in frustration. He was so close to his goal but this chasm appeared uncrossable and dangerous. The tumult of the waterfall muffled other sounds but not the movement of many terramesh guarding the hidden entrance to the turbines. There was nothing Darian and Belial could do but observe from the precarious safety of the chasm ledge.

42

Encircled by howling terramesh, the depth of the gorge lay hidden by a spectral mist, glowing with a venomous green hue. Darian resisted the urge to nudge a stone over the edge to test the depth of the abyss. A suicidal impulse, the terramesh were on guard and would rip any intruder to shreds of bloodied flesh and splintered bone in seconds. What manner of man was this, to create these nightmarish fusions of demonic spirits and artificial flesh? Who raised entombed foul entities from deep within the earth in a spell that used grave dirt from an unbaptised infant's burial and fresh human blood to mould forms for them to inhabit? Crude in design deadly in intent, controlling wraith was child's play to such a man. Of all the rivals seeking the Technomicron, this was the one Darian most feared.

Belial held him back firmly from the narrow ledge leading to the abyss, he recognised the green clouds, Lethe-mist, breathe too much in and all human nature's quirky impulses were set free to self-destruct. Darian would do more than nudge a stone over the edge under the influence of the stuff, he would leap down to his death.

A voice reached across the swirling vapour, well-cultured, aristocratic reeking of old privilege and duty. A voice honed by Eton public school and Oxford University, a life spent creating confidence and poise with an underlying arrogance to make a leader of men. The haze parted briefly revealing the tall, upright form of Sir Edgar Quibbe, the British prime minister. Though the voice seemed vaguely familiar, Darian could not have been more surprised if it had been the Queen herself addressing him.

'You are a long way from Parliament, Sir Edgar,' said Darian. 'Should you not be back there debating the war with the Ashanti or considering levying some irksome tax or another –

not that I have ever paid any.'

The answering silence stretched on, once again hidden by the mist.

'I suspect it is too late to start paying it now.'

Again no answer across the chasm, Quibbe appeared to be waiting for the intruders to make the next move. The sensible one would be to leave, but Darian's curiosity was in full flow, what in the name of Hades was the British prime minister doing in a mysterious cavern deep beneath the Aetherium generators?

'You are a most remarkable man, Cyrus Darian. No matter what obstacle I threw in your way, you and your little gang overcame it. The clumsy brute force of the Mechmen, the fanatic zealots of Satarel – even using the greed and overvaulting ambition of my man Villance to destroy you all came to nothing.'

Quibbe's voice was no longer fully human, a demonic rasp undercut his speech betraying his true origin – Hell.

'You even managed to stay one step ahead of the Lady, no mean feat for her wiles and determination are considerable.'

'Hello Orias.'

Belial stood beside the alchemist, 'May I introduce you to a nobody from Hell. Little more than a guttersnipe meddler in the plans of human magicians. A bottom feeder in the hierarchy of the Infernal Realms.'

Quibbe's voice roughened to a guttural snarl, all trace of humanity purged by his anger, 'A nobody that was able to give you quite a fright in that London alley. A nobody who will soon command the power of the Technomicron, *Prince* Belial.'

The lack of respect in his voice triggered an answering snarl of fury in the demon.

Ignoring the prince, Quibbe continued, 'So who will be so high and mighty once I have the book and will drain Heaven and Hell of all their souls? The Earth will become a breeding ground for more power, each human death adding to my greatness.'

'Why do they always have to do this?' Darian ventured to the demon with an extravagant yawn. 'Megalomaniacs, human or whatever insist on boasting about their nefarious plans. Tedious in the extreme.'

'Tedious and pointless,' Belial replied. 'You do not have the ability to fuse the Technomicron with the generators. Or even to find a way across the chasm to confront us in person.'

A mistake. On some unseen, unheard signal, all the terramesh squirmed around and flew to the opposite side of the abyss and formed a living bridge for Quibbe/Orias to cross by stepping on their backs with the supreme confidence of his demonic nature. He remained in the outward form of the British prime minister but hellfire blazed in his eyes, his face contorted with upward curving tusks like a wild boar.

'This little piggy ...' began Darian but was silenced by a glare from Belial's own fiery eyes. 'Not now my friend, this is not an adversary a human dare mock. Even you. Especially you.'

'Spoilsport,' Darian muttered back, he had never seen Belial so on edge.

By now Quibbe had reached their edge of the abyss, a smirk too large for his human face distorting his features further. 'I may be lowly in the pantheon of Hell but I have a great advantage over you Prince Belial. You are one of the Fallen, tormented by a cruel corruption of the universal love you were created with. You love this man. That makes you weak. I have no crippling flaw, I can know only hatred and the sweet joy of spreading despair among these verminous primates.'

As Quibbe talked, his terramesh were gathering, surrounding them.

'Cyrus,' the demon implored, 'run – run for your life!'

It was too late, any escape route, even to suicide by leaping into the abyss now cut off. The Terramesh's clumsy, ill formed heads twisted and turned some exposing yellow tusks, brutal grinding and crushing weapons with no chance of a merciful swift death by sharp fangs. Their ill matched tiny eyes disturbingly human in form, all turned to focus on Darian.

'Of course, you can still save your paramour, Prince Belial,' Quibbe continued, gloating, 'return to demonic form and you will easily overwhelm me and my children. You have such infernal power as a High Prince of Hell, there is nothing I could do to stop you.'

The look of dismay on Belial's face betrayed him, he had no intention of returning to his cursed Fallen form and had planned to remain at Darian's side forever. And Quibbe knew that.

'Lucifer misses you, as does Sammael and all the other corrupted Angels. They want you back. Indeed, they demand that you come back.'

Quibbe had gone too far with his mocking. Belial knew no Fallen Prince would deign to speak with this loathsome underling. Nor would they object to his time spent on Earth. There was no redemption, no forgiveness for the Fallen; it did not matter where Belial served out his eternal punishment.

Clammy earthen limbs enfolded Darian, the stench of corruption causing his gorge to rise. Now the Terramesh held him, just a little more pressure and they would crush him to a pulp within seconds.

'I knew if you survived all that the others threw at you, Darian, you would still come for the book.' Quibbe's confidence soared, all his plans coming neatly into fruition. 'It is your relentlessly predictable nature that betrayed you, endlessly curious, stubborn and wilful. Being denied the Technomicron was all the bait I needed to get you here with the Prince.'

'Yet you did your best to kill me,' Darian managed to wheeze through his crushed lungs.

'Did I?' Quibbe replied with a grunting sound signifying his amusement. 'Or did I respect the considerable skills of my greatest opponent? Indeed I did my best to protect you against our mutual rivals. Villance's betrayal was an unexpected turn, I appointed him to protect you. But the lure of the false grimoire at Fortune's castle was too much for a man of such greed and ambition. That trap had been set for Crimm-Smyth and Fogue, not for you.'

Darian was not convinced, but lying was second nature to demons as it was to him. It didn't matter, none of the past mattered now, this was the start of the end game, he had no doubt the real grimoire was here. The future of humanity no less would be decided in this high vaulted marvel of British engineering.

Quibbe threw back his head and raising his arms to the roof with what Darian considered rather unnecessary drama and in his own demonic voice summoned his followers, 'My babies, take them to the book.'

With a deep grunting sound wordlessly mimicking Quibbe's voice, ten huge Terramesh dragged themselves across the floor, above them swirled many wild-eyed wraith, their spirit forms weaving in and out of each other making counting their number impossible. At the margins lesser creatures chattered and squabbled, Breeth and Blaggers following the summons.

Darian recoiled at the stench, an amalgam of the foulest corruptions of the Earth and the brimstone of Hell combined into one roiling miasma. He turned to Belial, 'Never thought I'd be nostalgic for the London Particular. That's a posy of sweet violets compared to this infernal stink. How can you stand it down there?'

'I couldn't,' Belial answered, his voice grim as he weighed up his options. 'Why else do you think I hang around with you? The most vexing human I could ever have encountered out of all the millions of you primates infesting this world.'

Time for a gamble – the last thing Darian wanted was for Belial to shake off his human form. 'Because you love me?' The alchemist kept the tone light hearted, bantering, but the flicker of intense pain across Belial's beautiful face was just what he wanted to see.

Another gamble to keep Belial human, Darian lent forward as much as the chains binding him could allow and kissed the demon on the lips, a step further in the dangerous dalliance than he had ever dared before. Darian tasted the sweetness of the Fallen Angel and the foulness of the eternally punished demon, felt the corrupted love, once innocent and embracing all humanity now focused on a destructive, carnal obsession. So cruel, yet again Darian questioned the need for such a hideous punishment. He pulled back sharply before the corrosive effect of Belial's returning kiss damaged him. Darian needed all his wits about him now.

Quibbe caught the interaction between his prisoners and threw them apart with a swing of his fists. There would be time for these fevered emotions very soon, when he forced Belial into obeying him in return for the human's miserable life.

43

Sir Miles Hardwick, Britain's greatest inventor and now prisoner of the country's prime minister awaited the madman's return in the cavernous halls of the generator room. Chained to a pillar, he had plenty of time to study the surrounding marvel of grandiose design. Wide round steel columns soared to a high vaulted roof of multi coloured stained glass glowing in a complex design of occult symbols. Quibbe had created a profane cathedral, built to house the fusion of modern technology and ancient maleficent magicke. Vast panels of brass and copper inlaid polished wood gave the generator room a dignified air, a gravitas Hardwick found surprising in something so hurriedly built. But then he reasoned, the project had the Prime Minister working with the innocent approval of the Queen, Quibbe was able to galvanise a nation, its foundries, its brickworks, its manpower.

Beneath his feet the brass floor vibrated with the sound of vast turbines draining the Thames of water ready to drive their engines, the metal leviathans poised, hissing, preparing to unleash their power. Hardwick studied the floor of the chamber inlaid with swirling occult symbols made from gold, silver and platinum, others were created in precious crystals and gemstones etched into the metal. He wished Darian was here, damn his eyes, to interpret the symbols though he knew they could not mean anything benign.

The innermost circle of the chamber held a crystalline structure on a black marble plinth identical to the one he'd seen at Fortune's castle. Set in its centre, the grimoire waited, a deceptively simple tome of faded vellum and parchment. Above it was a complex structure held by jointed copper fingers, an intricate metal filigree designed to intertwine and fuse with the book. The delicacy of the tracery in stark contrast to the massive structure surrounding it.

At least he was alone, his stomach aching after a pummelling from Quibbe's henchmen. It was totally unnecessary brutality. He had already succumbed to the chloroform from their abduction from the quayside. He had gone to Southampton to say goodbye to Athena Dedman. Her distress at losing her father compounded by an uncertain financial future could not have been helped by the sudden disappearance of her only English friend. His abduction had been brutally efficient and swift, one minute he was pleading with her to change her mind, to abandon plans to board the Oceanic and stay in London as his wife, the next he was gone.

The henchmen who had chained him here were human but Hardwick had seen the lurking shapes of Quibbe's other familiars including the revolting mockery of life the Prime Minister had called his Terramesh. Nightmares that shuffled awkwardly along the ground hauling their malformed bodies on stubby vestigial limbs. Yet though without wings, they could take to the air and fly. For a man of science and technology, this defied all reason even by the skewed standards of the supernatural.

Hardwick groaned as a foul stench announced the arrival of some of Quibbe's minions, sadly not the humans but the odious Terramesh. Two approached him and split open his chains with their boar-like tusks, they raised themselves up onto two legs and dragged Hardwick towards the inner circle. Clearly the culmination of Quibbe's master plan was approaching. As were a party of more Terramesh, preceded by swirling Wraith.

Hardwick's eyes flared with a mixture of relief and alarm at seeing his companions as they were dragged into the chamber in the painful grip of the monsters. So, they too were prisoners, but what was that to those two resourceful reprobates? Darian and Belial represented hope of escape but were also the final pieces of Quibbe's diabolical plan to harvest and harness spectral energy for himself. Quibbe needed him to get the generator's mighty engines working in harmony, ready to fuse with the grimoire and release the spell to control all the souls of the dead.

As a lower denizen of Hell, Quibbe needed Belial to handle the Technomicron, once the power was engaged it would no longer be a handwritten grimoire created by a long dead mage, its new form would reduce any normal human to ash. And Darian? Hardwick assumed he was here as leverage to get the demon Prince's cooperation. Quibbe was playing a dangerous game at every level – something only an insane entity would contemplate. Whether he succeeded or not, the power of the Technomicron could cause disaster and loss of life on an unthinkable scale. Somehow they must stop Quibbe. Hardwick was prepared to sacrifice his own life to sabotage the monster's plans but would Darian? Highly unlikely. And all Belial had to do was to return to his princely form and all hell would literally be let loose. Hardwick had never felt so human and so vulnerable.

Sir Edgar Quibbe, a man who once dined with the American President, the Czar of Russia and most of Europe's royalty was now salivating as the culmination of his plans fell together, a drool of yellow-green ichor poured from his distorted mouth and pooled on the metal floor.

'It is perfectly simple my unwilling accomplices, Sir Miles Hardwick will attach the grimoire to the power source while it is still just a book of ancient spells. Then he will start up the generators to the strength I command. When the energy courses through the book, Prince Belial will fuse the two sections together to form the Technomicron at which point, he will hand it to me. For this simple act of co-operation, you will then be rewarded with your lives.'

Ever predictable, Hardwick challenged his captor, 'And if I refuse?'

'Sacrificing yourself for the good of mankind is the sort of selfless act I expected you to make, your lordship. You may be weak and dissolute but you are still an English gentleman. So, I have given myself a little extra insurance.'

Quibbe turned, revealing a new addition to the chamber, the vivid blue shop front from a Moroccan souk, festooned with gleaming brass and silverware, rich coloured wool rugs and glass inlaid lanterns. From its beaded door way stepped a beautiful, dark-eyed harem girl clad in diaphanous lilac voile, her face barely hid by a sequinned veil. She held a long, curving knife at the throat of Athena Dedman.

'What a bloody, treacherous bitch!' Hardwick swore.

'I say, there is no need for such profanities, old man,' Darian replied amicably. 'That is my sweetheart you are maligning. If it wasn't for the circumstances, I'd be forced to call you out.'

Quibbe bowed to the Lady. 'Well done my dear. Our business transaction has worked out most agreeably. At the first sign of Lord Hardwick failing to do his task, cut the woman's throat.'

'Do what the old boar wants,' Darian muttered to the distraught inventor. 'Things do not always work out how people, or demons want.'

Hardwick had worked alongside Darian long enough to recognise a clue in his words, he must be up to something. Please God, let the fellow be up to some nefarious plan to save the day. Darian did not do nobility or self-sacrifice but a world controlled by Quibbe where even the dead were slaves would be odious to him. Surely he would try to stop Quibbe if only to save one particular lost soul that Darian adored, his not so well kept secret.

Hardwick glanced across to poor Athena. He had no doubt of the Lady's ability to carry out the threat to her life. There was nothing for it but to do his part in the creation of the monstrous Technomicron. He walked to the crystal set on the plinth and studied the book's cover for clues to where the metal lattice would connect.

'Do not fear making a mistake, my Lord,' Quibbe slavered. 'The book will tell you when you are wrong.'

Hardwick took his time, eventually finding a logical pattern to follow. Removing the grimoire from its crystal resting place, relieved only to feel fragile, dusty vellum in his hands, he gently removed the copper attachments and began to fit the book within the metal framework. Three sections of the tracery fitted onto the book with a hiss of satisfaction, another was misplaced – Hardwick's hand snapped back stung by an agonising display of supernatural pique.

He stood back and took a deep breath to recover, a move misinterpreted by the excitable Quibbe. 'Back away one more step and the woman dies.'

Hardwick swore under his breath and glared with hatred at the Prime Minister. 'I have not stopped, Quibbe. But I swear on all I hold sacred, if you or your shapeshifter bitch harm one hair on Miss Dedman's head, I will pursue you both through all eternity.'

He ignored the monstrous being's snuffling contemptuous mirth and forced himself to concentrate on the book. Sweat poured down his face as he did his best to work out the last fittings, finally succeeding but not before receiving three more punishing jolts. He looked across to Darian and Belial, hoping to see some clue in their eyes that all would be alright but saw nothing to give him hope.

'Hardwick, go to the generator controls and on my mark set the turbines to build up to maximum power. My Lord Prince, time to fulfil your duty.'

Even before the subterranean gears and pistons began to turn, the cold, tense air in the cavernous chamber grew humid, fetid with the stench of the Terramesh. Agitated wraith flew around and above the captives, baring their long razor teeth desperate to attack but held back by the force of Quibbe's implacable will. The force of the thunderous power beneath their feet shook the chamber like an earthquake, the booming rhythm of the pistons like the heartbeat of a vast leviathan.

A pulse of concentrated power began to build in a large spherical blue crystal above the book. Hardwick's hands were on the controls but he pleaded under his breath for Belial to stop this insanity, to forgo the weakening human form and use his incredible demonic power. Why wasn't Cyrus pleading with him? Was his selfishness so complete?

Instead the demon remained in the form of a beautiful youth. He took the book in both hands triggering ecstatic wailing and screeching by Quibbe's creatures. He held it high up to the crystal and stood tall and unyielding as a discharge of blue fire shot into the book, enveloping it in a plasma ball of violent energy. One lightning bolt after another hit the grimoire as the power surges built in ferocity but Belial withstood the assault, his long hair flowing behind him from the electrical storm, his amber gold eyes turning to blue flame. Yet he did not transform, Hardwick's hopes dying with each surge of baleful force.

'It is done.'

With Belial's words, Quibbe ordered the power switched off, his heavy hands shaking with anticipation. 'Hand me the book, Prince.'

Belial's long pause sent shock waves tremoring through everyone in the chamber. The prospect of such power in the hands of one of the seven High Princes of Hell was far worse than the weaker and potentially defeatable Quibbe.

Belial held the book tightly to his chest, unharmed by the flickering blue flames that still danced across the newborn fusion of technology and magicke. Desperate, Quibbe grabbed the alchemist, his only pawn left in his gamble for power. Belial would be unmoved by the death of millions of humans but he cared for this one.

'Imagine what I could do with the Technomicron,' Belial's voice was commanding, enthused with the overwhelming pride that caused his downfall. 'A power to control all the souls of man, for now and forever. That would make me greater than Lucifer, than Sammael, greater than ...'

Quibbe moved fast, his meaty arms engulfing Darian in a crushing embrace, one tusk drawing blood from his throat. 'This is how this ends, Prince, you give me the book, I give you back this human alive.'

Despite his best efforts to abide by his strict upbringing steeped in stoicism and courage, Hardwick began to whimper as the fearful consequences sank in. The doomed, one-sided relationship between the demon and Cyrus Darian was now pivotal to the future of humanity. Such madness. There was nothing he could do but watch the drama play out. His heart went out to Athena, still in the clutches of the she-devil, the knife firmly held against her throat. With all the focus on Belial and Quibbe, he had to try to save her.

Darian was unable to speak, his face turning blue as Quibbe's grip tightened, the blood flow from the throat wound spilling over the monster's arms and pooling on the floor. The sight of this heavy blood loss quenched the blue flames in Belial's eyes as Quibbe's gamble paid off. With a snarl from the depths of his tortured soul, the demon handed the still burning hot Technomicron over. Quibbe gave a clumsy, capering dance of triumph around the chamber clutching his trophy as the demon ran to Darian's side, desperately trying to staunch the flow of blood from the alchemist's throat. All vestigial illusion of Quibbe's patrician human appearance dissolved in a swirl of foul smelling smoke and Orias in his true lumbering monstrous form became fully revealed. A slavering beast-like shape covered in barbs and bristles with a heavy skull bearing curving yellow tusks and three pairs of horns.

Orias opened the book and began to intone the chant that would give him the power to command all human souls but within seconds realised something was wrong – something fundamentally flawed in the procedure. The book remained static, inert, all flames extinguished. His three pairs of small crazed eyes blazed with confusion and anger. Darian struggled to his feet, somehow managing a smile. 'You have in your … er … hand, a fancy version of a basic necromicron … which will only respond to a human necromancer … which, Quibbe, old chap, you clearly are not.'

Orias threw back his heavy head and howled his fury and frustration to boom and echo throughout the mountainous chamber.

'No need to make such unseemly noise, my porcine friend, I

can read the words for you.'

Hardwick stopped in his tracks, his mind unable to comprehend the depth of treachery, Darian was capable of many low actions, taking advantage of poor Athena's poisoned state for one, but this? Surely not this.

Orias paused, silenced by the human's words. It must be trickery yet without the necromancer's voice, all his plans had come to nothing. It had to be done. He beckoned Darian over but the man was too weak to move and so with reluctance, Orias took the book to him. 'No tricks.' He snarled, one club-like fist poised ready to crush Darian's skull at the first sign of wrongdoing.

His hands shaking, Darian took the book, doing his best not to bleed over the words, without which the book was impotent. At last, after all these months of obsessing, searching, of enduring injury and loss, he finally had the Technomicron. This was a time of choice. All he had to do was utter the ancient words etched with blood and ink into the Persian mage's skin and the awesome power of the Technomicron would be all his. No human born would ever wield such sway over the fate of billions alive and dead. A tempting thought. For a crazed megalomaniac. But what use was the baleful thing to him? It could not reverse time, could not bring the dead back to life and therefore ultimately it was useless to him. He had achieved his goal, he had beaten his rivals. He had won. Was this the time to be sensible? To do the right thing for once?

Why not. He had no interest in enslaving the energy of the souls of human dead. Where was the fun and adventure in that? By Hades, the wretched tome needed destroying. For once he had to be on the side of the angels.

A burning sensation at his throat reminded him of the phial, the parting gift from Aayushi, the ancient Indian oracle. He remembered her insistent words of knowing the right time to use it. This must be that time. Had to be! It was now or never.

He began to utter the spell, slowly and pretentiously tempering his pronunciation with a deliberate guttersnipe accent, gambling Orias would not know the subtle difference in the same human language – ancient Farsi. But using the false incantation bought him enough time to break the glass phial and allow all the tears to pour onto the book. The speed of the Technomicron's dissolution was shocking, one minute it was an object of terror, the next a disintegrating mess of corrupted skin. Orias grabbed the book in shock only to see it fall in tattered flakes through his lumpen fingers. Before the enraged creature could exact his revenge, Belial picked the alchemist up and ran out of the raging creature's reach.

The Lady released her prisoner and threw her the knife before shouting, 'Over here, quickly! Into the Emporium before this place blows itself to pieces! Run!'

Belial needed no second command and bolted into the shop carrying the stricken Darian. Hardwick hesitated at first, his forsworn intentions were never to have anything to do with the renegade alchemist again.

'Don't be a darned fool.' Hardwick spun around at the feel of a woman's firm hand on his shoulder. Athena! Stronger and braver than ever, she kissed him on the cheek before grabbing his hand. 'Please, forget that rogue, he's not worth your anger. But you must come with me if you want to live.'

Astonished and overjoyed, Hardwick let a determined Athena lead him into the souk shop front before it disappeared. In a shimmer of silent energy, the Emporium disappeared and went elsewhere in an instant.

Left alone with only his panicking creatures, Orias attempted to start the ritual to open the portal back to Hell. But the swift destruction of the Technomicron had dire consequences. The power it unleashed still existed but with no concentrated point of focus or purpose, it whirled around the chamber in a ball of frenzied blue plasma. Each ricochet off the chamber walls caused a massive explosion, chunks of molten metal rained down setting fire to the wood panelling. Terramesh caught in the conflagration screamed in agony as their artificial flesh burnt swiftly to a cinder, the Wraith still trapped by Orias's spell of command could not escape but whirled and flailed in the volcanic heat unharmed by the flames but tortured by their unwilling entrapment. If Orias left without releasing them, the wraith would remain forever in this chamber or where it once stood.

Beneath them, without Hardwick's hands at the controls, the turbines began to turn again, powered by a sudden surge of an angry river, rebelling at its control and confinement. It generated a runaway build up of energy and the cathedral built for the madness and uncontrollable ambition of one of Hell's lowliest denizens prepared to blow itself and a large area of London's outlying towns and villages to oblivion.

Orias roared with fury, in flesh form he had no immunity from the inferno and shuffled to the turbine controls across the red hot floor. Unable to manage the controls with his clumsy beast claws, he reluctantly returned to human form and as Sir Edgar Quibbe did all he could to avert the disaster. With hands raw with burns from the hot metal, he turned wheels and hauled on levers until the pressure eased and the blades slowed their blur of reckless, destructive speed. It was too late to undo all the damage and as the whirling blades lost momentum, their rhythm became disjointed, uneven. One blade sheared off and crashed into another creating a catastrophic disintegration of the turbine tower. What had taken months to build now collapsed in seconds, all of London could hear the deafening sound of the structure's collapse, undermining the second edifice and bringing the metal titan crashing down to its knees.

The control chamber beneath them first collapsed in on itself from the shock wave, then became submerged beneath the hundreds of tons of falling debris entombing Orias and the captive wraith. Great chunks of broken masonry tumbled down from the mound flattening anything in their path including the first human casualties of the enfolding disaster. Rising heavenwards, mushrooming dense clouds of burning hot dust, debris and steam hid the turbine towers last dying moments from the horrified citizens of London before descending to hurtle down across the city forcing the people to bolt for their lives to the nearest shelter.

Then an all encompassing silence.

It would be some time before anyone could hear the screams of the wounded and dying, the shockwaves from the project's destruction had robbed the citizens of London of their hearing. For most victims, that would gradually recover, a restoration accompanied by the pain of burst eardrums. Ironically, the London Particular, its foul density further enhanced with the detritus from the toppled titans would claim more lives, those with already damaged lungs choking to slow, painful death on the fumes.

The country's most ambitious building project, feted around the world, had ended in a spectacular disaster, another nightmare for London and loss of life.

Whether trust and respect for the Establishment who ignored all advice and built the doomed turbines would ever return was another question for the future to answer.

44

The Emporium decided the adventurers needed a break from the chaos and destruction overwhelming London, especially as they had caused it. What they had prevented was of course far worse but it did no harm to lie low in more pleasant surroundings. The Lady agreed with the spirit of her shop and gave Darian's team a choice of anywhere they desired with reassurance the Emporium would return for them, if they wished it. A generous offer they were too exhausted to question. One possible sign of the Lady's goodwill scampered on sharp talons from beneath her skirts and leapt up to Darian's shoulders. Thoughtfully, she had brought along his dragoncat.

A lovestruck Hardwick wanted to take Athena to the romantic city of Venice but could not suggest something so forward without a chaperone. A dilemma. One that was not unsolvable. At Darian's suggestion, made tongue in cheek but one enthusiastically embraced by Athena, the Emporium took them to a charming row of Regency town houses in St John's Wood. There at the most imposing home, Darian introduced them to Lady Arabela Grayshott, who as Darian expected, was delighted at the chance of an adventure in Venice.

Athena and Hardwick were instantly charmed by Lady Arabela's dainty figure dressed in the latest mode and her sparkling blue eyes, her intelligence and ready wit. It also helped that she was fluent in both French and Italian. Lady Arabela was the perfect choice. She would make a delightful travelling companion.

While Arabela's maids packed for her journey and Athena and Hardwick were admiring a collection of eighteenth century miniatures of her illustrious ancestors, Darian took her to one side, well out of earshot.

'Thanks Libby,' Darian whispered. 'That's a big favour I owe you.'

'Oi! Less of the Libby,' the pretty minx replied in a tone of mock scolding, 'An' this is no 'ardship, I aim to bag me an Italian Prince!'

The past traumatic events had slightly changed Athena. She had lost some of her hauteur from realisation of her loneliness and vulnerability. But not enough to lose the opportunity to be a companion to a real English titled lady. Someone of impeccable morals and status who could help Athena integrate into society should she become Lady Hardwick. Thank goodness Darian had not lumbered her with some appalling skivvy or streetwalker as a chaperone. Some standards in society must never be allowed to slip.

With the humans' plans made, that left only an uncomfortable Belial who could see the alchemist wanted time alone with the Lady, comforting himself that their amorous trysts fuelled by love, hate but primarily lust, were always short lived. He could wait, earth time passed like the blink of an eye to one used to eternity. The Lady was a passing diversion for Darian, exciting, intoxicating but impossible to sustain a long-term relationship without one of them killing the other.

He chose to return to London and Darian's home, to take care of it and Misha and deal with unfinished business.

Belial, unless dragged back screaming in protest to Hell, intended to be a permanent fixture in Darian's life. He knew that nothing would come of it, nothing should, for the moment Darian succumbed to the demon's love, the alchemist's soul would not just be damned, it would be utterly destroyed. Yet for Belial, the torture of his eternal punishment in Hell was as nothing compared to not being with Darian. It was still worth it to be no more to him than his sidekick, an ever loyal companion in adventure, though it tore more jagged rents in the demon's crippled heart. Belial would just have to compensate for all this pain and repressed emotion by being more evil to any humans that crossed him and Darian. Or those who hadn't and whose only crime was to be human. He had no tears of angelic love for humanity. They had permanently dried up during the Fall.

His renewed reign of unpleasant behaviour would start with the Brethren of Satarel. What was it Darian had threatened them with? Having their heads boiled while they were still alive? Primitive and a little crude for one of Belial's expertise in devilry but why not? It would pass the time pleasantly until Darian returned from bedding the Lady.

Lost to the night and the shadows, an urban dog fox trotted through Highgate cemetery, following a familiar path through the lanes lined with small humble gravestones and the magnificent marble sepulchres of the rich. He paused, one foot raised, alert to danger. He was not alone, a predatory beast larger and fiercer than the fox blocked his well worn route. Something large, angry and not of the world he knew. Not with so many confusing smells merging in one beast, the fox recognised shrew, rat, dog, pigeon, cat and other fox odours but there were many musky, feral scents he did not.

Alarmed, the fox slunk away in the opposite direction and therefore was spared becoming the focus of the beast's frenzy of impotent fury and grief with no target for its rage beyond the silent inhabitants of the graves it destroyed. It had been so close, within scenting distance but its prey was not here, the trail had gone cold. How could that be? It was fast, clever and knew many tricks. It hauled a concrete angel from above a tomb and smashed the carving's serene head against the ground, pulverising it to grey dust.

Eventually, exhaustion stilled the beast and it rested within a carved stone mausoleum as large as a peasant's hovel. Curled up on the dry bone, grave dust, it waited. It had learnt to exist as many forms and now it must learn to be patient.

45

Darian edged closer to the slender beauty in bed beside him, a light sheen of sweat glistening on her dark brown skin. Were any women more beautiful then those of Somalia? Looking at the naked splendour of the woman beside him, Darian thought not. Her eyes closed, a slight, sweet smile of contentment lit up her perfect features. With her regal bearing, she could have been a reincarnation of the Queen of Sheba, but was yet another facet of the Lady. All past strife between the lovers forgotten for now and in celebration of their truce, they had made love all through a night full of passion and emotion. For once it was not just their usual pleasurable, combative sex and though Darian knew the edginess and danger of their relationship would return, for now they enjoyed a rare peace and serenity.

The Lady stirred, her large, almond-shaped eyes of darkest brown remained soft, loving as she trailed a finger across his features. 'I wish it could always be like this between us.'

Darian took her hand and kissed it. 'So do I, *Tesora*, but we can change appearances but never our true nature. We are nature's alley cats, society's despised outsiders. We prefer to live alone, mate and part, bite and scratch each other over tasty morsels. We will never settle for a tame life, purring on a cosy cushion by the fireside.'

A flicker of genuine sadness passed over her eyes then her old, independent poise returned as she rose to dress. A waft of warmth made the white gauze drapery dance as the intoxicating scents of North Africa filled the room on a khamsin breeze.

'What is the hurry?' Darian pulled her back down onto the rumpled white cotton sheets, covering her with his body. 'The world and all its intrigues and discoveries can wait for once.'

Laughing, she agreed by pulling him even closer, delighted

to see his stamina and enthusiasm remained undaunted by the energetic night just passed.

'Just one question before I lose my body and mind to you again,' Darian murmured kissing the lush, narrow valley between her breasts. 'That Dedman woman, she wasn't really ever your prisoner, was she?'

'Of course not,' the Lady replied, her fingernails lightly scratching along his spine from neck to hips, then lower – much lower. 'She is my pupil, my protégée. A very quick and eager learner.'

Bugger, thought Darian as he prepared to pleasure the Lady again, that meant another dangerous female out there for him to avoid, only this one, he suspected would be like a Black Widow spider, one who having mated with him once, now intended to kill him. On these matters, he was never wrong.

Aftershock

Nothing could bar their way, even their own strong wills. Ignoring the chaos and pain of the stricken city, they walked from every corner of London. Immune to solid debris, oblivious to choking dust, they came seeking their master. An army of earthbound souls summoned by the brief flash of power of the doomed Technomicron moved through London, converging as one outside a Mayfair town house. The malign book could not summon the dead from the afterlife, but it had trapped those who had not moved on.

Whatever motives caged them on the earthly dimension; revenge, grief, mischief, confusion, they were as nothing to the clarion call of enchanted servitude. They had no power to break free, to rebel, or dissent. They were his.

They waited, patience their only gift, some had already wandered the earth for thousands of years, what was a few days, weeks, years more? As they gathered, too many to number, the area of Mayfair around them became charged with freezing spectral energy that even the most insensitive living human could feel without knowing why. Those given the gift or curse of genuine mediumship stayed as far away as possible, too overwhelmed by the weight of so many unhappy, imprisoned souls.

Pet dogs and cats fled their homes, carriage horses refused to pass through, preferring to bolt through the streets in the opposite direction. The few scraggy pigeons left in the dying trees flew away. Rats relocated to less eerie locations. Only breeth and blaggers bothered to prowl, ignoring the spectres.

Mayfair's wealthy inhabitants either stoically put up with the inexplicable chill or moved to their country homes until someone in authority sorted it out.

But if the man the enslaved spirits sought was not there, this was not a cause of concern to the patient ghosts. He would be soon, drawn to this centre of his universe, his haunted home that once belonged to a succubus he'd slain within its walls.

Though he did not yet know it, an army of the dead waited for Cyrus Darian.

About the Author

Raven Dane is an award-winning fantasy author based in the UK. Her published works include the highly acclaimed *Legacy of the Dark Kind* series of dark fantasy/sci-fi crossover novels (*Blood Tears*, *Blood Lament* and *Blood Alliance*).

However, Raven's skills in fiction don't end there. Her comedy fantasy *The Unwise Woman of Fuggis Mire* - a scurrilous spoof of high fantasy clichés – was met with great enthusiasm by the reading public. In more recent years Raven has met with critical acclaim for her steampunk/occult adventures *Cyrus Darian and the Technomicron* and *Cyrus Darian and the Ghastly Horde*.

Cyrus Darian and the Technomicron was the winner of the best novel award at the inaugural Victorian Steampunk Society awards 2012.

Raven also has many short stories published in anthologies including one in *Full Fathom Forty*, a celebration of 40 years of the British Fantasy Society, and the first annual of ghost stories from Spectral Press, called the *13 Ghosts of Christmas*.

Further works include poetry, published in an anthology of pagan verse.

Other Telos Titles
By Raven Dane

THE MISADVENTURES OF CYRUS DARIAN
Steampunk Adventure Series
1: Cyrus Darian and the Technomicron
2: Cyrus Darian and the Ghastly Horde
3: Cyrus Darian and the Beastly Breath

Death's Dark Wings
Stand alone alternative history novel

Absinthe and Arsenic
13 Horror and Fantasy Short Story Collection

Other Published Novels

LEGACY OF THE DARK KIND SERIES
Thrilling Vampire Series
1: Blood Tears
2: Blood Lament
3: Blood Alliance

The Unwise Woman of Fuggis Mire
Comedy/Fantasy Sland Alone Novel

Other Telos Steampunk and Horror Titles

FREDA WARRINGTON

Nights of Blood Wine
Vampire Horror Short Story Collection

PAUL LEWIS
Small Ghosts
Horror novella

STEPHEN LAWS
Spectre

RHYS HUGHES
Captains Stupendous

DAVID J HOWE
Talespinning
Horror Collection of Stories, Novels and more
Shrouded By Darkness Ed. David J Howe
Urban Gothic Ed. David J Howe

SAM STONE

KAT LIGHTFOOT MYSTERIES
Steampunk Adventure Series
1: Zombies at Tiffany's
2: Kat on a Hot Tin Airship
3: What's Dead PussyKat
4: Kat of Green Tentacles
5: Kat and the Pendulum
6: And Then There Was Kat (Forthcoming)

THE JINX CHRONICLES
Dark Science Fiction and Fantasy, dystopian futre
1: Jinx Town
2: Jinx Magic
3: Jinx Bound (Forthcoming)

THE VAMPIRE GENE SERIES
Vampire, Historical and Time Travel Series
1: Killing Kiss
2: Futile Flame
3: Demon Dance
4: Hateful Heart
5: Silent Sand
6: Jaded Jewel

Zombies in New York and Other Bloody Jottings
Horror Story Collection

The Darkness Within: Final Cut
Science Fiction Horror Novel

Cthulhu and Other Monsters
Lovecraftian Style Stories and more

TELOS PUBLISHING
www.telos.co.uk